FRENCH VANILLA & FELONIES

a Cambria Clyne mystery

Erin Huss

To the great and marvelous people of The Apartment Management & Maintenance Support Group.

Acknowledgements:

I first want to thank Gemma Halliday for bringing this book back to life. Working with you and your team has been a dream. Wendi Baker, thank you for your superb editing skills and knowledge. And to everyone else at Gemma Halliday Press for bringing this book back to the shelves, thank you!

To my husband, Jed. Your unwavering support and love mean everything. To my children, Natalie, Noah, Ryder, Emma, and Fisher, you are my motivation in all things. Thank you for letting me be your mom.

Thank you to my mother, Barbara Stotko, for continually telling me I could do anything; my dad, Tim Hogan, for your endless support; Tyler Hogan for being the best brother an annoying big sister could ask for; my stepdad, Mark Stotko, who met me as a teenager and still wanted to marry my mother; my best pal, Katie Ledesma, for losing sleep while going over plot twists with me; Cody Christiansen for being my go-to lawyer; Christina Christiansen for being the sister I always wanted/needed; my in-laws, Janean Huss, Rod Huss and Julie Huss, for taking me in and allowing me to use the Huss name. I wear it proudly.

I want to thank my beta readers, all those who read the first few (terrible) drafts and the final one—Jordan Elliot, Brittney Zeedik, Katie Ledesma, Barbara Stotko, Tia Howard, Julie C. Gardner and Lucy Woodhull. Thank you to Sam Young for taking a young, relatively inexperienced apartment manager and allowing her to manage your flagship property. Thank you to Ashley Stock for the author picture and early-on beta reading. Iris Handy Peugh, thank you for *Crap-o-la.* I want to thank all the readers of The Apartment Manager's Blog, some who have been with me since 2009. To Michelle Crump, Kris Salvesen, Beth Chamberlain, Lisa Griffin, and all those who helped launch the first edition, thank you for your support. I feel like I wouldn't have the confidence to write if it weren't for my grandma, Melba Raynaud. She told me from a very early age I should be a writer. Look Abuela, I finally listened!

PROLOGUE

———

Here's the thing, we are all varying degrees of crazy. You know it. I know it. If aliens are in fact spying on us like every bum on Sunset Boulevard says they are, then they know it too. When in public, you hide the crazy in order to conform to what society deems "appropriate" behavior. Some are better at this than others. When you get home, within the confines of walls and away from watchful eyes, you can let your crazy run free without worry of judgment, public persecution, or jail time. Home is where you can dance naked. Safely satisfy your strange fetishes. Where you can role-play or engage in conversation with yourself, out loud, about *Star Wars* or *Harry Potter* or *The Real Housewives of Orange County* and no one will judge you for it.

It doesn't matter if your home is rented or owned. If your home is an apartment in Compton, a mansion in Beverly Hills, or a cardboard box under a freeway overpass—home is where your secrets are held. It's where you can let your freak flag fly high and proud!

This is what keeps my job interesting.

As an apartment manager, I'm privy to all of it—the freak flags *and* the secrets. Whether I want to be or not.

Trust me. It's not a job for the thin-skinned, weak-stomached, or easily offended.

It's a job for me…or at least I thought it was. Until I stared down the barrel of a gun and was arrested for a murder I didn't commit.

Now, I'm not so sure.

I hear accounting is nice.

CHAPTER ONE

———

Seeking an on-site Apartment Property Manager for a charming 40-unit community. Applicant must have excellent organizational skills and a calming demeanor.

"Calm down!"
Honk.
"You're not the only one in a hurry."
Hooonk.
"Go around!"

The silver BMW roared past me. I turned to deliver a mad glare, but Captain Douche was too busy looking at his phone to notice.

"Pay attention to the road!" I yelled to his rear bumper. "Honestly, no one can drive in this city." I flipped down my visor. The zit in the middle of my freckled forehead pulsed in the tiny mirror. "You really couldn't have waited until tomorrow?" I asked the zit.

I reached over and grabbed my makeup bag, smothered the monstrosity in concealer, added a touch of gloss to my lips, and mascaraed my lashes into tiny tarantula legs. I had to look my best today. One more week of unemployment and I'd be left with no other option than to become a phone sex operator by night who flips burgers by day. I had applications for both jobs in case this interview led to yet another dead end.

Hooonk!

"Take it easy." I flipped the visor back and continued maneuvering my dented Civic through the crowded streets of Los Angeles. I grabbed the past-due phone bill out of my bag and double-checked the directions scribbled on the back.

Right on City Court.

I looked up as the street sign for City Court drifted by my window.

"Crap." I made a hasty U-turn, which inspired another cacophony of horns. A man wearing a dirty Spiderman costume weighed in on my poor driving habits by flipping me a double-fisted bird. Even if I didn't come *that* close to him or his overflowing grocery cart.

My hand automatically went up as a feeble apology before I made the sharp turn.

And there I saw it. An imposing ten-story building. A cobblestoned walkway led up to a pair of whimsical wrought-iron doors. Brilliant red and yellow flowers were strategically dispersed throughout the lavish landscaping. A sign, welcoming those who were clearly richer than me, hung above a glistening koi pond near the entrance. It was beautiful.

I parked under the sign pointing to the leasing office, shoved the phone bill into my bag, and polished off the pint of French Vanilla wedged between my thighs. Ice cream was my go-to coping mechanism—and I'd been doing a whole lot of *coping* lately. I crawled over the center console and passenger seat to exit the car. The driver's side door had been stuck shut since an expensive meeting with a runaway dumpster a few months ago. It was annoying and awkward, especially on the days when I managed to squeeze my butt into a pair of skinny jeans. My little Civic still managed to get me from point A to point B (usually), and that was all I could afford to care about.

As I stepped onto the sidewalk, I flattened the front of my dress with my hands and brushed off the lint clinging to my thighs. I had on an Anthropologie dress worth more than my car—the one designated for interviews and first dates only because it minimized my butt, elongated my waist, was dry clean only, and the navy color matched my eyes. Sadly, it hadn't been getting much action in the last—*oh let me see*—four years.

Rolling my shoulders back, I took a deep, calming breath. The irony that I was about to interview for a job as an apartment manager when I was nearing eviction from my own apartment was not lost on me. It had been six months since I was laid off. Finding a job when the qualifications portion of your résumé ran three deep wasn't easy. Neither was being a single mother. The phone call for this interview couldn't have come at a better time. Decent salary, apartment, utilities, medical benefits, and bonuses—it was the perfect opportunity to get Lilly and me back on our feet. I only hoped my lack of apartment management experience would be overshadowed by my obvious desperation.

Setting my focus on the whimsical doors, I charged toward—*oomph!*

There was a step.

A big step.

A step I didn't see until my hands and knees were plastered atop the scorching cement and I was staring at it.

"Are you OK?" A pencil thin, tube top–donning brunette stood over me, sucking on a Tootsie Pop.

"I think so." I peeled myself off the ground and brushed away the chalky debris coating my knees. "That step came out of nowhere."

The brunette flipped her long ponytail over her shoulder. "Yeah, it happens a lot. Like, that's why they put up the sign." She pointed her sucker to the caution sign with a person about to plunge to the ground like I had just done. "But it doesn't seem to help. I totally see people trip here, like, all the time."

"Do you live here?"

"Nope, my Boo lives next door."

"Next door? There's another apartment complex on this street?" Panicked, I checked my watch. The interview was scheduled to start in five minutes. Story of my life—I was never late. I was always *almost* late, enough to be a frazzled, sweaty mess when I did arrive.

She pointed her sucker toward a row of tall shrubs. "Yeah, it's over there."

"Dang it… Thank you!" I yelled over my shoulder as I ran to the foliage fence blocking the neighboring apartment building. This one was smaller. Two-story with gated parking to the left. Pots filled with succulents lined the chipped brick walkway that led to a pair of sad-looking brown doors. No welcome sign. No koi pond, but a mud puddle near the entrance had a cloud of tiny insects hovering above it.

I dug out the instructions from my bag: *10, 405, Exit SM, Sepulveda, right on City Court. Apartment building on the right. Ask for Joyce.* That was it. That was all I wrote. No apartment name. No address. That would make too much sense.

I ran back to the first apartment complex. Standing between the two buildings, I shaded my eyes with my hand, trying to decide which one might house Joyce. The first building was much nicer. So I turned and ran toward the second one, because running toward mediocrity felt more natural.

When I reached the doors, I rested my hand on the rusty knob. *You've got this,* I told myself. *You are a strong, confident woman with better-than-average abilities and a kid to feed.* I took another deep breath, pushed open the door, and entered...1988?

I blinked as my eyes adjusted to the pink and blue striped wallpaper. A glass coffee table was surrounded by an overstuffed peach leather couch and two floral-printed armchairs. Below my Payless pumps was teal carpet, followed by yellow linoleum with a repeating brown octagon pattern across it. The track lighting gave the room a yellowish, hazy tint, and a ceiling fan clinked with each turn of its golden blades, pushing the stale, nicotine-laced air around the ugly room.

To my right was an enclosed office with a waist-high counter (also teal) overlooking the lobby. A frail old woman with scarlet hair sat behind a desk, her hands clasped and brown eyes on me.

"Hi. Are you Joyce?" I asked, hoping she'd say no and direct me to the spa-like resort next door.

"I am," she answered in a barely audible rasp. Despite the hundred-degree outside temperature, she wore a sweater, which hung loosely around her bony frame. Just looking at the cashmere caused my sweat glands to produce in double time.

"I'm Cambria Clyne. I have an interview with Patrick for the apartment management position. His secretary told me to meet him here at noon."

"You sure you really want *this* job?"

"Yes, I do," I answered slowly, unsure of what that was supposed to mean.

She regarded me for several awkward seconds before speaking. "OK then. Up to you." She stood on shaky legs and shuffled up to the counter. The two-foot journey looked painful. "Nice to meet you, Cambria. I'm the current manager." I took her proffered hand. Her palm was cold, but her eyes had a hint of warmth to them. "Patrick should be here in a bit. Would you like me to show you around while you wait?"

"That would be great, thank you." I smiled.

Joyce motioned for me to walk around the counter to the door that separated the lobby from the enclosed office. I followed her through the cramped space, squeezing past a row of tarnished filing cabinets and an L-shaped oak desk. She opened the door behind the desk, and—*bam!*

The nicotine air punched me in the lungs, knocking me back against the doorjamb. It was as if I'd walked directly into a cigarette. I placed my hand over my chest, mentally apologizing to all my vital organs.

Joyce stood in the middle of a square kitchen. The blue tiled counters were piled high with boxes and rolls of bubble wrap.

"Once we're gone, this would be your apartment," she said, fanning her arm out like Vanna White. "If you get the job."

I nodded in appreciation and took a gulp of air through clenched teeth, hoping they'd work as a filter. The lack of oxygen caused my head to beat in time with my heart, but I wasn't about to let a little cancerous air stop me. I *desperately* needed the income.

The kitchen looked out to a spacious living room with Smurf blue carpet and two long windows overlooking a courtyard. Asleep in the middle of the room was an old man with a beer in one hand, remote in the other, and *The People's Court* playing on the television opposite him and his purple recliner. Not just any old purple either—a two-toned mauve and lavender corduroy chair with a coordinating couch and love seat. Clearly, someone was colorblind.

I followed Joyce down a short hallway and into a bedroom.

"This is perfect for an office or guest room," she said, sliding the mirrored closet door open to reveal a space larger than my current bathroom.

"I actually have a daughter, and she'd love this room." Truth is, I would too. I'd been sharing a room with Lilly since the day she was born. The *Frozen* décor wasn't doing me any favors in the love department.

"Are you married?" Joyce rasped.

I shook my head.

"Interesting..." She rubbed her chin. "How old is your daughter?"

"She's three going on sixteen," I answered with an exaggerated roll of my eyes.

Joyce let out a laugh that quickly turned into a procession of dry, hacking coughs. She placed her veiny hand on the wall for support as her coughs morphed into more of a gurgling sound. My joke wasn't *that* funny. Nor was it original, and certainly not worth dying over.

I placed my hand on her back, feeling the ridges of her spine under the cashmere. "Can I get you something?"

She took a slow, gravelly breath then brushed off my concern with a wave of her hand. "I'm fine. Don't fuss. Let's move on." She let out one more cough before pushing past me.

I trailed behind, worried Joyce may not make it through the tour.

We next entered a room slightly bigger than the first with an attached walk-in closet and bathroom. Despite the smoke and the blue carpet and the yellow popcorn ceilings, I was in love. To have that amount of space, in a neighborhood I could never afford otherwise was unfathomable. On *Rent or Run* (a trusty app tenants use to rate their apartment building and let prospective renters know if they should rent there or run away) the place had 5 stars for safety, 5 stars for management, and a 4% run rate. Since moving to LA, I'd never lived in anything lower than 80%.

I was moving on up!

A little paint and oxygen would turn it into the perfect home.

"Joyce, I love it." Then, because my mother had taught me the way to any person's heart was through compliments, I eyed a massive oak armoire and added, "This is beautiful, by the way."

"You like it?" she asked, not masking her surprise. "I'll be sure to give it to you when I move."

I feigned excitement. "Really? Wow. You're so kind." I smiled, eyeing the monstrosity I now apparently owned.

I followed Joyce down the hall, past another full bathroom and into the living room. The old man was still lifeless in the chair. "How long have you been working here?" I asked, looking around and mentally arranging my own furniture.

She pulled a pack of cigarettes from her back pocket along with a lighter. "Almost…let's see…it's been about twenty-five years. This retirement is well overdue." With a shaky hand she positioned a cigarette between her pale lips and lit it.

I may vomit.

"OK…there are forty units," she continued, emitting a fresh batch of smoke. "You can take a look around. Just don't go in the third courtyard—ever. Never, ever go there. Trust me." She handed me three pieces of paper with her cigarette hand. "Then come back and fill these out." Ash broke off the end of her cancer stick and rolled down the front of the application.

I opened my mouth, about to ask why the third courtyard was off-limits, but she opened the front door before I could get the words out. My need for air overcame my manners, and I dashed outside, seeking refuge for my burning lungs.

I will never take oxygen for granted again.

After several deep, appreciative breaths, I shot an apologetic grin in Joyce's direction. My exit could be deemed rude, yet an arch of her penciled-in brow and stifled smile told me she took no offense.

"There's a picnic table by the pool you can use to fill out the application." She used her cigarette-free hand to point the way. "Bring it all back once you're finished, and remember, no third courtyard." The stern shake of her bent forefinger drove the point home.

Note to self: After job offer, get more third courtyard specifics.

I walked along the cement pathway, exploring the open first courtyard. There wasn't much in the way of color. Brown doors. Brown fascia. Tan walls. Brown staircase leading up to the brown second story. Greenish-brown grass. Greenish-brown shrubbery. Yet, it was clean. Not a single piece of trash or graffiti. No barred windows. No couches in the walkway. It wasn't the koi-pond apartments next door, but it was better than the armpit I was about to be kicked out of.

I strolled through a short ivy-laced breezeway and found the picnic table next to the pool. Taking a seat, I began filling out the application. It wasn't too difficult, and I nailed the first page—name, birthday, social security number, current employer, and previous employer. Unfortunately, a questionnaire was attached.

Please explain how you would handle the following situations:
1) The tenant in Apartment 5 and the tenant in Apartment 6 don't get along. The two call you daily to complain about the other, and both refuse to move.
2) You notice the tenants in Apartment 6 have a constant flow of visitors. The visitors tend to arrive and leave within minutes.
3) The tenant in Apartment 19 plays his drums during the day. The neighbors complain constantly and have threatened to move.

I had no idea how to correctly answer any of these questions. Sure, I could use common sense, and I had enough common sense to know there were legal forms and procedures to follow before one can start passing out eviction notices like candy. I just didn't know what those were.

Self-doubt slithered through my mind like the soul-crushing serpent it was. I should have stayed in college. Everyone warned me when I had taken the year off to find myself that I wouldn't return. They were right. All I'd learned during my quest for self-discovery was that VH1 played an entire season of *America's Next Top Model* in a single day. My one-year hiatus had quickly turned into seven. I'd already moved out to LA from my hometown of Fresno and gotten myself knocked up by the time I realized the value of a degree. I found a job as a barista and worked my way up to manager. I was doing

OK until the owner decided to sell the property to support his new girlfriend.

I gnawed on the end of the pen, staring down at the ashy questionnaire, when out of nowhere a pair of work gloves plopped down in front of me. I jumped, dropping my pen, and gazed up at the stranger sliding onto the bench across from me. I froze, unsure of why this random, albeit very attractive, man had shown up. The Universe was not typically this generous.

My eyes ventured down his tan shirt, past the wisps of blond hair peeking out from behind the button-up collar, to the word *Maintenance* embroidered in blue above his shirt pocket. This, coupled with the paint specks scattered across his dark blond hair, plus the gloves on the table, gave me reason to believe he worked there.

Obviously, espionage should have been my chosen career path.

"Do you need help?" the stranger asked, flashing a perfectly straight white-toothed grin.

"Um…" *Breathe, Cambria.* "Sure," I answered in a voice three octaves higher than my own. I found his scruffy jawline and unkempt hair wildly attractive. A tiny scar under his left nostril made him look edgy in an I-fell-down-when-I-was-a-kid kind of way. I cleared my throat, realizing I was staring. "Hi, I'm Cambria," I said, more even-toned. I then shot my hand out like an idiot.

He slipped his hand into mine. His strong, callused grip caused my insides to dance and flip and flutter and beg for more. It was the most physical contact I'd had with a man in years.

"I'm Chase," he said, prying his hand out of mine. He removed a notepad from his shirt pocket. "What unit are you in?"

"Huh?"

"What unit are you in?" he repeated, this time slower.

"I don't live here. I'm interviewing for the apartment management job." I held up the application in case he didn't believe me.

He scrunched his cute face and looked around. "Joyce said there was someone sitting at the picnic table who needed my help."

Note to self: Send Joyce a thank you card.

He looked around the empty courtyard until his stunning green eyes met mine then ventured downward. I pretended not to notice him checking me out but felt myself blushing anyway. "Not sure if you knew this," he said. "But you have a little something..." He pointed to my chest.

I looked down to see the French Vanilla dribbled down the front of my dress.

"Ah, bleep," I said under my breath.

Chase planted his forearms on the table, leaning forward. "Did you just say *bleep*?"

"Oops, yeah, I probably did." I blushed again. "I try not to cuss in front of my daughter, and now it's sort of become a stupid habit." I pulled a package of tissues from my bag and began dabbing the spot.

Now I had an ice cream stain dotted with tissue residue. Great.

Chase laughed. "Wait, you replace profanity with *bleep*?"

"Um...*yes*." I pulled the elastic band out of my hair, releasing my Einstein-inspired dark mane. I tamed Einstein down to a side ponytail and slouched my shoulders. Trying to cover the spot. "Better?"

His face said *no,* but his mouth said, "Sure." And I liked him even more for it.

He slipped the notepad back into his pocket. "What did you need help with?"

I could think of a hundred and two ways he could help me. None of which would be appropriate to ask for, having only known him for about a minute. I glanced at the questionnaire. "Well, I'm curious, how might you handle a tenant who was getting a lot of foot traffic? I'm assuming it's drug-related."

Chase made a *V* with his brows. "Why?"

"There are questions like this on the application. I haven't been an apartment manager before, and I want to get them right."

"I'm not sure. I've never been a manager." He ran a hand through his hair. I resisted the urge to reach over and do the same. "Maybe record all the information in the apartment file?"

I snapped my fingers and pointed at him. "That's a good idea. Then I would call the police once I've gathered enough evidence. Like, who are the visitors? How long do they stay...?" I began writing my answer. "I think the police code for that is, like, 10-50 or something."

Chase shrugged.

"I watch a lot of crime shows," I explained. "I need to get this right because I *really* need this job."

"I'm not sure how much help I can be. But I'll try." He rested his chin on his palm and watched me scrawl down my answer.

"Can't you give someone a three-day notice if they are being loud, or do you have to give them a certain number of warnings before you give the notice?" I asked.

Chase shrugged again. "They told you about Kevin, right? That'd be more concerning than foot traffic."

"Who?"

"He's the owner's son who lives here. He can be a real *bleep*."

My light bulb flipped on. "Does he happen to live in the third courtyard?"

He nodded *yes* then returned his chin to his palm.

"I take it he and Joyce don't get along?"

"You could say that."

I looked past the pool and out to the third courtyard. All I could see from where I sat was another courtyard for Lilly to play in, Chase's left bicep deliciously bulging under his sleeve, and, at the top of the back stairwell, a black door. There appeared to be red paint dripping down the front, and the window beside it was boarded up with fresh wood.

Strange but...*meh.*

It's LA.

I'd encountered every shade of strange since moving here.

If there was anything concerning happening in the third courtyard, it would have been reported on the Rent or Run app. People love to complain.

It would take a lot more than a black door and an unruly teenager to stop me from taking the job, if I were offered it. I still had to get through an interview, and if there was one lesson I'd learned during my employment drought, it was that I was a terrible interviewee. I'd been practicing though. Watching dozens of YouTube videos on what to say, and more importantly, what *not* to say. I prayed I'd be able to come across as poised, skilled, and normal.

I hurried through the questionnaire without further input from Chase, who was summoned away by a bathroom emergency. His presence served only as a physical motivator anyway—and what a physical motivator he was. A cute co-worker could offset whatever was happening with Kevin.

I think.

I should probably get more specifics on that.

When I swung open the lobby door, Joyce was seated in the floral armchair. She looked to have aged during the time I'd been gone.

"Here she is," Joyce announced, sounding as if she had swallowed sandpaper. "This is Patrick." She motioned toward a tall man with a cul-de-sac of brown hair sitting on the couch.

Patrick half stood and held out his hand. I shook it, hoping he didn't notice my sweaty palms. A casual wipe on his pants afterward told me he had. Great.

"Have a seat." He plopped back down and began rummaging through his briefcase.

"Here, take mine," Joyce offered, sliding off the chair. "I'm going to get some packing done."

"Thank you." I slipped into the floral atrocity, feeling like a child waiting in the principal's office. Nerves crawled through my stomach and down to my intestines, butterflying around in my gut. Authoritative figures had this effect on me. It didn't matter how many deep breaths I took or positive thoughts I had—my nerves still managed to get the best of me.

Joyce leaned down. "Good luck. I'm pulling for you," she wheezed into my ear before shuffling back to her apartment.

"You have the application?" Patrick asked. He struck me as a no-nonsense type of guy with his stern face and permanent stress lines around his eyes. He wore khakis, a checkered shirt, a silver band on his left ring finger, and stark white Nike running shoes. His attire reminded me of Forrest Gump.

I handed him the application and watched as he sat back, crossed his Nike over his knee, and read through it. At one point he squinted and looked closer with a scrunch of his forehead. Perhaps moving the drummer in Apartment 19 next to the arguing neighbors in Apartments 6 and 5 wasn't the right answer. I thought the two could bond over their shared hatred of their new neighbor. Then I'd give the drummer a three-day notice to find a new hobby. Seemed like a creative win-win to me.

Patrick tossed the application on the coffee table and grabbed a yellow notepad. "First, you pronounce your name Came-bree-ah not Cam-bree-ah, right?" he asked with a click of his pen.

"Yes. The correct pronunciation of my name is Came-bree-ah." Then, for no apparent reason, I added, "I'm named after the city I was conceived in. Just two teenagers on a little road trip, and bada-bing-bada-boom, here I am."

Whyyy?

Obviously, my nerves had taken my mouth hostage.

Patrick made a noise I believed to be a stifled laugh or a burp. I wasn't sure. I bit my lip, afraid I would ask. He made note of my stupidity on his notepad then continued to ask sharp questions regarding my previous employment and how I might handle situations that seemed unlikely to ever occur. I stammered through, fidgeting with my thumbs, trying to use the whole "think *before* you speak" notion I'd been practicing. When we finished, he placed the notepad on the coffee table and rubbed his temples with his forefingers.

"I will say this," Patrick began. "I was impressed with how you answered the questions on the application. You seem like a 'think outside of the box' kind of person. That's a good quality for this job. I like that you've had some management experience. I spoke to your references yesterday, and they all sang your praises."

I'd used my grandma as a reference.

"I need to tell you this," he continued. "The owner's son lives on the property."

"Oh, I know about Kevin," I hastily interrupted, too desperate to recover from the whole "bada-bing" incident to remember my manners.

Patrick's eyes grew in diameter. "You know about Kevin?"

I nodded. "Chase told me *all* about him, and it's not a problem." His gaping expression told me I might have redeemed myself from the unfortunate "bada-bing" incident.

"That's good to know," he said. "I still have a few people to interview today and will be making my final decision tomorrow. Thanks for coming in."

"My pleasu-roo."

Stop talking, Cambria.

CHAPTER TWO

———

Applicant must be dependable, punctual, and able to multitask without becoming easily frazzled.

I rolled Lilly out of my arms and onto the bed. She flopped over without stirring. The sequins from her Cinderella dress caught the reflection of the light streaming in through the blind slats on the window, causing rainbow specks to dance across the far wall. The display was a little too cheery for my current mood.

I twisted the blinds shut and snuck out. The heat-swollen floorboards squeaked with each careful step. Transferring a sleeping toddler without waking her required ninja-like abilities, a skillset my clumsy self did not come by naturally. I was determined, though, knowing that being productive during Lilly's hours of operation was near impossible. I urgently needed the extra time to stress and sulk and shovel ice cream into my mouth.

It had been one week. *Seven days* since my interview. A park-like courtyard, free rent, two bedrooms, safe neighborhood, and a sexy co-worker: The job was tailor-made for my needs. Then I had to open my mouth and share my conception story of all things.

Bada-bing-bada-boom?

The memory was mortifying. I shook my head as I crept down the hallway, eyeing the dirty laundry tower in the corner of the bathroom. I was wearing a red lace thong I'd found buried in the bottom of my drawer. A memento of a time when a thin piece of fabric shoved up my crack seemed sexy and didn't cause chafing. Now it meant I was out of clean underwear.

With a sigh of defeat, I grabbed my laptop from the hall closet and headed to the living room. As uncomfortable as my wedgie was, it was more doable than laundry. I dragged the cord behind me as I weaved through the sea of toys scattered across the scratchy, vomit-colored carpet. If my mother were here, she'd fall into her routine speech on how I was way too young and far too pretty, with way too much potential, to still be squished into a flea-infested apartment with bars on the windows, homeless women fighting over my trash, a toilet that only occasionally flushed, a neighbor who was frequently visited by his parole officer, and upstairs neighbors who sounded like they tap dance twenty-four hours a day.

She would then take the two-step journey from the living room to the shoebox-sized kitchen, point to the collection of empty ice cream containers lining the counter, and do her signature eye roll. She had this ability to get her entire iris shoved so high up into her lids that only the whites of her eyes showed. It was unnerving. I didn't know she had blue eyes until I was out of adolescence.

When I told my mom I was pregnant, she rolled her eyes so far back into her head I thought she was having a seizure. Her reaction had less to do with the fact that I was unmarried, barely made over minimum wage, and couldn't keep a houseplant alive (although I'm sure it didn't help), and more to do with my determination to raise my baby in Los Angeles. I'd impulsively moved to LA a year earlier with my best friend, Amy. My mother, bless her controlling heart, was upset she wouldn't be able to effectively manage the situation from afar.

However, I had a secret, and the four-hour drive cushion made it easier to keep. I didn't like to think of it as a lie but more of an omission of one detail that would break my father's heart, please that woman he insisted on marrying (my parents divorced when I was eight), and kill my mother.

Cause of death: mortification.

It happened when Amy and I were bar crawling our way down Third Street. Amy had landed the role of Smiling Girl #4 in a toothpaste commercial, and that had to be celebrated—and celebrate we did. We ran into an attractive-enough group of law students who insisted on buying us drinks. The free-flowing alcohol proved a challenge to my system, but I was never one to back down from adversity, and I didn't want to be rude. Both adequate grounds for stupidity.

We laughed. We sipped. We flirted. We gulped. We danced. We glugged. Based on the YouTube video, I serenaded everyone with what was supposed to be Shania Twain's "Man! I Feel Like a Woman!" but sounded more like a Jabba the Hutt impersonation.

After a few (or ten) drinks, one of our almost-attorney fellas caught my attention. Tom Dreyer. Tall, very tall, tousled dark hair, glossed-over hazel eyes, and a side-smirk that had me seeing hearts and flowers and fireworks to the point where I questioned if I were solely under the influence of alcohol. I'd never been a one-night-stand kinda gal. But, hey, there was a first (and last) time for everything.

I walk-of-shamed my red lace-thonged butt out his door the next morning with a hangover that lasted nine months. When I told Tom, he got all lawyer-y on me and demanded a paternity test. Which of course came back positive. I'd been too busy battling morning sickness to have the opportunity to hook up with anyone else. Then he swore. He cried. He cursed. He sobbed. He attached the F-word to a variety of different nouns. Then, he accepted it.

Now, here's where my secret comes in. It was one thing to have a child out of wedlock. It was an entirely different thing to get yourself knocked up while in the midst of a drunken stupor by a guy you'd known all of two minutes. Which is precisely what I did.

When I told my parents, I may have insinuated Tom and I were in a loving, committed relationship. Even though we weren't. Not that I didn't try. Several times. Tom never reciprocated. He did me one worse. He put me in the friend zone. The *Friend Zone*. It's the Alcatraz of zones—escapable only by death. I was devastated. In the midst of my heartbreak, I may have insinuated we broke up. I may have also implied the reason was that Tom had finally come out of the closet. My parents had met him twice and never questioned me on it. It got my grandparents off my case about not getting married first, and honestly, I didn't want my parents to hate Tom for rejecting me then proceeding to stomp on my heart as he slept his way through Los Angeles and Orange County. There was also some Ventura County and San Diego in there. Bottom line: Almost all of Southern California's single ladies had seen Tom naked at some point.

My parents loved the idea of Lilly being raised by a straight mother and gay father, and before I knew it, my mother started marching in parades, and my father started donating to LGBT charities. The lie took on a life of its own, and three years later, my life would be a whole lot easier if Tom would do me a favor and be gay for real. Lying is exhausting.

The saddest part of that story, aside from the fact that my fake relationship with Tom was the last relationship I'd had, was that Smiling Girl #4 was edited out of the commercial. Poor Amy. Those veneers were expensive.

I opened my laptop. A reflection of my puffy eyes and freckled face stared back at me from the dark computer screen. I'd never considered myself a beauty like Amy. I was attractive enough. My deep blue eyes were a nice contrast to my nearly black mane.

"God gave you those striking eyes to take the attention away from your hair," Grandma Ruthie used to say. She was right. I definitely had something to work with. However, glaring back at me was a pale twenty-eight-year-old with a massive zit on her nose to match the one on her forehead. It was anything but cute. If I were to have sprung for the seventeen-inch model, the screen would've been able to fit Einstein in as well.

I wiggled my finger on the mouse pad to erase the image and clicked over to my email.

Thirteen new messages. Most from clothing stores taunting me with fall sales. Two were from my dad—one informing me of his success with a particular sexual enhancement drug. Gross. Another apologizing that he had been hacked again. Nothing from Patrick, and no replies from the batch of résumés I'd sent out.

I felt queasy, miserable, and lost. Melting into the couch, I hugged the brown fake leather while yielding to another sickening wave of anxiety. *Why is adulting so hard?*

The front door flung open and crashed against the wall. The entire apartment shook as if a 4.2 had just rolled through. I jumped off the couch, ready to attack my insolent intruder. *You wake my kid, I kill you.*

Tom stood in the doorjamb wide-eyed and stock-still. I dropped my arms. *Lilly is asleep. What is wrong with you?* I mouthed.

Sorry. Pie is lure door docked, he mouthed back.

"What?" I whispered.

He traversed the threshold in one long step, stopping inches from where I stood, and bent his six-foot-five frame in half, his face close. Too close. I hadn't brushed my teeth all day. Oops.

"Why is your door unlocked?" he whispered.

"Shhh." I sprayed the inside of my hand with my Funyuns breath. "If she hears you she'll never go back down."

We paused and waited for the high-pitched shriek of a toddler abruptly woken. The only noise came from Mr. and Mrs. Nguyen, my sweet next-door neighbors who were both hard of hearing. Through the paper-thin walls, I was privy to every conversation they shouted and every show they blasted. They were watching *Jurassic Park* with Vietnamese voice-over.

Screeching dinosaurs. No screaming Lilly. Disaster averted. I swiveled my attention back to Tom. "Why don't you knock?"

"Sorry." He held up a bag from Ben & Jerry's and flashed his bleached smile. "I brought ice cream."

"Forgiven." I snatched the bag out of his hand and padded back to my spot on the couch. Inside was a Salted Caramel Core waffle taco. Chewy brownie bits and salty sweetness churned together and piled in a buttery-crisp wafer. *Mmmmmm.* Ice cream taco is my favorite kind of taco.

Tom dumped himself down on the couch and used Lilly's Barbie castle as a footrest, throwing his hands behind his head and stretching his long body out. "How long has Lil been asleep?"

"It's Lil-eee." I pushed his feet off the toy with my leg and unwrapped my taco.

"You're in a good mood."

"Sorry. I'm in the midst of a meltdown," I professed in between bites.

"No news on the job?"

I shook my head.

"I'm sure something will work out," he said casually. Stress was not in his vocabulary. No matter the situation, he assumed everything would "work out in the end" without worrying one step of the way. It was a completely foreign concept to me.

"I'm sure it will," I humored, wiping caramel off my mouth with the back of my hand. "What's with the ice cream anyway?"

"I was in the area and thought you and Lilly might want to split it." He leaned over and eyed the nearly empty package once containing my treat. "Or just you."

"Aw, that's *sweeeeet*."

He laughed. "I'm sorta seeing a girl who works there, and she hooked me up."

Curse you, Alcatraz friend zone.

"I've got something else to cheer you up." He reached into his back pocket and pulled out a coupon for a free burrito from a restaurant I'd never heard of. "I helped the guy who owns this place, and he gave me a couple of these. Looks good." Tom's clients showed their appreciation for his law abilities with free car washes, oil changes, haircuts, and even landscaping (which was of no use to him. He has a two-bedroom apartment in Mar Vista. He took a houseplant instead, which he killed. We're better parents than gardeners, I swear.) Cash would be a nicer form of gratitude, except Tom was a criminal defense attorney at a small firm with low-income clientele. He also had this thing about only representing innocent people, which, in my opinion, was just lazy lawyering. He should challenge himself and take on rich criminals, perhaps a money-laundering CEO who'd throw money at Tom to keep himself out of jail. Of course, Tom wanted no part of that. He had a moral agenda to uphold, and it paid peanuts. Or in this case, burritos.

All that schooling and all that student debt, and in the end, he was as poor as me (before the no-job situation). If only

I'd gotten knocked up by a lawyer with a desire to make money, then maybe my child support check would cover the electric bill.

I shoved the remaining bits of ice cream into my mouth, letting the salty caramel dissolve on my tongue before swallowing. The taco hit my intestines like a brick. I may have overdone it. I placed the bag down just as my sweatpants began to vibrate. I grabbed my phone from between my underwear and the elastic waistband of my sweats.

An unrecognizable number flashed across the screen. My stomach flipped. I raced to the bathroom and shut the door. "Hello," I answered with a smile.

"You have a chance to lower your debt," a recording announced.

Smile gone.

I hit *End* and shoved the phone into my pocket. It began to vibrate again. I knew it was the same recording. During my employment drought, I had entered every online sweepstakes I could find and didn't win anything except nightly solicitors wanting to lower my debt or refinance my nonexistent mortgage.

I placed the phone back up to my ear. In my most annoyed voice, I said, "Hellooo?"

"Hello?" a man's deep voice replied.

I pulled the phone away from my ear and looked down at the screen. A 424 area code. My heart regurgitated into my throat. "Hello?"

"This is Patrick from Elder Property Management."

Palm, meet forehead. "Hello, Patrick! How are you doing this day?"

"I'm doing fine. I'm calling because I would like to offer you the apartment manager job."

...

"Hello?"

...

"Cambria? You there?"

...

"Cambria? Hello?"

"Um, yes. Sorry. Yes, I'm here. That's...wonderful!"

"I'd like you to start Monday. That'll give you five days with Joyce before she moves. We should be able to get her apartment turned over by Sunday. I realize that doesn't give you much time to move. Due to the short notice, I'll cover a lease-breaking fee on your apartment and a little extra cash to help with the move."

"I'm on a month-to-month, so that shouldn't be a problem." I was getting kicked out anyway. "There's one thing though." *Breathe, Cambria.*

I had to calm my enthusiasm and rationalize my thoughts. I wanted this job. I *needed* this job. There was one issue I dare only raise now that I had the job. Patrick sighed into the phone.

"Thank you so much for offering me the position. I would love to accept the job. However, I have a daughter—she's three—and the amount of smoke is a concern. I'm hoping you'll consider changing the carpet at least."

"Oh, the smoke." He sounded relieved. "We'll be doing the whole works on the apartment. Carpet, paint, counters. I've already discussed this with our new maintenance man, and he said he could get rid of the smell, and then we'll air out the lobby."

"New maintenance man?" My heart sank. "What happened to Chase?"

"He is the new maintenance man."

Happy jig.

"Now," Patrick continued. "I would prefer for you to train alone. Once you move in, I'm fine with your daughter being there during office hours."

I may have peed my pants. "Patrick, I promise I'll do an exceptional job. Thank you for the opportunity." It felt like my chest had been pumped full of helium.

"Thank *you* for taking it," Patrick said with an odd fluctuation of his stern voice. I was too high on excitement and relief to be bothered by the implication. "Have a good day."

"You too." I hung up.

Yes!

I threw my arms up in silent victory and smacked my hand on the shower rod. Causing it to crash into the tub. Taking my shampoo, soap, and Lilly's bath toys with it. Lilly screamed. Now I had to put a frightened toddler back to bed and clean up my grubby bathroom. But who cared? Life just took a major upswing toward fabtabulousness. Which isn't a word.

* * *

"But totally should be," Amy conceded when she arrived early Monday morning. "I think it should be our new mantra."

I opened the front door wider for her. All I could see was the top of her blonde and pink bun piled high on her head over the mound of clothing and shoes cradled in her arms. The girl had the figure of a ruler. Unless she had a pair of magical Spanx in there, I doubted I'd be able to squeeze into any of her doll-sized clothes.

"I love that idea. We should bedazzle it on some shirts and start a Facebook page. *The Fabtabulous Females of Los Angeles*." I laughed at my wittiness. Amy did not. "Too far?"

"You lost me at bedazzled."

"That's the best part."

"Let's concentrate on the task at hand before we start adding rhinestones to stuff." She emptied her load onto my bed and spread out the clothes. She had on a pair of denim shorts that looked like Lilly cut them, all frayed and stringy, and a black tank top with a pink bra strap sliding off her shoulder. She was roughly eighty-percent leg, five-percent torso, and the rest was all boob. I was the Ethel to her Lucy. The Mary Ann to her Ginger. The Patrick to her SpongeBob. I was the typically scripted shorter, less cute, rollier best friend. I provided the comic relief and the logic. It was a role I was comfortable with.

"If I'd known you were planning to bring your closet, I would have come to your place instead." I leaned against the doorway, watching her hold up a shimmery, low-cut shirt, eyeing it with a tilt of her head. Amy had always been my go-to stylist when more than a Target Mossimo shirt and jeans were required.

Amy and I went back a long way. We'd bonded back in third grade over Lisa Frank pencil boxes and our mutual love of the monkey bars. Sometime during that year, while hanging upside down from the bars, the tips of her blonde braids touching the sand and my Einstein hair remaining unmoved (it tends to look the same whether I'm upright or upside-down), we pinky-promised to remain best friends forever. Even in high school, when she was president of the drama club and I was on the soccer team, we remained close. Sleepovers every Friday and Saturday nights, shoving notes into each other's lockers, we even went to sophomore homecoming together. (We weren't exactly what you would call popular. We had each other, so it didn't matter—too much.)

Some years ago, while watching a *Project Runway* marathon, Amy sat up, having an epiphany of sorts, and announced we were moving to Los Angeles to pursue her acting career. She didn't ask me to come along, nor had I asked if I could. Neither of us questioned it. We did everything together. I'd long since dropped out of college, and she was working as a waitress, a job she hated. "What do we have to lose?" she had asked, and I couldn't think of anything. So off we went.

Maybe it was because we were both only children, or maybe it was because we were both the same kind of crazy. Either way, we built a lasting friendship seasoned with trials, tears, and an ocean's worth of Diet Coke—as well as the occasional makeover.

Amy tossed the shimmery shirt back on the bed. "I brought everything because I wasn't sure what state your hair was going to be in." She turned around, and her clear blue eyes widened in exasperation.

"What?"

She grunted and dug through the pile again, pulling out a white shirt that looked as if it belonged to Lilly. "We need to pull attention away from what you have happening on top of your dome." She pointed to Einstein shoved into a knot on the top of my head. "Here, try this on."

She handed me the shirt, and I held it up to half of my chest. "This is not going to fit."

"Trust me. I'll have you looking like an apartment manager in no time."

"Do you even know what an apartment manager is supposed to look like?" I pulled my oversized shirt over my head and shimmied my way out of a pair of yoga pants that were stained with the remnants of every meal I'd eaten since Friday.

Amy shrugged. "Not exactly. But I have a good idea of where I'm going. Plus…yikes. Cambria, honestly." She took a step closer, shaking her head. The diamond stud in her newly carved nose caught the overhead lighting. I went cross-eyed looking at it. "When was the last time you plucked that brow? You realize there are supposed to be two, right?"

After an hour of tweezing, blow-drying, and bobby pinning, Amy stepped back to admire her work. "Voilà!" She kissed the tips of her fingers and tossed them into the air. "Perfection. You know I'm not doing this every morning, right?"

"I know," I whispered, barely able to squeeze the words out. The Spanx Amy talked me into were not conducive to breathing. Dots danced in my peripheral vision. "I wanted to look good on my first day. That's all."

"Suuuuure you did." She leaned in and yanked one more hair off my face with her tweezers.

"Ouch!"

"OK, now you're done." She tossed the hateful instrument back into her bag. "I've gotta get going. I have an audition in"—she checked her phone—"fifteen minutes. I'll come back and grab my stuff later. Tell the cute maintenance guy I said hi. Love ya." She kissed the air and bolted out of the bathroom. "Bye, baby," I heard her say to Lilly, who was lying on the couch in a *Mickey Mouse Clubhouse* trance.

I hoisted myself off the toilet seat and turned around to get a look in the mirror. I was wearing the *tight* white shirt, tucked into my own *tight* black pencil skirt—the one everyone said I looked good in. But I hated the skirt because it made my butt look three times bigger than it already was. Apparently, that's a good thing. Small gold hoops dangled from my ears, which complimented the gold chains drooping down my chest. Einstein was tamed into a tight bun at the nape of my neck, and my feet were crushed into a pair of Amy's red stilettos. My face was creatively painted on, which deviated from my usual mascara, lip gloss, and blush routine. I didn't look like an apartment manager per se. More like a librarian who moonlights as an escort. If I wasn't almost running late, I might have changed.

As it was, I hustled out as fast as my skirt and stilettos would allow, scooting Lilly along, feeling frazzled and clumsy. Three steps out the door and I was in Mrs. Nguyen's apartment dropping Lilly off. Mrs. Nguyen worked from home as a seamstress, and Mr. Nguyen (I couldn't pronounce their first names for the life of me, so we kept it formal) worked mostly as a mason and sometimes as a pedicurist at his cousin's salon. They were both in their sixties and barely spoke English. And they were the sweetest human beings I'd ever encountered. We referred to them as Lilly's SoCal grandparents, since my parents were in Fresno and Tom's were in Tahoe. They'd been helping me with Lilly since the day she was born. Having them next door would be the only thing I'd miss about living in what I'd lovingly nicknamed Crap-o-la Apartments.

"I love you." I kissed the top of Lilly's head and brushed a dark curl behind her ear. Her heart-shaped face, sparkling hazel eyes, and pouty lips always made it hard to say good-bye. "Be good," I warned.

"She good. Go, go." Mrs. Nguyen waved me off, drying her hands on the apron tied around her waist. "You be late. Go!"

"*Tạm biệt!*" Lilly yelled after me as I ran down the stairs. She'd become quite fluent in Vietnamese thanks to her SoCal grandparents.

As soon as I drove out of the parking garage, my car was pelted with tiny raindrops. Lucky for me, there was enough Aqua Net on my head to keep Einstein from reaching Phil Spector status.

Unlucky for me, no one in LA can drive in the rain.

My Civic moved along at a sluggish pace behind all the drivers going at sloth speed while they marveled at the wet stuff dripping from the sky. I even saw a news van parked near an exit. A female reporter stood in front of the camera wearing a yellow poncho, gesturing to the strange phenomenon foreigners referred to as "a light mist" and we Southern Californians called "Armageddon." Any deviation from warm and sunny turned the freeways into parking lots.

I compiled a mental list of reasons why I dared to be late on my first day while racing toward the sad brown doors. Traffic didn't seem a suitable answer. There was always traffic.

I was in a terrible car accident, and despite the fact there isn't a scratch on me, I almost died.

I stopped to help another because I am a responsible samaritan.

I was looking at the surrounding apartment buildings, you know, checking out the competition.

Oh, that's a good one.

I grabbed the rusty knob, using my momentum to push open the door. It was locked. I bounced off it like a rubber ball and stumbled backwards, barely missing the mud puddle.

I used my purse as an umbrella, searched around the stucco archway for a doorbell, and found one hidden behind a plant. It took two rings before Joyce appeared, engulfed in a fluffy pink robe and her hair still in curlers. She hadn't drawn in her brows yet, and her face was crinkly and pale. "Good morning, Joyce," I said sweetly, pretending my heart wasn't hammering in my chest.

CHAPTER THREE

———

The Lessor will be hereinafter referred to as "Landlord," and the Lessee will be hereinafter referred to as "Tenant." The parties to this lease agree to the following:
Tenant agrees to refrain from all felonious activity while on the Premises. This includes all Common Areas.

"Morning. You're early," Joyce said. I was ten minutes late, but who was I to argue? "Come on in." She opened the door wider, allowing me enough room to scoot past her. "You look *nice,* but a pair of jeans and a shirt will do if you want. Patrick isn't picky about wardrobe."

My face went cherry. I pulled at the hem of my skirt. "Sorry."

"Don't be sorry. Maybe letting the girls out will help you rent apartments." She was serious. I forced a chuckle, pulling at the top of my shirt. Willing it shut to no avail. "Check the machine while I finish getting ready, and then we'll start."

Joyce shuffled back to her apartment, closing and locking the door behind her.

Time to get to work.

I mentally cracked my knuckles and took a seat on my *new* (to me) chair, behind my *new* (to me) desk, in my *new* (to me) office, ready to...*sweet mother of all that is rotten.*

"What is that smell!" I said, out loud, to myself.

Blech.

Desperate to find the source, I sniffed under the desk. In the filing cabinet. Behind the computer. Inside the trash can. Under my arm...

Giving up, I cracked a window, went back to the desk, and searched around for a pen and pad of paper. The answering machine was easier to locate, given it was twice the size of my head and at least as old as Joyce.

You have five new messages.

Message received 7:45 p.m.

Joyce, it's Larry. Yeah, hey, my toilet stopped working, and I need Bob to come take a look at it. Soon, please, 'cause I gotta go. Thanks.

Message received 8:35 p.m.

Joyce, it's Silvia. I don't normally complain, but the tenant in Apartment 32 is urinating on his highly visible upstairs balcony. It's incredibly rude and disturbing, not to mention unsanitary.

Message received 2:15 a.m.

Trent would rather spend his only weekend off with his ex. So, let me know what I need to do to get him off my lease.

Message received 2:19 a.m.

I haven't seen my kid in a few months, and Alexis is getting all volatile over nothing again. She threw a pot at my head.

Message received 5:45 a.m.

It's Kenneth. Sorry to call early...but I was on my way out when I saw...there's...uh...with a spider web!...

End of messages.

I stared at the primordial machine, my lower jaw nearly resting on my cleavage, unsure what to make of Alexis and Trent and Larry and...what happened to Kenneth? The message was hard to hear. He was out of breath, his voice muffled. I leaned over and pushed *Play* to listen again.

Messages erased. You have no new messages.

Oops.

A chime echoed through the lobby, and a woman appeared behind the counter. It was the tube top brunette from the day I interviewed. This time she wore a red bandana as a shirt.

She snapped her gum. "I know you, right?"

I blinked, in an attempt to erase the image of Larry peeing off his patio from my brain, then stood and met her at the counter. "Yes. I'm Cambria. I fell down next door."

"Ooh, right, right, right. You, like, work here?" The Valleyspeak accent was strong in this one.

"I do now," I said. "I'm taking over for Joyce."

She pouted her glossed bottom lip. "So sad. I like her. My Boo will be totally bummed."

"What apartment does your Boo live in?" I asked.

"He's in Apartment 39." She plopped a folded-up rental application onto the counter. "I printed this off the website." *We have a website?* "I'm moving in with him. Yay me." She clapped. "Joyce said if I wanted to live here, I have to, like, have an application in or whatever."

"That's correct." I had no clue. "I'm sorry. I didn't catch your name."

"Wysteria, with a *y*. It's totally my work name, so you can call me Alice, 'cause that's, like, my real name. It's on the app." She pointed a freshly painted crimson fingernail at her name. The *i* dotted with a heart.

"Nice to meet you, Alice. I just need a copy of your driver's license," I said, reading the directions on the top of the application. I went ahead and skimmed through the rest of the paperwork. All the information appeared to be in place. Previous rental history, contact information, employer...The Palace. Occupation: striptease artist.

Surprisingly, I knew of The Palace. I'd interviewed there, thinking it was a restaurant. And it is: a topless one.

Alice handed me a folded copy of a student identification card from a college I'd never heard of. Which meant nothing. There were over fifteen junior colleges and trade schools in the area. At least that's what my mother said at the end of every conversation. "I totally left my license at a club and haven't gone to the DMV yet. Please don't tell my Boo. He gets really mad when I lose stuff, and he's totally sick with a gnarly cold right now." She held up a Vons bag filled with remedies and smiled until her bra started singing. "Oops. Hold on a sec." She pulled her phone out of her cleavage and answered. "Hi

Boo…no, I'm on my way right now." She pointed to my shirt and mouthed *Super cute. I totally want.*

I gave a thumbs-up.

She opened the door. "I told you I was going to go get some stuff… I'm walking back now… Don't worry…" I could hear Alice arguing with Boo until the door shut behind her.

I glanced down at my shirt—it was threatening to pop open with my next breath.

Thanks, Amy!

The door creaked open behind me, and Joyce shuffled in. Her eyebrows were back on, her pale cheeks rouged, and her red hair was looking extra voluminous and highly flammable. Not a good combination for a woman who smokes as much as she does.

"Any messages?" Joyce said as she took a seat on the other side of the L-shaped desk.

"A few." I returned to my *new* (to me) chair.

"That's the first thing you'll do every morning. Never bring the phone into the apartment with you at night. Trust me. You get people calling at two in the morning wanting to look at vacant apartments. If someone needs to get ahold of you, they'll call the emergency line, and that is directed to your cell phone… Why aren't you writing this down?"

"Oh, sorry." I sat up straight and poised my pen. "I'm ready."

"Good," she continued. "Speaking of emergencies, don't ever call Patrick unless it's a big one. He likes his managers to handle everything. The less work he has to do here, the happier he'll be, and in your case, you want to make him really happy."

I dropped my pen. "Why is that?"

"Because the only reason you got the job is because the two other applicants Patrick offered it to both turned it down. So here you are."

Well, that's a comforting tidbit of information.

"Do you know why he didn't want to hire me?" Not that I had to ask. *Bada-bing-bada-boom!*

"Could be because the maintenance boy put up such a stink about you not working here. Or was I not supposed to tell you that?" Joyce brought her hand up to her chin. The track lighting turned her skin translucent and her bulging veins a purplish blue. She thought for a moment before reaching her conclusion. "Nope, I was not supposed to say anything. Chase specifically told me not to. Forget it."

It felt like a bus had just rolled onto my chest, parked, and unrolled a convoy. "Joyce, I can't forget about it. Why would Chase say anything? I spent ten minutes with the guy. He doesn't even know me." Surely she had to be talking about someone else. Chase wouldn't do that. He was kind, loving, compassionate, hot, and an amazing, toe-curling kisser...or at least he was all those things in my imagination. I'd only met him once, and he'd already been tattooed on my brain. It said *I Lust Chase* in Lucida Handwriting twelve-point font right across my striatum, and tattoos are a pain to remove. I would know. I had one laser treatment to try to remove the dolphin permanently stuck to my lower back, but the pain rivaled childbirth, and the cost nearly killed me, so I opted to live with Flipper forever.

"It's my fault, really. I thought if you met him you'd be more inclined to take the job. Now forget about it. That ship has sunk." She swiveled her chair around and yanked open the filing cabinet, removing a manila folder.

That ship has sailed? Or sunk? Either way, I guess the ship was gone. What a disappointment. I wanted to sail on that ship.

I slumped into the chair. "Why did the two other applicants turn down the job?" I asked.

She swiveled back to the desk. "Kevin stories I suppose."

Right, Kevin. I thought back to the black door. Seemed like as good a time as any to broach the subject. "Can you tell me more about Kevin?" I asked.

"Kevin is...interesting."

"What do you mean '*interesting*'?" I pressed.

"I mean, you'll have to hike that bridge when you get to it."

Joyce clearly struggled with idioms.

"Should I *hike* back to his apartment and introduce myself today?" I asked.

"*Nah*. He's gone and won't be back until Friday. I'm sure you'll get a chance to meet him." She smirked, as if remembering a joke. "Now, what did the messages say?"

Messages? Oh, the messages. I cleared my throat, attempting to remove the basketball-sized lump now wedged in there. "Trent wants to spend the weekend with his kid, so Alexis threw a pot at his head and would like him to move out. Larry is peeing on his patio because his toilet is broken. Kenneth called. He sounded out of breath. Something about a spider web then he hung up. And Alice, who goes by Wysteria, dropped off an application so she can move in with her boyfriend in Apartment 39."

Joyce nodded along, as if this were an everyday occurrence. "I've been asking Wysteria to bring in an application for a while. Be sure you have a copy of her ID then send it all over to Patrick. He doesn't rush roommate applications, so it may be awhile. Alexis and Trent have been having problems since she started snooping on his Facebook thing. Don't worry. They'll be fine. I'll call Kenneth back while you write out a maintenance report for Larry's toilet."

"That's it?" Even at Crap-o-la Apartments no one had been caught peeing on their patio. Having sex, sure. Peeing, nope. "Should we write Larry up? I mean, what are we going to do about him using his patio as a urinal?"

"Fix his toilet." She handed me the maintenance notebook. "Fill out an order, and give it to Bob."

"Bob? Why Bob? What about Chase?" Did he hate me so much he'd rather quit than work with me? What could I have said to him? Such a waste of Spanx.

"Normally, Sundays and Mondays are our days off. He won't be around much until Friday anyway. He starts full…" Joyce's voice trailed off. "You smell that?"

"Yes!" I said, thankful. *Phew.* I was worried the odor was permanent. "I can't figure out where it's coming from though."

Joyce yanked open the bottom drawer of the desk and dug around until she produced a sandwich bag of gray and green fuzzy mush. Gross.

I pinched my nose. "What is that? Or, what was it?"

"Tuna. Was Saturday's lunch. I forgot about it." She dropped the stale fish into the trash can, tied the trash bag, pulled it out, and dropped it onto my lap. "Dumpster's in the carports. Hurry back. We have a lot to cover in a short period of time."

* * *

The carports horseshoed the building with a single, narrow space marked for each apartment. A rickety gate guarded the entrance, squawking the arrival of each car as it passed through. The rain had stopped, turning the ground into a slimy terrain of oil and debris. The driveway looked to have been paved sometime during the Vietnam War and not touched since. My heels slid into the cracks veining through the asphalt, and I hurried across, trying not to get hit by one of the many cars speeding over the bumpy terrain. It was a real-life game of Frogger. I managed to make it to the other side with only a scuffed toe.

Fifty points for me!

The dumpster was large, at least six yards wide and one person deep. Much bigger than the one at Crap-O-La. They must take their trash dumping around here seriously, I thought.

The mammoth of a trash can was pushed up against the maintenance garage. Just seeing the word maintenance brought my blood to a boil. What could I have said to make Chase not want to work with me? If the other two applicants hadn't turned down the job, I would have been screwed. It didn't make any sense. Maybe I was drooling? Maybe he didn't like that I had asked him for advice? Maybe he was just a butthole? I had no idea but had every intention of finding out, soon. In the meantime I pointed my nose to the sky and strutted past the garage, even if it was closed and even if Chase was nowhere near it. It was good practice.

I threw open the lid to the dumpster and swung the trash over the side, with a quick glance down before I released...*is that?*

I gasped.

A button flew off my shirt and hit the side of the dumpster with a *ping*.

An assortment of wallets were scattered along the bottom corner of the bin. They appeared to have spilled out of the black backpack lying beside them. I counted twelve wallets in total. All looked new and quite expensive. I wouldn't have given one or two wallets any thought, but twelve? It wasn't right. Why would someone throw away so many good wallets?

With a quick glance around to be sure no one was watching, I dropped the trash bag and hoisted myself up, resting my stomach on the side of the bin, teetering like a human seesaw, and...*oomph!* I would have face-planted at the bottom of the bin if the backpack hadn't broken my fall. It smelled like dead rats and gym socks, but still better than the office.

I awkwardly moved into a catcher stance and began gathering the wallets into a leathery mountain. Each still had identification inside, along with gym passes, Vons Club cards, meal cards from Café Rio, unopened condoms, and business cards. No credit cards, debit cards, or money. I scanned the IDs in search of a familiar face. All belonged to California drivers, and all addresses were located in the Los Angeles area. All were male, and none looked familiar.

These were stolen, I realized. Someone stole the wallets, took all the cash and credit cards, and then dumped them in here. What other explanation could there be?

The bin was about half empty (or half full if you're optimistic), so these would have had to be tossed recently. The rickety gate only opened with a transmitter, and the pedestrian gate required a key. It couldn't have been someone passing by, looking for a quick place to dump his or her stolen goods.

I turned my attention to the backpack. Unlike the wallets, the backpack looked worn, the coloring faded and the stitching frayed. The pain shooting down my face told me it wasn't empty either, and being that it hadn't detonated when I landed on it, chances were it wasn't an explosive.

Realizing I was now dealing with a potential crime scene, I figured I should probably stop getting my fingerprints all over the evidence. I grabbed a Popsicle wrapper that was stuck to the inside of the bin and used it to unzip the backpack. Irrational decisions traveled through my mind by way of rocket, while logic voyaged by donkey. It wasn't until the backpack was open flat and I was staring down at the contents that logic finally did stroll in.

A handful of zip ties and a black ski mask—both scandalous items on their own—were minimized by the handgun in the middle of the pile. The dark tarnished barrel sparked a fear deep in my Spanxed gut.

A small, blue rectangle lid stuck out from behind the mask. I knew what it looked like, although I had to be wrong. That would be absurd. However, the entire morning had been absurd what with urinating residents, malicious maintenance men, quarrelling couples, moldy tuna, five a.m. calls about a spider web, and now a gun in the dumpster. So, really, anything was possible.

I covered my pointer finger and thumb with the sticky side of the wrapper and, ever so lightly, grabbed the blue lid and pulled.

What. The. Hell?

I was right. It was exactly what it looked like.

"Hey, you down there! What do you think you're doing?"

Startled, I let out a high-pitched yelp, which echoed around in the tin bin. I grasped my chest and heaved a sigh of relief when Joyce's little head appeared.

"You're that pressed for cash that you need to start dumpster diving?" From my squatted position, everything south of Joyce's nose was hidden. The sunbursts of wrinkles around her squinted eyes told me she was smiling. Pleased with her wittiness. "Wait, is that yours?"

"No! *No...no...no...*I found it in here. Look." I gestured to the open backpack and wallets.

Her little eyes went wide. "Stay right there," she instructed, as if moving was an option. My skirt was too tight, and my heels were too high. Leaving the dumpster would require the delayering of clothing. With one missing button, I was halfway there anyhow.

Metal scratched along the asphalt, followed by a deafening bang against the outside of the bin. Ouch!

Joyce's head and upper torso appeared, with her curved, arthritic hands holding the side as she bent down to get a better look. "You found all this in here?" Her smoker's breath came right at me and filled the tiny quarters.

Blech!

"Well, what's the verdict?" Joyce asked.

With my nose buried into the crook of my elbow, I said, "Huh?" but it sounded more like, "Honk?"

"What is it?"

"Honk?"

"The test, positive or negative?"

Oh, that. I held the blue lid of the pregnancy test between my plastic-wrapped fingers and flipped it around. It answered Joyce's question with a tiny *YES* printed in the middle of the display.

"Well?" Joyce pressed, her eighty-year-old eyes not able to make out the small print from her step stool.

"It's positive," I affirmed.

"That's good. I guess. Now you know, so you can get out of there. Tenants kept calling to say a prostitute was going through our trash. Now I get to tell everyone they don't have anything to worry about. It was just their new apartment manager." She laughed herself into a coughing fit.

I waited for her to start breathing again before saying, "Joyce, this is serious. We could be looking at some incriminating evidence here."

She actually rolled her eyes at me. "If you want to survive as an apartment manager, you're gonna have to start loosening up. Or take a Xanax. Benadryl helps too. It's just a pregnancy test, not worth jumping into trash cans or screaming over. Bob found one floating in the pool not that long ago."

"I didn't *scream.* I yelped. And that's disgusting. But it's not the pregnancy test, Joyce. It's everything else. The zip ties, the stolen wallets, the gun—"

"Gun?" I had her attention now.

"Yeah, gun." I used the pregnancy test as a pointer. "See? Gun."

Her jaw dropped half an inch. "In all my years…"

My legs were going numb. "Can you call the police while I put everything back… Ouch!" A bag of trash landed on my head and spewed its contents down my back. I almost threw up. Why wouldn't you look *inside* the dumpster before tossing your trash in?

Some people can be so inconsiderate.

"Hi, Ty!" Joyce hollered to the owner of (what I hoped was) the chocolate milk running down my shirt. "Ty and his wife just had a baby girl last week," she told me.

"Yeah, I guessed that." I plucked the dirty diaper off my head. "Can you go call the…" I noticed a shoe sticking out from under a pile of trash bags. A Nike sneaker. A very nice, very new, very expensive-looking Nike sneaker. The bottom white, the swoosh a vibrant blue.

Great.

"Looks like our thief also fancies expensive footwear." I grabbed the shoe with my popsicle stick fingers to show Joyce, except it was caught on something.

One more yank and I realized the shoe wasn't caught on anything.

It was attached—to a person.

Now seemed like a really good time to scream.

CHAPTER FOUR

———

Tenant understands that Landlord does not provide security patrol, security system, or surveillance video on the Premises or Common Areas.

Within minutes of my uttering the words "I...f-f-f-f-ound a d-d-ead p-p-p-person and a-a- pregnancy test!" to the police dispatch operator, there were sirens, marked and unmarked police cars, caution tape, a full team of detectives, and a handful of paramedics—even though I was quite insistent on the phone that the body I found in the dumpster was in fact dead.

Like dead, dead.

No pulse.

No breath.

Cold to the touch.

Dead.

And, trust me. I may have been hyperventilating, but I thoroughly checked for signs of life. Which was difficult. The body—a short, stout male with white hair, crinkly skin, Nike jumpsuit on—was facedown, buried in trash, and quite heavy. Impossible for me to flip over. Especially while wearing my hooker clothes.

Note to self: Jeans and a T-shirt are definitely the right attire for the job.

After the crime scene had been secured, I was pulled aside by a detective named Angela Spray. I stood there with my skirt on crooked, my shirt barely hanging on, my red stiletto straps draped over my fingers, and my nerves shattered as I recounted how I happened to fall into a crime scene.

Detective Spray nodded along. She was a no-nonsense

type of gal wearing a three-sizes-too-big gray suit, like she'd recently lost a great deal of weight but couldn't be bothered to buy new clothes. Behind her, I watched another detective drop the wallets into a bag with a latex-clad hand before he walked back to the cluster of police cars and dark SUVs. The flashing lights brightly alternated against the building. Red then blue then red then blue then red then blue. It was a scene right out of *CSI: NY*, minus the hot actors.

A group of concerned-looking residents were gathered far enough to not be in the way yet close enough to hear what was going on. *"Who was it that died?...Someone who lives here?...Is that the new manager?...What is she wearing?...Is she the one who found the body?"*

Detective Spray cleared her throat, reclaiming my attention. "So I have this right, you were already *in* the dumpster when you found the deceased?" she asked.

The group of residents gasped.

"...She was in the dumpster first...Why was she in there?...Isn't it obvious. She was going through our trash, looking for valuables...Like a dumpster diver?"

Great.

"Yes, like I said, I *fell* in," I replied, in an exaggerated hushed voice, hoping the detective would mimic my tone.

No such luck. "And you found the wallets and pregnancy test first, correct?" she bellowed.

"Did she just say the new manager is pregnant?...Yes...Oh my gosh, you can totally tell..."

Why are so many people home?

Doesn't anyone have a job around here?

Geesh.

I scanned the crowd for Joyce and spotted her speaking to a detective. Her face was drawn, eyes tired, and she was still slouched on her step stool—just as I'd left her. After I found the body, she had turned a grim shade of gray. Worried I'd have two deaths on my hands, I got her situated on the stool before I scuttled off to call the police.

"You don't think the body is someone who lives here, right?" I asked Detective Spray. *Please say no. Please say no. Please say no.*

"I'm sorry. They haven't released the victim's name yet," she said. "You didn't get a look at his face?"

I gave a feeble shake of my head. A soy sauce packet fell out of Einstein. We both watched it sail to the ground with a splat.

Er, I wonder what else is in there?

Done with her interview, Joyce shuffled over and placed a hand on my shoulder for support, waiting for her breath to return before speaking. "Twenty-five years," she said between breaths. "And this is the first time I've had a resident die on me"

"How do you know it was a resident?" I asked.

"I got a look before they took him away," she said. "It was definitely Kenneth Fisk from Apartment 21. There's no mistaking that face, looks like the rear end of a rhino."

What a lovely visual.

"God bless his soul." Joyce crossed herself.

Even though I'm not Catholic, I made the sign of the cross for poor—

"Wait! Kenneth?" I said, mid cross. "How many people named Kenneth live here?"

Joyce stared up at me. "Well none now!"

Helpful.

I turned to the detective. "Kenneth left a message this morning on the answering machine. Something about how he was on his way out and there was a spider web. He sounded out of breath." Was the phone call a cry for help? Could the last words out of Kenneth's mouth have been 'spider web'?"

"What time was the message?" Detective Spray asked, her voice perked.

"It was early, just before six I think."

"Is it still on the machine?" she asked.

"It is…crap. I erased it." I mentally slapped my forehead.

Then I physically slapped my forehead because, ugh, why did I have to touch the machine!

To be fair, I had no idea Kenneth would turn up dead an hour later.

But still, erasing the messages was well worth a forehead slap (or two).

While I smacked my head, Detective Spray turned her attention to Joyce. Not that I blamed her. Between the dumpster diving, head slapping, message erasing, and hooker clothes, it's not as if I came off as credible.

Spray further questioned Joyce about Kenneth. His character. Temperament. Did he get along with the neighbors? When was the last time she saw him alive? Did he have visitors often, if at all? I stood beside Joyce, with a supportive hand on her back, and listened as she described in her raspy voice who the man in the dumpster was.

Turned out Kenneth Fisk was your average Joe Schmoe. A retired train insurance salesman. He was quiet. Paid rent on time. Single. In the ten years he lived there, Joyce could not recall a time when Kenneth requested a guest parking pass. He drove a Honda. Got along with his neighbors. Ordered pizza on Friday nights. Chinese on Thursdays and subscribed to the LA Times Sunday paper. The last time Joyce saw Kenneth alive was Saturday morning, when he came to the office to pick up a package—a pair of new Nikes along with exercise clothes. He told Joyce he had begun training for a turkey trot he and his sister planned to run next month.

Not that anyone deserves to be killed and dumped. *However,* it would make me feel a teensy bit better if there was an obvious reason. Like if Kenneth was an antagonistic puppy kicker. Or one of those people who don't put shopping carts away.

But no, he was a pizza-eating turkey trotter.

"Could it have been an armed robbery gone wrong?" I asked Detective Spray. Given the wallets, gun, and mask, it seemed a reasonable explanation.

"If it was then why would there be a pregnancy test?" Joyce said. "Who in the middle of an armed robbery situation thinks, 'I haven't had my period in a while. I should probably check on that.'"

"You never know. People are idiots," Detective Spray chimed in.

"Great. I'm glad these idiots are breeding." I sighed, looked over at the group of residents still watching, and did a quick abdominal check to see if any were pregnant. Didn't appear so. Still, "It should be fairly easy to determine who did this, right?" I said to the detective. "You have a urine sample of the killer."

"DNA is not that simple," Spray said matter-of-factly. "There are many factors."

Ugh. Factors.

Stupid factors.

I hate factors.

Almost as much as I hated that answer.

The answer I wanted was, *"Absolutely, we should have an arrest made by morning. Don't you worry about a thing."* Because how could I bring my daughter to live there if random Joe Schmoes were being knocked off?

The detective eventually left to go converse with her colleagues, leaving Joyce and me alone. Wrapping my hand around my neck, I rolled my head from side to side. My shoulders ached, and the bus was still parked on my chest, and I smelled like, well, I smelled like a smoky dumpster. This is not how I anticipated my first day going.

And it wasn't even over yet.

Joyce was deep in thought, staring at the bag of trash on the ground. The one I never did throw away. "You'd have to be an idiot to live here and toss a dead body into the community bin," Joyce said to me.

"You heard the police officer. People are idiots."

She nodded in agreement. "That is true. That is so true..." Her words trailed off and hung in the air like a raincloud above us.

"Have you ever had a robbery around here before?" I finally asked.

Joyce shrugged her bony little shoulders. "Not on my watch."

CHAPTER FIVE

———

Tenant agrees not to engage in disturbingly loud activities that may nauseate other tenants on the Premises.

In an attempt to calm our frazzled nerves, Joyce and I spent the remainder of the day sitting at her kitchen table. Me, eating an entire gallon of French Vanilla ice cream (or two). Her, smoking an entire package of Marlboro Lights (or two). Part of me wanted to go home early. The other part of me knew I was being paid hourly during my training period and, despite all that had happened, I was still broke with a toddler at home. So I stayed and listened to Joyce tell stories about when she first met Bob (who was still asleep on the recliner), growing up in Chicago, and how she became an apartment manager to pay for her son's college tuition.

The distraction was nice.

We took a short break to go over unclogging a garbage disposal with the end of a broom when Apartment 8 tossed a used condom into theirs (I didn't ask questions). Then Joyce and I assumed our positions at her table while I listened and she talked about anything and everything except Kenneth Fisk and the police still crawling around the property.

When the clock struck five, I gathered my belongings with a tired head, a heavy heart, and a mild case of emphysema. I was ready to go home, get my baby, and take a long shower (or three).

"Before you leave," Joyce said just as I opened the door. "Patrick wants you to fill out a detailed time card during your training."

My shoulders fell. "What do I write? Unclogged garbage

disposal, processed an application, found a dead body, ate ice cream."

"Something like that. And, here." Joyce dropped a key ring into my palm. "Lock up the office when you're done," she rasped.

There were at least forty keys of all shapes, colors, and sizes shoved on the small ring. None were labeled. "How do I know what key goes to what?"

She touched a gold one with her bent forefinger. "This opens everything. I have no idea what the rest do."

"Thanks. That's *helpful?*" I'd already forgotten which one she pointed to.

"See you tomorrow." She started for the door.

"Wait, Joyce."

She grunted. "What is it, kid? It's been a terrible day and *People's Court* is about to start."

"Right. Real quick. You never told me what Patrick said when you told him about Kenneth Fisk?" He had called when I was outside taking an oxygen break.

With a relenting sigh, Joyce lowered herself into the chair, her movements slow and painful-looking. "He said we'll have to wait for his next of kin to pack up his apartment and release it to us before we can re-rent it."

"I *meant*, what did he say about Kenneth Fisk being murdered?" Who cared about his apartment!

Or...*er*...I guess I should. Being an apartment manager and all.

Joyce propped an elbow on the desk. "He said, 'That's sad.'"

That's sad? I was hoping for more of a *let's-invest-in-high-powered-security-cameras-and-twenty-four-hour-patrol* kind of reaction. Crap. I dropped my bags and took a seat with my time card still in hand. "Do you think it's safe to bring Lilly here after what happened?"

"Of course," Joyce scoffed, as if I were being absurd. "This is a great neighborhood, and now the place is safer than it was before."

"Come again?"

"A couple of years ago, there was this restaurant near the

Grove that Bob and I used to go to. It was a real fine place with good pastrami sandwiches. Then several customers got salmonella, and I think one person died... I can't remember. But the Health Department came, it was on the news, and a lot of people stopped going. But not Bob and I. You know why?"

"Ummm...*why*?"

"Because it was the safest place to eat in town. Of course they were going to be on their best behavior because they *knew* the Health Department was watching them. We continued to go and enjoy our pastrami and never once got sick."

"So you're saying that..." I paused, unsure how this story was relevant. "I'm sorry. I'm not getting the correlation?"

"It's the same idea. What criminal is going to come near this place now that we're on the police's radar? My theory is Kenneth went out for an early morning run, saw a hooligan-type on the property, called the office to report, was mugged while on the phone, fought back, was killed accidentally, and tossed in the trash. What idiot is going to come back to the scene of the crime?"

She made a good point. Took a while to get there, but she made it. "What does that have to do with a spider web?"

"He walked into a web."

"Oh." Made sense. Kind of. My mood lifted—a little. "What ever happened to the restaurant?" I asked.

"It closed down."

Oh.

Joyce tapped my hand. "Focus on the job and keep Patrick happy, and you'll all be just fine."

*Keep Patrick happy...*I'd almost forgotten about the whole third-choice, Chase, Kevin situation. "What else did Patrick have to say about what happened?"

"He asked why you were dumpster diving."

"I wasn't dumpster diving," I said to her, for at least the fifth time today. "Would you stop saying that. I need to impress Patrick, not give him more reason to think I'm crazy."

"Potatoes. Tomatoes. Doesn't matter. If you want to impress him, all you've got to worry about is your bottom line. Keep this place full and your residents happy, and you'll keep Patrick happy. Vacancies cost money, and mad tenants turn into vacancies."

"Got it."

Full occupancy + Happy residents = Happy Patrick.
Happy Patrick = Employed Cambria.
Too bad I flunked algebra.

"Anything else?" Joyce asked.

I had about a hundred more questions, but it *was* five o'clock, and *People's Court was* on, and it had been a traumatic day. "That's it for now," I said.

"I'll see you in the…" Joyce's voice trailed off. Her eyes fixated on something outside the large window next to the desk.

"What's wrong now?" I turned around. A woman stormed through the breezeway. Her pink robe flapped behind her like a cape as she treaded toward the office. "Who's that?" I asked.

"It's Silvia Kravitz." Joyce sighed with a shake of head. "Say a prayer she hasn't heard about poor Kenneth. And for goodness' sake, if she doesn't say anything, don't offer up that information."

A chime echoed through the lobby, announcing a visitor, followed by the sharp tapping of heels across the linoleum floor. A woman with ten-too-many facelifts appeared. It was the love child of Gollum and Joan Rivers. Her silk robe hung off one shoulder, revealing the thin strap of her red nightie. On the other shoulder a parrot sat so still that I questioned if it were alive or a prop.

"Hello, Silvia, this is Cambria, the new manager," Joyce greeted from her chair.

Silvia's bulging eyes met mine, and I smiled. "Hello, nice to meet you." I walked up to the counter and held out my hand. Silvia eyed it suspiciously and slowly placed her fingertips into my palm, as if waiting for me to kiss the backside of her hand.

I shook her fingers instead, eyeing the unmoving parrot. Silvia reached over to the sanitizer propped next to the brochures advertising a *spacious studio*, gave it two pumps into her palm, and began slathering it on.

"Is there something I can do for you?" I asked.

Silvia groaned. The parrot repositioned him or herself on

her shoulder. "It's happening again. Look what it's doing to Harold."

"Who's Harold?" I asked. She gave me a look, trying—and failing—to move her brow. "Oh, is…is he Harold?" I pointed to the parrot.

"You know I'm not one to complain." She looked over my shoulder at Joyce for backup, but Joyce remained silent. "It's every day. Morning, noon, and night. It's…" She leaned in closer. "It's unnatural," she whispered.

"Unnatural?" I whispered back.

She nodded. "Unnatural." She reached into her pocket and pulled out a saltine cracker, took a small bite, and then handed the rest to Harold. He grabbed it with his claw and attacked it with his beak, sending crumbs down Silvia's chest and into the wrinkled cleavage peeking out from her nightie.

I looked back at Joyce, who was now doing a crossword puzzle. "Can you elaborate on what is so unnatural?" I asked Silvia, keeping my eyes away from Harold, who was now picking the cracker crumbs out of her cleavage.

"No!" She closed her eyes and placed her hand over her chest, forcing Harold back to his spot on her shoulder. "Come with me right now. You can hear for yourself what we have to put up with. Because Joyce refuses to see for herself." She clapped her hands together. "Come, come."

I turned around and mouthed *What do I do?* to Joyce.

She shrugged. "I'd follow her if I were you. But be careful. Harold bites."

Harold bites?

Silvia's silk robe rustled behind her as she walked through the complex, her heels clacking against the wet pavement. Harold perched himself backwards to better keep a tiny eye on me.

We passed the pool and arrived in the third courtyard. It was my first time in the banned area. It mirrored the first, except for the detective standing in front of Apartment 21. I scanned the area in search of a spider web, spider, something eight-legged…nada. Instead, my eyes landed on the black door again. Apartment 40. From here, I could see the *Forty* was sprayed in red, dripping paint. I squinted, trying to read the weathered note taped above the doorknob.

Management never...

Silvia snapped her fingers in front of my face. "Concentrate, new apartment manager." She flipped her bleached hair and trotted forward. I caught one more glance back. The *Forty* looked as if could be the title to a horror movie, a really gory one. Goose bumps prickled down my arms and up my neck.

"Apartment Manager!" Silvia yelled.

I jumped, so lost in thought I forgot about Silvia.

"Apartment Manager, hurry up!"

Happy residents. Happy Patrick. Employed Cambria. Happy residents. Happy Patrick. Employed Cambria...

I took the stairs up to Silvia's apartment. She stood at the door with her arms crossed, foot drumming, face frozen in shock. She pointed down to my feet. "Those have to be removed before you may enter my home, always."

"Of course," I obliged, and yanked off Amy's stilettos. My feet sprang back to life. Feeling slowly returned to my toes as they sank into the plush tan carpet. It felt heavenly. It smelled heavenly—fresh lilacs and vanilla. Cool air wafted from the air conditioner stuck in the window. The apartment looked staged for an open house. The furniture firm and untouched, vacuum lines perfectly spaced along the carpet. A bookshelf containing framed photos of a beautiful brunette posing in a garden, posing in a swimsuit at the beach, standing with Muhammad Ali, and another of her with an actor I recognized, but I couldn't remember his name. I guessed the woman in the pictures was Silvia, with her original face on.

She placed Harold on his perch next to the couch and snapped around to face me. "Well?" she asked.

It's like she was speaking in code. "Well..."

"Listen."

I took another step in, eyeing Harold. I heard muffled voices. I followed them down the hall into the bedroom, where the sound became painfully clear—and was followed by a repeated thumping against the wall.

Oh, please, no.

"Can you hear that?" she shouted over the husky moans coming from the other side of the wall. Two oil paintings hung above the bed and swayed with each thrust, threatening to swing off the nails holding them to the wall. "Do you see how disturbing this is?"

I saw. I heard. I agreed. I found myself nodding my head along with the rhythmic humping.

"Go talk to them. Maybe they'll listen to you. It has to stop, or I'll move! I'll do it. I hear you already lost one resident today. Can you really afford to lose me as well?"

The sexing couple was now screaming. It was awkward. "I will make a note and speak with them later when they aren't so…busy."

Boom!

One of the paintings swung off the nail and landed on the bed. "That means they're done. You can talk to them now. Go. Go." She clapped her hands together.

"Right, OK. I'll go do that." *Is this really happening?*

I grabbed my shoes on the way out and took the four-step journey to the neighboring apartment. I stared at the door, thinking of all the things I would rather do than speak to strangers about their loud, unnatural sex life.

I raised my hand and knocked twice. The door creaked open, and an old, old woman poked her head out, her short, thinning gray hair pointing in every direction.

You have got to be kidding me.

I forced my mouth to move. "Um…I'm the new apartment manager…and…um…*hi.*"

The woman opened the door wider, allowing me a full glimpse of the white sheet wrapped around her sagging unmentionables. "Hey, hon, look. It's the new apartment manager," she yelled to the old man sitting in a recliner wearing nothing but boxer shorts, smoking a cigar. "Say hi," she scolded. The man raised his hand, not taking his eyes off the fishing show he was watching. "I'm Clare, and that's Bill. I was about to bake you some welcome-to-the-neighborhood cookies except I got a little distracted." She smiled—*Oh hell, where are her teeth?*

I looked at the floor. "That's actually why I'm here. Your bed backs up to your neighbor's bedroom, and if you could keep that in mind, that would be great." I hoped she understood my point, because saying sex in front of a toothless grandma required more maturity than I currently possessed.

"Hon, your snoring is bothering the neighbors again!" she yelled to Bill.

"Oh, it's not the snoring," I quickly added and leaned in closer. "Do you have a large headboard?"

Next thing I knew, I was standing at the foot of her bed—a wooden bedframe with four tall posts that nearly touched the popcorn ceiling. She readjusted her sheet. "See. It's just average size."

That's what she said.

"It's not the size, more so the sound when it crashes against the wall," was my roundabout explanation. Grandma stared at me. I gave the foot of the bed a hard shove with my thigh, causing the headboard to slam into the wall. I then gave it three more steady shoves to drive the point home.

Grandma made an *O* with her wrinkled lips. "I can fix that." She grabbed a throw pillow from the chair next to the bed and shoved it behind the headboard. I gave it another hard thrust. The pillow kept it from ramming the wall.

"That seems to work. Now if you could, you know, try to keep it...*quiet*...that would be helpful."

"I'll try my best," she said with a contrite smile, readjusting her sheet again.

CHAPTER SIX

_____

Tenant agrees to observe a speed limit of no more than five MPH while driving in the carports.

That night, I lay in bed with the *Frozen* blanket pulled up to my nose. Lilly sprawled out next to me, deep in REM cycle, while I stared up at the stiff peaks and bumps of the ceiling. Cars zoomed down the busy road, their headlights flashing across the popcorn as they passed one after the other in a constant rhythm. Sirens wailed, feet pattered along the sidewalk, and the occasional drunken outburst followed by a scuffle commenced outside my window—hence why 80% of LA's renters said to *run* away from this place.

My body yearned for slumber, but my mind wasn't about to surrender. It had more important things to do, like repeating everything from Kenneth to the gun to the zip ties to the pregnancy test to the detective to nearly naked Grandma Clare to Chase to the black door to being third choice. Every detail, every smell, every possible theory played out in my mind like a never-ending bad movie.

The thing was, nothing about the crime made sense! Granted, I wasn't a detective, but to my amateur sleuth mind—nothing about the crime made sense! For one, it rained. It rarely rains in California. So when it does, the oil rests on the surface, causing a foamy, slippery, grimy residue. The bottom of Kenneth's shoes were white. If he'd gone for a run or even walked across the driveway, his shoes would have a scuff, a pebble wedged between the grooves, a thin film of grime! Unless his killer replaced his shoes before dumping him. Which seemed unlikely. The more plausible scenario was that the murder took place in Kenneth's apartment or thereabouts. The killer would then have had to lug the body to the dumpster—unseen—just before dawn. In the rain. On wet, slippery asphalt. And it's not like Kenneth was in stellar physical shape either.

Also, who goes through a great deal of effort to conceal a dead body under trash bags but then carelessly dumps a backpack filled with incriminating evidence along with a DNA sample right beside it?

And what did any of this have to do with a spider web?

And who the hell was pregnant?

These sorts of thing happened on television, *not* in my reality.

Could I bring Lilly to live in a community where someone had just been murdered?

I wrestled with this question.

The truth was, murder aside, the apartment was located in a *much* better area than my current apartment. Case in point, my neighbor was currently getting high right outside my door.

Of course, there's a hefty difference between smoking pot and killing someone.

I thought about what Joyce had said. Based on the contents of the backpack, the likely scenario was that Kenneth was robbed. The killer snuck in behind a car or jumped the fence then snooped around for valuables left in vehicles. Found nothing of interest, went inside the third courtyard, ran into Kenneth who was up, stretching, preparing for his trot. He saw the killer and called Joyce to let her know someone was trespassing? Or maybe Kenneth attempted to apprehend the criminal while on the phone, and the killer panicked? Either way, the end result was murder. And the person responsible was— hopefully—long gone (or better yet, arrested). The place was now on the police's radar. It wouldn't be safe to return to the very spot he (or she) dumped all his evidence.

Right?

If only I could shake this feeling that something heavy was lurking around the corner, waiting for me to get comfortable before revealing its ugly head. Was this feeling intuition or paranoia, though? It had always been difficult for me to differentiate the two. I had a habit of sprinting to the absolute worst possible conclusion then sticking to it, unable to let go even if I wanted to, hostage to an exaggerated mind and the continual *what-ifs*. Some would call this a fatal flaw—and those "some" would be every guy I'd ever dated.

Sometime around dawn, I convinced myself I was being overdramatic—again—and quitting my job would be nothing but a wasted opportunity to better our circumstances. Everything was going to be fine because I couldn't afford for it to turn out any other way. Therefore, dwelling on the possibilities was a useless endeavor.

Instead, I spent most of the sleeping hours scouring the help wanted ads (for backup) and watching instructional YouTube videos on how to escape a hostage situation (specifically using zip ties). I then checked the news to see if any armed robberies had been covered. Nothing. Only gang shootings, stabbings, and hit-and-runs had been highlighted on the *Los Angeles Times* website. Plus a news story of a woman who released a jar of bed bugs into her apartment manager's office as revenge. That's when my mind slipped back into the pessimistic realm of thinking, so I turned off the computer and took a swig of Benadryl.

The next morning, after a few deep breaths, I rolled out of bed and dressed in the recommended jeans, along with one of my many solid-colored Mossimo V-necks. With newfound determination, I was ready to apartment manage like no woman had ever apartment managed before.

I arrived (on time) for the next few days, eager to learn as much as Joyce was willing to teach me. Which wasn't much. More stories. More ice cream. More secondhand smoke with the occasional job talk thrown in, like when Joyce said "be friendly, but don't make friends" and "do for one as you would do for all." Which may have been Yoda quotes, but I took what I could get.

On Thursday Kenneth's sister, Scarlet Fisk, arrived to collect her brother's things. Scarlet had gray hair, a straight nose, and eyes like a Basset Hound. Based on the picture in Kenneth's file, she was the female version of her brother.

There'd been no news about the investigation since the detectives returned the apartment keys Tuesday morning—and even then it was "here you go, thanks."

I was eager to grill Scarlet for information, but it seemed a teensy bit insensitive to blurt out *"Sorry for your loss. Do you know how he died? Has an arrest been made? A suspect named? Did your brother have any known enemies? Secretly interact with the mob? Gangs? Mexican Mafia? Trade on the black market?"*

Instead, I stood there while Joyce and Scarlet chatted, and waited for the subject to come up naturally.

But it never did.

The two talked about the weather, retirement, the economy, how expensive California is. When Scarlet muttered, "I still can't believe Kenneth is gone." I decided to take that as my cue to blurt out:

"Sorry for your loss. Do you know how he died? Has an arrest been made? A suspect named? Did your brother have any known enemies?" I left out the Mexican Mafia, mob, and black market until, you know, it came up naturally.

Scarlet blinked a few times. "No," she said slowly. "They haven't said anything to me about an arrest or a suspect. Kenneth was quiet but a very nice man. He didn't have any enemies that I knew of."

"Does spider web mean anything to you?" When I Googled 'alternate meaning of spider web' I was shown several variants—none of which made sense in the situation.

Scarlet's eyes went from me to Joyce and back again. "It means that a spider was there?"

Joyce rammed her bony elbow into my rib—a not so subtle hint to shut up.

Easy for her to say (or…er…nudge). She was moving out. I was moving *in*.

"Did the police say anything was missing from his apartment?" I asked, while rubbing my rib.

"The door was locked, and there was no sign of forced entry or of a struggle," Scarlet said. "If I notice anything missing I'm supposed to let them know."

"Did they tell you how he was killed?" This question evoked another elbow to the ribs from Joyce.

"He's still at the coroner's office and—"

"Never mind all this," Joyce interrupted, giving me a

sideways glare. "Scarlet, dear, you let me know if you need any help."

Scarlet took Joyce by the hand. "I will. Thank you so much for your kindness." She gave me a quick wave good-bye before leaving.

As soon as the door closed, Joyce shook her bent forefinger at me. "There's no need to interrogate the poor woman. Her brother was just murdered."

OK. I felt bad. I could have been more tactful in my questioning, but still, "I need to know what happened."

"No, you don't. You're not a detective. You're not investigating the case. You're an apartment manager. You take care of your residents. Stay out of their personal business. Let the police do their job," Joyce said, still waving her finger around. "Got it?"

"Got it," I replied, reluctantly.

"Good." She dropped her hand and shuffled back to her spot at the kitchen table and lit another cigarette (her sixth one today). She puffed out a circle of smoke with practiced precision and heaved a sigh of relief, as she often did when reunited with nicotine.

"Let's get back to work." She patted the seat beside her. "I was just about to explain to you the difference between a thirty-day notice and an eviction. But first, have I told you about our new place?"

And this is how the remainder of our training went.

I suspected retirement was more difficult than Joyce was letting on. She had devoted twenty-five years of her life to the care of the property and the residents who had lived there. Her avoiding all things pertaining to the actual job was a defense mechanism, or so I thought. A way for her to deal with Kenneth's murder and the finality of retirement. Because of this, I was sensitive and didn't press the issue. I was a fast learner and confident in my BSing abilities. Once she taught me about rent collection, I'd let Google cover the rest.

I imagined her emotions would surface on her last day. I imagined a lot of well-wishes from the residents, maybe some thank-you cards, gift baskets, tears, hugs, maybe a crochet blanket from naked Grandma Clare. In my head I was going to have to shoo her off the property. Force her to leave.

That was not the case.

When I arrived Friday morning, Bob was at the helm of their Oldsmobile, donning a driver's cap with his gloved hands resting at ten and two. Joyce sat in the passenger seat, the seat belt strapped over her shoulder and a houseplant in her lap.

"But...but...Joyce," I stammered, shocked. The plan was for her to stay until closing. How was she going to get a proper send-off if she wasn't even there? It was rent day, and I didn't have a clue how to even do rent. Plus there was the not-so-small-task of dealing with Kenneth Fisk. I had no idea what to do once Scarlet turned in the keys and paperwork. "Well," I continued, finding the words to properly express my appreciation. "I first want to say thank you so much for everything, and I promise—"

"You're welcome," she interrupted, reaching for the door and pulling it closed. Bob slammed on the gas, rubber burned, and the car smoked and screeched before disappearing down the driveway.

Joyce was gone.

Kind of fast.

CHAPTER SEVEN

―――――

Tenant acknowledges that Landlord is neither a physician nor a psychologist and is not qualified to give medical advice at any time, nor does he or she want to.

"OK, fine. Where's Joyce then? Because she'd never do this to me," the resident from Apartment 3 asked, cupping the edge of the counter, her knuckles turning white.

"I told you, Joyce left this morning. I'm the apartment manager now. According to your lease, the rent is due on the first. I'm not sure how asking you to pay the rent on the apartment you are renting is so offensive to you."

She released the counter and stood up straight, hands on hips, head cocked, angry face on. "That's fine. I'll talk to my lawyer about this."

The front door swung open, and Mickey, my new (to me) upstairs neighbor, walked through. An older, round man with dark hair and thick scars running down his dark forearms. "I'll kill you. I'll take you to hell and bury you there," he mumbled to no one in particular while Apartment 3 hammered on about her lawyer. I leaned over to see if a Bluetooth was in either of the man's ears. Both were empty. "The government is gonna take it..." he continued as he walked to the other door and swung it open. "Gonna take it..."

"This is beyond ridiculous." Apartment 3 was still going. "Fine! Whatever. I can tell you're going to be *that* kind of manager." She slapped her wallet on the counter, clicked her pen, filled out a check, yanked it from the binding, crinkled it into a ball, and tossed it at me.

It bounced off my forehead.

I unraveled the check wad and: "It's dated for the fifteenth? If you postdate a check, it's still considered late."

I thought her head was going to implode.

But before it could, the front door swung open again. In came Scarlet pulling a dolly piled with boxes.

I ran to hold the door open for her, leaving Miss *I-have-a-lawyer* in the midst of a mental implosion.

"Thanks. This is the last of it." She held out the paperwork we'd given her yesterday along with the apartment keys.

"You're done already?" I squeaked in surprise. That was fast!

"Kenneth didn't have much. I took a few things and scheduled for the Donation Truck to come pick up the rest. They'll be here Friday afternoon." She kicked her dolly to an incline and readjusted the bag on her shoulder. "My address and phone number are on the paperwork if you need me."

"Hello?" Miss *Let-me-chuck-my-postdated-check-at-your-face* raised her hand. "We were in the middle of something here."

"Hold on," I told her. Then I shifted my attention back to Scarlet. "I want to apologize if I came across as harsh yesterday. My intention was not to make you feel worse. I only wanted to know what happened."

"You and me both." She pulled her bag up her shoulder again. "The coroner's report came back. Kenneth was strangled, and the police don't have a suspect, and they don't appear to be in any hurry to find one." She chocked back a tear.

"*Hell-ooo!*" hollered Miss *I-am-the-center-of-the-universe*.

"Hold on!" I snapped. My gosh! The job listing wasn't joking when it said applicant must have the ability to multi-task without becoming violent (or was it flustered?) either way, I was almost there.

Back to Scarlet. "Please let me know if there is anything I can do to help with the investigation or whatever you need," I said, and I meant it.

"All I want is justice for my brother."

"Me too." I reached around the dolly and gave her a hug.

We then said our good-byes, and I held the front lobby door open while she wheeled her dolly through.

I watched her walk down the uneven bricks, toward her car. Kenneth Fisk was strangled to death despite the gun beside him?

"Hello!" Miss *On-my-last-nerve* interrupted my thoughts. "You interested in doing your job today?"

Ugh. Right.

I assumed my position behind the counter. "Where were we?"

"You were denying my legal right to a grace period," she said.

"Right. Yes, there's no such thing. Rent is due on the first."

"I'm sure my lawyer would be more than happy to fill you in on the law."

Man, she was annoying, completely irrational, and...*hmmm?* I leaned over the counter to peek at her stomach.

"Oh my gosh!" Miss *Doesn't-appear-to-be-pregnant* scoffed. "Are you checking me out?"

"Er...*no.*"

"This is just...no... I'm not doing this." She threw her hands up then turned around and left. Taking her wadded-up check with her.

Who knew collecting rent would be so difficult?

As the day continued, I heard everything from "my grandma died" to "a gypsy stole my money." Larry, in Apartment 32, couldn't pay his rent because of his hemorrhoids. I didn't ask for specifics, but he shared them anyway. I was ready to pay his rent for him if he would stop talking about it!

Blech!

When five o'clock arrived, I quickly flipped the locks on the lobby doors before anyone else could storm in. I'd successfully made it through my first rent day, collecting nearly half the rents. I hoped the rest would be waiting in the drop box, with the late fees attached, when I returned Sunday (aka Moving Day).

All ancient equipment powered down. Lights off. Einstein retamed. Two layers of lip gloss applied, and I was ready to tackle the last two items of business before I scurried home to finish (and start) packing.

One) deal with the maintenance man.

Two) check out Kenneth's apartment.

Chase had arrived in the morning with a crew of men recruited from the Home Depot parking lot. Within minutes the carpet was gone, the walls were primed, and the toilets and sinks were trashed. We had not exchanged pleasantries since he was far too busy doing his job and I was far too busy Googling how to do mine. I was ready for him though.

During my shower the night before, I prepared a cleverly scripted speech expressing my anger in an eloquently condescending way. I held up a bottle of Pantene as Chase's proxy and told it I was an honest, hard worker and even if he attempted to sabotage this job for me and my small, defenseless, hungry child, I was not one to hold a grudge (which was mostly true sometimes). I reminded the shampoo I was now its boss, but I did it with a glower that said "watch your back" and a hair flip that said "I'm too good for you." Then I sauntered off (well, as much as I could in my tiny shower), swaying my booty in a way that said "Mmm hmm, coulda had this and blew it." Oh, it was good. I took another shower in the morning to perfect my glower.

I had seen the hired workers leave, but I knew Chase was still working because *he* had to check in with *me* before he could leave, because *I* was *his* boss.

Mwhahahahaha.

I stepped into my apartment. The last time I'd been there was shortly after Joyce had peeled out of the parking lot. So much had already been accomplished. The Smurf carpet was now a plush pecan color. Cream linoleum covered the dinette and kitchen floors, the walls were a shiny eggshell, and the tiled counters were now bare wood, ready for the laminate.

I strolled down the hallway, amazed at the difference. I peeked into the first bathroom. The uninstalled toilet sat near the door, and the sink was in the bathtub. It was still so surreal to think I'd get *two* full bathrooms. *Two.* A luxury I hadn't had in my entire adult existence. The smell of freshly applied paint and newly installed carpets temporarily abolished all thoughts of murder, black doors, spider webs, guns, naked grandparents…and replaced them with pure, childlike excitement.

I'd been treading for so long, barely able to keep my head above water. Now it was time to swim. This was the fresh start I'd been waiting for.

I stepped across the hall into the master. With my hands clasped over my heart, like a child at Christmas, I looked around. My stomach bubbled with all the possibilities. I had a bedroom all to myself.

Only me.

Just mine.

All mine.

Mine. Mine. Mine.

All…by…my…self…

It was a notion far more depressing than I'd anticipated. A tinge of loneliness stabbed at my heart.

As promised, Joyce's massive armoire towered in the middle of the room. I ran my hand across the smooth surface, tracing the dark, natural swirls with my finger, deciding if I should paint it, stain it, or trash it. I yanked open the cabinet doors, releasing a batch of hoarded nicotine. I coughed and gagged and slammed it shut.

Trash it. Definitely trash it.

While waving my hand in front of my face, warding off the offensive smell, the squeal of a drill pushing a screw into the wall caught my attention.

Showtime!

I peeked into the master bathroom and saw Chase standing on a step stool, holding a bronzed light fixture against the wall with one hand while the other worked the power drill. Drywall dust coated his hair and stuck to the scruff on his face. He was intently focused on his job, and I was intently focused on his bicep.

I sincerely believed I'd find him repulsive after what he'd said. Unfortunately, he was just as attractive as the day I met him, if not more. Suddenly, all my anger soared out the window, and my insides started to hyperventilate. I turned into one of those annoying girls who forgot their convictions the moment a cute boy arrived. I was a total cliché, and it didn't bother me, which totally bothered me. I was nothing but a giant ball of contradictions, but I couldn't move because my legs were all watery, so I stood there staring like an idiot.

Chase stepped down and admired his work, crossing his arms over his chest. I wanted to run away, go look for my convictions, and staple them to my forehead so I wouldn't lose them again, but I couldn't tear my eyes away.

Finally noticing my wobbly presence, Chase turned and delivered an infectious grin. I wanted to slap him and kiss him and fire him and… *Ahhh! Get a grip, woman!*

"Hello," he said

"Hello," I said back.

"Hi," he said.

"Hi," I said back.

It was tantalizing conversation.

"How are you doing with everything?" he asked.

"I'm doing fine, and you?"

"Good. I just finished," he said.

Finished? I glanced up at the fixture. It was upside down and crooked. The caulking around the toilet was thin in some parts, thick in others, and mostly globby and smeared all over the floor.

Is that medicine cabinet on backwards?

I tried to open it.

Sure is.

Lilly could have done a better job. This was my fresh start, my chance to swim. How was I supposed to swim if I couldn't even open my medicine cabinet?

And just like that, my convictions returned, my legs resolidified, and my glower appeared. "Are you serious?" I asked in an eloquently condescending way.

He looked around, confused, scratching the scruff on his face and causing the drywall dust to fall to the ground. My legs started to go all liquidy again. I imagined him as a bottle of Pantene. "I'll be back tomorrow to finish the first bathroom…" I wasn't sure if this was a question or a statement.

"I'll also need you to finish this one," I said, glower still in place. "I'll send you a text with the items I'd like you to address, specifically, the giant armoire in my room that I need removed, please." Hair flip. Glower. Hair flip. "Now, before I leave, I wanted to discuss our working situation."

"Situation?" He looked confused.

"Yes, situation." Hair flip. Hair flip. *Ouch.* Neck kink. "I know you didn't want to work with me, and I wanted to assure you I have a very high—"

"Who said I didn't want to work with you?" He took a step closer, placing his drill on the paint-spotted counter.

"It doesn't matter. What does is—"

"No, it does matter. Who said that?" he pressed again, mirroring my glower.

I grunted. This was supposed to be a one-sided conversation. "Joyce mentioned it. It's not important—"

"Why would she say that?"

"Would you stop interrupting me?" I snapped. I was losing momentum. "I wanted to assure you I have very high standards regarding…stuff…" *Dammit.* I forgot what came next. "Please know I plan on working here for a long, long time. You can find someone else to maintenance if you don't like me." *Did I just say someone? Crap.* "Somewhere, somewhere else to maintenance," I quickly added.

Chase stared at me. I squirmed. He asked for permission to speak with an arch of his brow. I nodded my approval. "My buddy applied for the job as well, and I wanted him to get it, that's all. It wasn't personal. I don't even know you. I like working here. I don't think there's any *situation.*"

"Huh" was my response, because I couldn't think of a better one. During my rehearsal, the Pantene bottle never spoke of any friends. It never spoke at all. Joyce could have mentioned the friend. It would have lessened the blow. "OK then, well, glad we got that out of the way. I'll text you the items I'd like you to fix tomorrow. You may leave." I turned and sauntered off as planned except, crap. I sauntered too soon.

I back-peddled to the bathroom. Chase was staring at his phone.

"One more thing," I started, glower in place. "Kenneth Fisk's sister returned the keys to his apartment today. We'll need to get it turned over as soon as possible. That's all." I turned and sauntered off again, swaying my booty until I whacked it on the doorknob. Smooth.

My hipbone throbbed. I pretended not to notice and kept on swayin' until I was out of his sight.

Ouch.

CHAPTER EIGHT

———

*If the Leasee dies during the leasing period, the estate of the
deceased will be held liable for damages and cleaning costs,
should the estate fail to claim damage.*

I stood in the middle of Kenneth Fisk's studio apartment.
Scarlet had packed her brother's belongings into boxes and
labeled them *clothing, hats, kitchenware, books...* They were
stacked into a pyramid atop the bare mattress along with a lamp
and a few other household items like blankets and pillows, with a
handwritten note for the Donation Truck taped to the front of
kitchenware.

The apartment walls were naked. The cabinets empty,
aside from a bag of plastic forks. In the closet a lone wire hanger
dangled from the rod, and a pair of well-worn loafers lie on the
floor. I flipped the switch in the bathroom, and the light flickered
on. The tub had a dark ring around the inside and a thin bar of
Zest on the ledge. I found a paper taped to the back of the door:
Couch to 5K Running Plan. A nine-week training program for
beginners. The edges were wrinkled and paper crisp from
condensation.

I followed the high-traffic grooves in the carpet from the
bathroom to the bed to the living area to the kitchen and back
again. A perfect circle ten years in the making.

It reminded me of when I was a kid. My Grandma
Ruthie and I would spend our Saturdays at estate sales. We'd
walk through the homes of Fresno's recently deceased and dig
through the stuff relatives deemed worthless—knickknacks,
pictures, clothing, vases, wedding dresses. It was an eerie feeling
going through their stuff. Often, I'd get this feeling that the ghost

of the recently departed was looming over us, shaking his or her head in despair as strangers bought their possessions for cents on the dollar. Grandma Ruthie called this the "shivily wivilies"— when every hair on your body stands on end, the air feels heavy, and you have an acute feeling that you're being watched.

This is exactly how I felt in Kenneth Fisk's apartment. I had a bad case of the "shivily wivilies."

It was creepy.

Really creepy.

Not creepy enough to leave.

I continued through the apartment looking for what, I had no idea. The police had spent a full twenty-four hours in there—it's not like I was going to uncover anything incriminating. All I did find was a bag of trash under the sink, a cook book in a drawer, and a daily planner on the closet shelf. Other than that—nothing.

Nothing at all.

The boxes were folded not taped, making it easier to slip the items I found into the allotted donation box (also easier to snoop around). As promised, the *clothing* box contained just that—clothes. Jeans, shirts, Lands' End sweatshirts. The *hats* box didn't disappoint either—a bowler hat, well-worn Dodgers caps, and several straw fedora hats.

In the *books* box?

Books.

Lots of books. Mostly about trains. An Encyclopedia Britannica. The entire Twilight Series.

I opened the trash bag. Inside?

Trash.

Lots of trash.

Protein bar wrappers, a banana peel, takeout menu…stuff you'd expect to find in a trash can.

Next, I flipped open the planner to October. Last week, Kenneth had a colonoscopy. He was set to get his eyes checked this coming Thursday. DMV Friday. Lunch with Scarlet Saturday.

My conclusion: Kenneth Fisk was in fact Joe Schmoe.

There was even a novelty T-shirt with *Joe Schmoe* printed across the chest.

So who would want to kill Joe Schmoe?

Scarlet wanted justice for her brother. I too wanted justice for Kenneth Fisk. I also wanted a safe environment to raise my child and a peaceful place for my residents to reside (happy residents = less vacancies = happy Patrick = employed Cambria, or however that equation went).

I locked Kenneth's apartment and left. The sun had set, and residents were meandering home from a day of work—some carrying mail, others with bags of groceries, most staring at their phone. It was all very ordinary.

In the parking lot, asphalt crunched under my Converse sneakers as I walked to my car parked along the wall. The back lot was dim, and I used my phone to light the path.

Note to self: Check about parking lot lights.

It took several pumps of the gas, a quick prayer, and a few *bleeps* to get my car to start. Once it coughed to life, I was on my way. The front gate shook, rattled, and leisurely rolled open while I sat behind the wheel and waited. A silver hatchback with illegally black windows bounced over the railing and teetered across the driveway past me. I could just make out the outline of a person behind the dark window. I waved, unsure of what else to do. The car stopped.

I stared.

The person behind the dark window stared.

Then, with a pop of the exhaust pipe, the hatchback roared forward and took a sharp right turn into its assigned spot. Leaving a cloud of smog behind.

I glanced into my rearview mirror to catch which carport the car parked in.

Number 40.

Looked like Kevin was home.

CHAPTER NINE

———

Tenant agrees to use the emergency line for real emergencies only—Fire, Flood, Blood.

I took a mental break from all things murder related for the weekend. It was time to move. Despite the hundred-and-one-degree heat, a rental truck on the brink of exploding, and a cranky toddler, Tom, Amy, and I still managed to get all my belongings from one apartment to the next.

By the time we lugged the boxes and furniture from my old apartment to the truck, chased the woman who stole the items from the back of the truck, and then unloaded everything into my new apartment, we were beat.

Tom, as a kind gesture, took Lilly for the night so I could organize and unpack.

And unpack I did.

I unpacked an entire box of Oreos like a boss. I crushed the cookies, sprinkled them on top of three scoops of French Vanilla ice cream, and topped it with a spoonful of cookie butter, caramel, chocolate sauce with a swirl of whipped cream on top (it had been a long day...or...er...week). The sweet, creamy, chocolatey, buttery goodness rolled around my mouth and slid down my throat, bringing so much joy to my stomach. I relaxed on the couch, propped my sore feet up on an unlabeled box, and licked the chocolate leftovers off each throbbing finger.

One of the perks of being an apartment manager was free cable. My television was atop four boxes functioning as my entertainment center. I now had hundreds of channels of mind-numbing distractions at my disposal. An indulgence I hadn't enjoyed in years. *This must be how the other half lives*, I thought while watching reruns of *Law and Order.*

Not wanting to be completely unproductive, I grabbed a box marked *Lilly* and dragged it to her room. I then set up Lilly's new bed. A pink plastic toddler bedframe I had purchased for five dollars from an estate sale. It was gently used, only a few scuff marks, which became invisible once I pushed it against the wall. Her old crib mattress fit perfectly inside it. I arranged her stuffed animals next to her pillow and folded her princess blanket at the foot of the bed—the *Frozen* décor was all hers now. I couldn't wait for her to see it.

That was exhausting.

I hauled my tired body to the kitchen and set the alarm, flipped off the lights, and closed the blinds. The warning beep from the alarm echoed through the apartment while I heaved my mattress down the hall and through my bedroom door, dropping it on the ground with a loud thud. That mattress and I had had our fair share of moves. When I was eight, after my parent's divorce, it went with me to my dad's condo. When my dad married that woman (aka my high school Spanish teacher!), it came with me to my mom's apartment. It followed me to college then LA and all the random places I dwelled in between. It was with me when I lost my virginity during my first (and only) year of college. Alex Simon was the douche…*ahem*…I mean boy's name. He was my first real boyfriend. He was my first real love, or so I believed at the time. Three months later, the solid springs of my mattress held my devastated body after I discovered Alex had also visited Stacey's mattress and Courtney's and Isobel's and Leah's…

My mattress had been vomited on, strapped to the top of cars, shoved into moving vans, hung off the back of a truck. It was soaked in tears of heartache after Tom sent me to Alcatraz, tears of defeat when I lost my job, tears of joy when Lilly finally potty trained. The floral print had faded, the stitching frayed, and the springs were visible through the thinning fabric. It was actually kind of gross, I realized.

Note to self: With first bonus check, purchase a slightly soft, mostly firm, mostly new mattress.

Unable to muster the energy required to shower, I unsnapped my bra and pulled it out through my sleeve, dropped my jeans to the floor, and curled up in my new comforter—a housewarming gift from my mom. It had arrived Friday morning, priority mail, which had to cost a pretty penny—a penny I knew she didn't have.

"Some things are worth spending money on," she had said when I called to thank her. "And you moving out of that apartment is definitely one of them. You're far too pretty, with way too much potential, to be..."

The white fabric puckered every few inches, creating the most elegant, comfy, grown-up looking texture I'd ever owned. I cocooned myself in it, laying my head on the matching pillowcase, in my very own two-bedroom apartment, an apartment I wasn't about to be evicted from. An apartment that didn't have bars on the windows or neighbors getting high outside my door or parole officers frequently visiting or couches in the walkway. I even had a ceiling fan cooling the sticky air to a sleepable temperature. Installing the fan hadn't been on Chase's to-do list, but he'd taken it upon himself to do it anyway. I almost forgave him for forgetting to remove the ashtray-smelling armoire. Almost.

For the first time in a long time, I looked forward to a night of peaceful slumber, allowing my thoughts to turn to nonsense as I drifted...

* * *

Ring...ring...ring...ring...ring.
Is that my phone?
What time is it?
I rolled over and grabbed my cell off the box working as my nightstand. *The emergency line!* I bolted up and threw the phone to my ear. "Hello, this is Cambria," I answered, my hand over my chest, my breath hitched in my throat. I'd been the sole manager for three days. First a murder, and now the building was already on fire.

"Hello. You have a call on the after-hours emergency line. To accept, please press one," an automated woman's voice with a pleasant British accent instructed. I gulped and pressed one, anxiously placing the phone back up to my ear.

Three rings later and I was connected. "Hello, this is Cambria."

"Hi, this is Ty," the caller said. "Someone's in the pool. I wouldn't normally say anything, but I've got a baby trying to sleep."

Phew. No fire. "I'm so sorry, Ty. I'll go speak to them right now."

Pants on. Bra on...the floor. Phone in hand. Keys in pocket. Cold water on face and I was out the door. According to paragraph three on the fifth page of the *House Rules*, the pool closes at nine. It was nearly midnight. This, of course, was a major infraction. I strutted along the pathway, feeling quite important, ready to lay down the law. *This is my town now...or...er...community.*

My confident strut slowed to a walk...to a shuffle...to a stumble...to a complete...stop. I felt my eyes go wide as saucers. My heart skipped three beats. I was a braless statue carved of flesh, unable to move. My brain had yet to process what it was looking at.

Then, finally, my frontal lobe grasped the situation and screamed and recoiled and forced my eyes closed with a violent shiver of my body.

Penis.

A penis attached to a hairy man who was very wet, obviously cold, and much too old to be skinny-dipping. Maybe late thirties, early forties? He swayed around on the pool deck with a boogie board tight in his grasp. Then, the naked man stretched his board in front of him and slid across the pool. The hazy, underwater lights made the auburn hair covering the man (covering all the man) shimmer as he sailed to the shallow end.

The penis...*ahem*...man exited the kidney bean-shaped pool and ran back to the deep end. He had a skinny face, chicken legs, and a black tattooed snake wrapped around his scrawny arm. I was trying to keep my eyes above the abdomen.

I pushed open the pool gate, catching the attention of the skinny-dipper before he descended across the pool again.

"What apartment are you in?" I asked, trying to sound authoritative.

He scoffed as he got out of the pool. "What apartment

are *you* in?" the skinny-dipper countered while swinging his board under his arm, nearly falling over in the process.

I crossed my arms and took a wide stance. "I'm the apartment manager."

"Pfft, no you're not. Joyce is. Go away." He slid across the pool again.

I met him on the other side. "Joyce retired. I'm the new manager. And you're not allowed to be out here this late, and you're never allowed to be out here naked. Now, what apartment are you in, or who are you visiting?" *Please say you're a visitor.*

"Joyce retired?" he asked, grasping tight to the pool railing. "My prayers have been answered!" The board went flying into the pool, and before I knew it, the skinny-dipper was wrapped around me.

"Get off of me!" I yelled in panic. This hairy naked man could be Kenneth's killer.

Or not.

Hairy Naked Man was scrawny. No way he could strangle Kenneth. I could have easily taken HNM down. Before I could, an upstairs porch light flicked on, and a woman's head poked out. "Keep it down!" she yelled. The door slammed, light turned off, and I was still in the skinny-dipper's embrace.

"Get off," I repeated more quietly. I wouldn't want to disturb anyone again with my own problems, like being assaulted.

The skinny-dipper released me and took a step back, scanning me from head to toe with a disapproving shake of his head. "I never gave Patrick consent to hire a new manager. What's your name?" he asked, closing his eyes like he had just fallen asleep.

"No, what's *your* name?"

His eyes popped open. "What?"

I reached into my back pocket to retrieve my phone. This seemed like a good time to call the police. "Your name?"

He looked around to see whom I could be talking to. Realizing we were alone, he placed his hand over his furry chest. "Me?" He sounded offended. "Who am I? I am the owner of this entire property, that's who I am, and if I want to swim around here naked, I can."

Oh, please no.

"You're...you're...you're *Kevin*?" My voice rasped in my ears. It felt as if I had swallowed a bucket of sand. In my head Kevin was a teenager with a bad attitude. Not a forty-year-old nudist.

The porch light flicked on again. The same head poked out. "Would you keep it down? I'm trying to sleep."

"Yeah." Kevin nodded. "Keep it down, Apartment Manager." He flashed a sardonic smirk and leaned into the pool, grabbing the strap to his board. "Try to be a little more considerate," he said before walking off, the board scratching along the cement behind him.

I feel sick.

* * *

Ring...ring...ring...

"Hello," I moaned into the phone.

"Hello. You have a call on the after-hours emergency line. To accept, please press one," the robotic British voice answered. Again.

I pressed one and waited for the rings. "Hello, this is Cambria." I pulled the phone away from my face and squinted to see the time—two in the morning. It wasn't easy falling asleep after meeting Kevin. And Kevin *junior*. Does workers' comp cover hypnotherapy? I definitely needed a few sessions.

"Hey, it's Larry." His voice was shaky on the other end.

"Hi, Larry. What's wrong?" *Please don't be about his hemorrhoids.*

"I'm really upset. I was up watching TV, because you know I haven't been sleeping much because of the hemorrhoids. And Kevin came in and started eating my food. He ate the last of my Thin Mints! When I asked him to stop, he called me fat. And you know, that wasn't nice."

My frontal worked hard to catch up. "Kevin came into your apartment and began eating your food?"

"Yeah."

"Did you invite him in?"

"No, he just came in," he said without pause. "I've been

dieting since the doctor told me to drop some weight. He hurt my feelings. I know he's the owner's son, but he shouldn't be so nasty. I mean, Cambria, you've noticed I lost weight, right?"

As hard as I tried, I couldn't formulate a single rational thought. Larry appeared to be far more upset that Kevin called him fat than the fact he came into his apartment and ate his Thin Mints.

"You've noticed I lost weight, right?" he pleaded.

I'd known him all of three days. "For sure. You look great."

* * *

Ring...ring...ring...

"Whaaat," I whined into the phone, stealing a glance at the clock. *Four in the freaking morning.*

"Hello. You have a call on the after-hours emergency line. To accept, please press one," the annoying computer barked into my ear. She was a patronizing little witch.

I pressed one and waited. "What?" I answered.

"Apartment Manager, this is Silvia Kravitz. You know I don't normally complain, but some of us have to work tomorrow, and Harold is in a frenzy over here. I know he's allowed to do as he pleases—Joyce made that crystal clear—but can *you* ask him to do so more quietly?"

"Wait...what?" I pinched the bridge of my nose, steadying my thoughts. It sounded like Silvia called to complain about her bird, which would be utterly ridiculous, and also a huge relief. Anything not related to Kevin felt doable.

Silvia moaned into the phone, and Harold's wings flapped in the background. I imagined he was perched on her shoulder...or in her cleavage. "I *said* I have to work in the morning, just like a lot of people around here, and I can't if the owner's son keeps playing whatever it is he is playing over there. I get he's allowed to bend the rules, but this is getting excessive. Maybe he'll listen to *you*, because I'm going to move. I'll do it."

The phone was at my ear, but my mind was off somewhere else, like in Nevada, pounding on Joyce's door, ready to unload a string of expletives. This is why she peeled out of the parking lot. This is why she never talked about Kevin or the job. She wasn't sad about retiring. She was elated! I was the fool for not questioning her more about it.

I hung up. Pants on. Bra still on floor. Keys somewhere. Phone in pocket. I kicked the armoire on the way out.

Kevin's apartment bridged over the back walkway leading out to the carports. I charged up the stairs, wishing I hadn't forgone the bra. He was playing the saxophone or a clarinet or killing a cat. It was quite unpleasant.

I knocked. The door, obviously not fully closed, slowly opened...

My frontal lobe didn't even try this time. The scene before my eyes was too far out of the realm of rationality. Kevin had the same floor plan I did, with the spacious front living room, attached square kitchen, and little dinette area. The comparison ended there. His carpet had been replaced with black, scuffed rubber flooring. The walls were covered floor to ceiling with newspaper clippings—a random collection of headlines and articles that looked to have dated back to the eighties. Blue and pink swirls were spray-painted along the ceiling, with a disco ball mounted in the center. All the kitchen cabinet doors were missing, and the seventies-inspired yellow refrigerator was wrapped in a heavy chain with the words *LIVE EXPLOSIVES* written in Sharpie across it.

What would I do if a tenant were receiving an excessive number of visitors? That's what Patrick was worried about? How did this not make the questionnaire?

Kevin appeared from the hallway, wearing pink boxers and a pair of mismatched socks. A saxophone dangled around his neck. I could almost feel him slapping me from across the room. He lunged toward the door, stopping inches from my face. A mixture of garlic and cigarettes laced his breath. He lifted his finger up to my nose and spat, "You don't ever come into my apartment. You never come in here. Do you understand me?"

I stumbled backwards.

"Get out of my house, you ugly tramp!" The door slammed in my face.

Oh no you didn't!

The dying cat music returned. I knocked. He didn't

answer. I knocked again. The dying cat melody grew louder. You don't call me an ugly tramp and get away with it. I was many things—many, many things—but a tramp was not one of them. I banged with a closed fist, three steady beats.

The neighbor's door to the right opened. A blonde drowning in a Dodgers shirt stood in the doorway, rubbing her eyes. "Can you stop pounding on the door like that? Some of us are trying to sleep."

CHAPTER TEN

———

In regard to visitors, Tenant agrees not to invite unruly,
sociopathic, or felonious individuals onto the Premises.

To: patrickelder@eldermgmt.com
From: cambriaclyne@eldermgmt.com
Subject: Nudist Man-child

Dear Patrick,

Good morning. Last night, I received a call from a tenant letting
me know Kevin was using the pool, sans clothes, at midnight. I
asked him to leave, but he was quite belligerent. At 2 a.m. Kevin
broke into a tenant's apartment, stole their Girl Scout Cookies,
and then verbally assaulted the tenant. At 4 a.m. I received a
complaint that Kevin was playing a saxophone. When I asked
him to stop, he called me a "tramp" and slammed the door in my
face.
I have attached the contact information for several mental health
services. I'd be more than happy to make all the arrangements as
soon as possible, preferably today. The center in Brazil looks
nice.

Sincerely,
Cambria

I could deal with screeching parrots and sex-crazed
grandparents. I could even listen to Larry talk about his
hemorrhoids. However, I could not, nor would I, put up with
Kevin. I was desperate for the job, yes. I had an overdrawn

account, yes. I didn't have the funds for another apartment, yes. I...forgot where I was going with this...

Anyway, I couldn't leave. Therefore Kevin had to. And honestly, he needed to. Sane people didn't skinny-dip in a community pool at midnight or steal Girl Scout Cookies—you can only buy those once a year!

What kind of monster does that?

After clicking *Send* I rested my forehead against the hot surface of the desk. A migraine threatened to explode behind my tired eyes, and my stomach did a nauseating flip in anticipation. I abandoned the desk in search of the box labeled *drugs.* I was in need of two Excedrin and a Diet Coke and a tub of ice cream and a nap.

One step into the apartment, and my heart sank. Unlabeled boxes towered throughout the living room and kitchen—a daunting sight. I hadn't used any kind of packing system. Walking from room to room, I shoved whatever fit into the box I was carrying—silverware with the hangers, pictures with glass cups. I then pulled the tape gun across the top and started over. Occasionally I labeled the boxes holding important things, like the Excedrin. Except that box was not readily visible and was going to require some effort to locate. My arms felt like two anchors keeping me from drifting off toward the land of productivity.

Why is life so hard?

The *ding-dong* from the front lobby door thwarted my journey.

"Coming!" I unlocked the door. Tom stood before me, looking all rested and showered and dapper. Lilly bounced up and down at his side with her shirt on backwards, hair in a tangled mess, and remnants of breakfast stuck on her face.

Tom's restful appearance and our homeless-looking child sparked a rage deep in my weary core. I clenched my teeth so hard my jaw nearly popped. "Give me." I nodded to Lilly's go-between bag slung over his shoulder.

Tom carefully draped the strap over my outstretched arm, as if feeding a ravenous animal. "Up late celebrating the new job?" he asked, taking a big step back.

I grabbed Lilly's hand and led her inside. "Something

like that. Bye." I pushed the door shut with my thigh.

Lilly and I settled on the couch, her sucked into an episode of *Mickey Mouse Clubhouse*, me actively avoiding movement. It was clear this was a ship of fools and I was the captain, janitor, psychologist, and cruise director. *"Good morning residents, we have an exciting day planned for you. At nine thirty we have a game of Who Killed Kenneth Fisk? At noon, we'll play Anyone Here Pregnant? And Spider Web! What the Hell Does That Mean? Before dinner, there will be a tournament of Excuses Why I Can't Pay My Rent This Month. All games will be held on the Lido Deck. Clothing is required although not enforced if you are an offspring of the owner. Hope to see you there!"*

"Momma?" Lilly asked, snapping me back to reality. The Mickey gang sang their farewell song in the background. "Momma, where is my Minnie?"

"I don't know, sweetie. It's in one of these boxes." I licked my finger and wiped breakfast off her cheeks.

"Can you find her? Can you find her now? Puh-leeease?" Her big hazel eyes and long lashes tugged on my momma heartstrings.

"How about we go swimming?" I asked. My head pounded in time with my heart. Submerging my achy body in a pool of cool water felt like the best idea I'd ever had.

Lilly squealed. I winced. We found our bathing suits, I packed us a light brunch, and we padded off to the pool.

Lilly tiptoed into the shallow end, her arms spread out and shoved into pink floaties. I dropped myself in. The water lapped over the side of the pool and slapped the scorching cement while I sank to the bottom, watching Lilly's little feet kicking feverishly underwater.

I floated back to the surface and became a princess mermaid with Lilly. The heat was in full force, and the cold water felt heavenly. I pushed the thought of Kevin swimming naked in the pool—less than twenty-four hours earlier—out of my mind. *That's what chlorine is for, right?*

We swam. We splashed. One of us had a near meltdown over a bee in the pool. The other cried because her floaties were too tight. After a while we mermaided our way to the steps and exited the pool. I wrapped my towel high under my armpits to hide my too-tiny pre-baby bikini. Luckily, it was Chase's day off, and no residents were around to enjoy the view either. Not that I was ashamed of my body. I had grown to accept and love my stretch marks and new curves. I just loved it more when it wasn't bulging over the side of a two-sizes-too-small bikini.

I wrapped Lilly in a fluffy towel, and we parked ourselves on a lounge chair. Within minutes the sun had soaked up most of the chlorine dripping off our bodies. I reapplied sunscreen, protecting our freckled figures from the ultraviolet rays. Lilly sat in my lap snacking on goldfish crackers and apple slices. I leaned back, resting my head on the plastic backing of the lounger. The fresh air dulled my headache to a more manageable throb, and I allowed my shoulders to relax while soaking in the much needed vitamin D.

I turned and looked out to the third courtyard. I couldn't see the black door from my seat, and all was peaceful. *Kevin must be nocturnal.*

Poor me.

All I heard was the quiet footsteps of a man walking out of Apartment 36. He had a small brown bag and tucked it carefully under his jacket. *A jacket?* He looked over his shoulder and hurried out to the carports. I propped up on my elbow and watched as yet another man exited Apartment 36, same small brown bag carefully tucked into his arm. The man, late forties/early seventies/somewhere in-between, dressed in casual attire and flip-flops, also looked around the courtyard before exiting to the carports.

It struck me as odd, most certainly suspicious.

"Momma?" Lilly put her little hand on my cheek, forcing my attention. "Cracker, puh-leeease."

I dug into my bag and pulled out more goldfish crackers. Out of the corner of my eye, I caught another person, female this time, around the same age, walking through the courtyard. She stopped at each door, noting the number, until she came to Apartment 36. I leaned over and watched the woman enter the apartment.

You notice the tenants in Apartment 6 have a constant flow of visitors. The visitors tend to arrive and leave within minutes.

I refilled Lilly's cracker supply and threw the rest of our belongings into my bag. I swung Lilly onto my hip, bag over my arm, and pushed open the pool gate. It creaked and squeaked and moaned before slamming shut, loudly announcing our exit to the entire community. I rolled my eyes and continued to creep through the breezeway toward the third courtyard. Not exactly sure of my plan, I only hoped to get there unnoticed.

The door to Apartment 36 opened. I dropped behind the nearest bush and crouched down, trying to balance Lilly and my bag without falling face first into the thorny shrub. I peeked up and watched the woman leave with the same small brown bag. Like the rest, she handled it discreetly while looking around.

Apartment 36's door shut, and it was safe to get up. I could get up. I wanted to get up. But it became clear that the best way out of my position was to fall flat on my butt and proceed from there. The dirt clung to my still damp derriere, and I took my mud-butt up the first stairwell, eyeing Kenneth Fisk's apartment across the way. Apartment 21 (the building was not numbered sequentially. It drove delivery people crazy. The original architect was experimenting with mushrooms when he planned the building, was my guess).

As slyly as one can with a toddler on the hip and mud on the butt, I climbed up the stairs. "This is awkward," I mumbled.

"What's awk-wad mean?" Lilly asked.

"It's when something is uncomfortable," I whispered.

"What does uncom-for-tita-ble mean?"

"It means…not comfy."

"What does not comfy mean?"

"These are really good questions. Please keep them in your brain, and I promise I'll answer them when we get into that apartment up there, OK, sweetie?"

"Hey, Cambria!" Larry poked his head out his window and waved. His long, stringy gray hair dropped down like Rapunzel's. I waved back. Then Lilly waved. Then the resident from Apartment 7 walked by and waved.

Good grief!

I dashed up the remaining steps, opened the door to Kenneth's apartment, and closed it quietly behind us.

Lilly slipped out of my arms and ran around. Her little feet thumped from the living room area to the kitchen to the bedroom area then back again.

I really suck at this undercover crap.

Positioned at the window, I slid one vertical blind over to get a look down at Apartment 36. A skeletal woman waited at the door, one bone-thin hand shoved in her back pocket and the other knocking. The door opened, and a man around my age, maybe a tad older, with a small face, slicked blond hair, and round, gold glasses opened the door and motioned her in. Minutes later they reemerged, her with the bag and him with a fistful of cash.

I pulled out my phone, pointed it at the door, and hit *record.*

There is not enough available storage to record video.

"You have got to be kidding me," I said to the phone. I quickly went through my pictures and deleted as many as I could. Most pictures—OK, more than 3,400—were of Lilly's cute face.

Fifty pictures gone, I repositioned the phone on a new visitor waiting at the door and hit *record.*

There is not enough available storage to record video.

Fine. I snapped a few pictures and composed a text to *Cambria*, noting the time of arrival, the length of stay, and the description of each visitor.

"Can we go home?" Lilly asked, pulling at my towel, causing it to fall to my feet.

"I'm almost done, and then we'll go," I promised.

She slapped her forehead. It was cute. So I took a picture. Then I turned my attention back to my sting. *Is that...Chase?*

It was. He strolled along the pathway, his hips swaying deliciously with each step. His dark blond hair looked extra tousled and his face extra scruffy. I wondered if he ever shaved and what it would feel like to rub my hands across his scruff.

Focus, Cambria.

Since technology had failed me, a second witness would

be beneficial. I looked down at Chase while the phone rang in my ear. He stopped, reached into the pocket of his jeans, and pulled out his phone. He stared at the screen and hesitated. He *hesitated*.

He looked around first then answered, thankfully, because that would have been uncomfortable. "Hey, Cambria. What's going on?"

"Can you come up to Apartment 21?" There was a possible crime in progress, no time for pleasantries.

"The dead guy's apartment?"

"His name is Kenneth Fisk, and yes. Can you come?" Chase looked up at me. "Don't look up. Look at the ground." He looked at his shoes.

"Why am I looking down?"

"Because I'm trying to be discreet here. Can you come up to the apartment, slyly?" He looked up again. "Stop looking at me."

He used his hand as a visor. "I can't see you."

"That's good. Pretend like you're going to fix something in here. See you in a sec." I hit *End*.

About a minute later the door opened, and Chase slipped inside. He was much better at this covert crap than I was.

He looked at me then at the ceiling. "Where are your clothes?"

I imagined my face resembled a tomato. "Er, um, uh…" I bent down and grabbed the towel, envisioning how this could be construed. I called, asked him to meet me in a vacant apartment, and to do so discreetly. Then he finds me in a bikini. I cleared my throat. "I was swimming when I witnessed some suspicious activity back here."

"Suspicious?" He returned his eyes to my fully covered body.

"Very." I pulled the blind back, and we looked down into the empty courtyard.

Lilly tugged on Chase's shirt. "Bạn là ai?" she yelled with a wave of her hand.

Chase looked down, startled, and smiled. He dropped slowly to one knee, holding the window ledge for support. "What's your name? Wait, let me guess…hmm, is it Anna?"

"Nooo, it's not Anna." She giggled, shoving her fingers into her mouth like she did when speaking to strangers.

"No? Is it Elsa? Or wait, no, I got it. It's not...*Lilly*, is it?"

She released a full-face smile, orange cracker stuck in the gaps between her teeth, and nodded. I melted into a big puddle of mushiness right there. It was quite frustrating. It would be easier if he would commit to being a butthole or get ugly. Then I could stop liquefying in his presence.

Lilly offered Chase a cracker, and he popped it into his mouth. Not concerned with germs, as I would have been. The affectionate exchange was becoming too much. "OK now." I clapped my hands together. "Let's get back to work."

Chase winced and used the windowsill as a cane. I offered my free hand, the other clutched to the towel. "Would you like some assistance?"

He brushed off my help. "No, just an old injury." He rolled upright. "You teach your kid...is that...Vietnamese?"

"Yep. Doesn't everyone?" I laughed at my own wittiness, as I usually did. "Do you have kids?" Single guys weren't generally proficient in *Frozen.*

"No, nieces." He moved the blind slat over and looked down. "I'm still not seeing anything."

I glanced out the window. Alice walked through the breezeway. She wore a short-sleeved green shirt and jeans. With so many clothes on, I almost didn't recognize her.

"Can you tell me what's going on?" Chase asked, growing impatient.

"It's Apartment 36. I've seen several suspects coming and going, all carrying a small bag. I'm sort of a crime show junkie. So I sort of know what I'm doing. I think he's selling stolen goods? It makes sense, because if it were drugs, then why would he put it in a bag like that? If it weren't illegal, then why would everyone look so guilty when leaving? Why check the surrounding area if you're carrying, oh, I don't know, a bagel or something? Think about it. Joyce never came to the third courtyard, ever. Kevin is nuts, so anything else going on here is peanuts by comparison. It's the perfect place to run an illegal business."

Chase opened his mouth about to reply, but I wasn't finished.

"There was a gun, zip ties, mask, and wallet in the dumpster along with Kenneth. What if it all belonged to this guy in 36. Kenneth saw what was happening, threatened to expose 36, and was killed." I paused to take a breath—unraveling crimes is exhausting. "Not sure how a pregnancy test and spider web works into this...I haven't gotten that far."

Chase nodded along with my explanation. Stifling a smile. "Have you met Spencer?"

"Who?"

"The tenant in number 36."

"No, why. Have you?"

"He's really nice."

"It's a cover," I muttered.

Chase raised his unkempt brows high up his forehead.

I wanted to lick my finger and smooth the hairs back in place. Though that would be awkward. Almost as awkward as having this conversation in my bathing suit.

"I feel like you *may* be overthinking this. I'm not seeing anyone. Couldn't he be having a party?"

Now I was the one stifling a smile. "In the middle of the day? On a Monday? None staying for more than a few minutes? All leaving with a bag?" I was clearly more versed in criminal behavior than he was. "That reminds me—keep an eye out for any pregnant women around here."

"Why?"

"Pregnancy test in the dumpster?" I reminded him.

"If someone took a pregnancy test last week, would she be showing this soon?"

"Uh..." Good point, but still, "Some women show early." Heaven knows I did. "Do you think I've seen enough to warrant a call to the police?"

Chase ran a hand through his hair. "I think the best thing you can do is keep documentation in case you need it. And instead of camping out in dead people's apartments and spying, how about I keep an eye out when I'm here. I'll start watching crime shows if you think it will help." I couldn't tell if he was flirty-teasing or insult-teasing. *Should I be upset or aroused?*

This was the question every time I was around him.

"What are you doing here anyway?" I asked in an *uproused* kind of way.

Ha, good one, Cambria.

"I stopped by to grab some tools. I've got a big job I'm helping with for a different company. Speaking of which…" He checked his watch. "I've got to head out. I'll be here tomorrow, in case anyone commits any felonies you need help with."

"Ha-ha," I said, not really laughing, because it wasn't funny. *Who knows what will happen tomorrow?*

"Is it OK if I sneak out of here, detective?" That was definitely a flirty-tease. *I think.*

"You're dismissed.

CHAPTER ELEVEN

———

Tenant parks in the carport at Tenant's own risk.

Thirty-two-year-old Spencer Bryant had lived in Apartment 36 for two months. According to his file, he paid rent on time and hadn't made a single maintenance request. According to his application, he had excellent credit upon approval and was a local dentist. Not exactly your run-of-the-mill felon yet definitely a good cover.

In reality Spencer Bryant, DDS was a drug dealer. Writing illegal scripts and selling narcotics out of his apartment for money.

My new theory went like this: Kenneth saw the foot traffic coming and going from Spencer's apartment and was already suspicious. One of Spencer's clients had recently gone on a crime spree, stealing wallets, guns, pregnancy tests…whatever he could get his hands on to sell for cash. Early Monday morning, he brought that cash to Spencer's apartment, ready to buy OxyContin, Vicodin, lidocaine…floss? Whatever it is that a dentist prescribes. Kenneth Fisk, who was outside his door, stretching, ready for his morning trot, saw the burglar leaving Spencer's apartment. He called Joyce to let her know what was happening. When the burglar saw Kenneth on the phone, he came after him. The two got into a scuffle, and Kenneth was killed. The burglar tossed his backpack and Kenneth Fisk into the dumpster to get rid of the evidence, thinking no one would notice. Had I not jumped in—likely no one would have.

Still not exactly sure who was pregnant.

Or how a spider web was involved.

Also, the backpack looked to have been dumped later

than Kenneth...

What I *was* sure of was that Spencer Bryant had something to do with Kenneth Fisk's murder. But theories don't hold up in court. What I needed was proof.

I printed out my carefully crafted, extremely detailed, three-page incident report along with my theory and placed them both in Kenneth's and Apartment 36's file. I closed the rusty cabinet, swiveled around in my chair, and found a reply from Patrick on my computer.

To: cambriaclyne@eldermgmt.com
From: patrickelder@eldermgmt.com
Subject: RE: Nudist-Man-child

Cambria,

Thank you for the mental health information, specifically the one in Brazil you highlighted. I'll pass on the information. Don't hold your breath. Please note that Kevin's actions and opinions are his own and do not mirror those of my company or myself. Feel free to write out an incident report for his file instead of emailing me next time.

-Patrick

I read the email twice to surmise Patrick's tone, and it was not happy. Joyce warned me about bothering Patrick unless it was an emergency. If Kevin skinny-dipping and entering tenant's apartments to eat their food doesn't qualify as an emergency, then what does?

I typed up an incident report as requested and swiveled back around to the filing cabinet. The files were in order from Apartment 1 to Apartment 39. No Apartment 40. I yanked opened the cabinet below and found a file labeled *Kevin*. The papers were squished tight, filling the entire length of the drawer, with not enough give to fit one more. In the next drawer was another file labeled *Kevin*, not quite as full. I shoved my incident report in the back and grabbed the one before it. It was handwritten in Joyce's shaky writing and dated one month prior.

Incident Report

Early this morning (around 1 a.m., I think) I received a call from Silvia Kravitz. She was upset because Kevin was playing his music loud and scaring Harold (her bird). I explained his mental disorders to her. I had already explained this when she called the week before, but I felt it necessary to explain again. I told her it's best to leave him alone. I then received two more calls before I became fed up and called the police. Kevin was arrested. Released on bail the following day, he came into my office and was very upset. When I asked him to leave, he took my vase, the one I keep on the counter to put fresh flowers in. I asked him to return it because my son gave it to me for Mother's Day the year before he passed away. He didn't. Instead, he took it home with him. I walked to his apartment to ask for it back, and he threw it out the window, breaking both the window and the vase. I have quit my job and will be suing Kevin for the cost of my vase.

Update: I received a check for my vase and a bonus for my troubles. Kevin has entered rehab, and it's been promised to us that he will not be returning until after we have moved.

It was the last incident report Joyce wrote.

Joyce's son was dead, as was her vase, Kevin had a mental disorder and had just been released from rehab. And what did he go to rehab for? Alcohol? Narcotics...there was so much backstory to follow. It was like a giant onion—with each layer I peeled back, the more I wanted to cry. *What mental disorder was I dealing with?* "Mental disorder" had extensive implications.

What do I do with the information?

Did it change the situation?

No.

Did it change my perspective?

Yes.

In all the times we'd talked, in all the stories she'd told, Joyce had never mentioned her son had died. One afternoon she'd told me of a time when her son, Josh, was nine and decided he wanted to learn how to drive. He'd somehow managed to get the car out of the driveway and into the neighbor's living room. She'd told it with such a longing fluidity to her voice, like my own grandmother when she told stories of when she was younger, that I hadn't thought anything of it. I'd asked where he lived, and she had replied, "He's in paradise." For whatever reason, I assumed "paradise" meant he lived in Tahiti, near the crystal blue waters, white sandy beaches, and lush greenery. I'd only seen pictures, but it looked like paradise to me. I then said to her, "I hope you get to visit him very soon." Again, I was thinking Tahiti, not an eternal paradise in the sky. I guess paradise is a relative term, and it was hard to think on all four cylinders while trapped in a nicotine fog.

The baritone *ding-dong* summoned me from my thoughts. I slid the incident report back into Kevin's file and closed the cabinet. Tom stood behind the lobby door. He removed his aviators and flashed his signature side-smirk. "Feeling better?" he asked.

Feeling better?

No! One resident is dead. I'd inadvertently told Joyce I hope she'd die soon. Kevin has an unknown mental disability. I have a possible criminal living in Apartment 36. I was third choice, and I can't find my drug box.

"I'm fine," I said instead. "Come on in." I opened the door wider, allowing him entrance, and locked it behind him. "Lilly should be up soon from her nap. Are you on lunch?" I led him to the office and pulled out Joyce's old swivel chair for him.

"I had a break between clients and figured I'd come by and see how the unpacking was going." He took a seat, threw his arms behind his head, and stretched out his long legs, crossing his brown loafers. "I was going to ask for a tour this morning, except someone slammed the door in my face."

I rolled my eyes. "I didn't *slam* the door. It has a door closer preventing it from slamming." I gave him a so-there look and reached down to grab an extra gate opener from a box under the desk. "Here, take this. It'll open the gate, and you can use my apartment front door from now on." I slid it across the sleek wooden surface.

He managed to snatch the opener with one hand before it fell to the floor and slip it into his inner suit jacket pocket. He delivered a full-fledged smile, impressed with his own catlike reflexes. It was cute.

"Nice catch," I said. "Oh, and before I forget, can you take Lilly to the doctor Friday morning? They're going to squeeze her in first thing, and you're usually pretty light on Fridays, right?"

He moaned and went limp, as if suddenly stripped of all cartilage. "Why is she going to the doctor?" he asked, drawing out each word.

"When we got back from the pool earlier, she kept sneezing, and her snot had a yellowish tint to it. This could be the start of a major microbial infection." Examining Lilly's mucus had become a slight obsession.

Tom slapped his hands over his eyes with a relenting sigh. As part of our child support agreement, he's responsible for Lilly's insurance and all medical bills. An agreement he wouldn't have initially agreed upon had he known how much time I spend on WebMD.

"Fine," he surrendered. "I'll take her. She sneezed twice last night, so it's not a bad idea. I guess."

"Thank you. If it's not an infection, ask about allergies." I grabbed my phone. "I'll forward you this article about allergies in toddlers to show the doctor."

"Cam?"

"Huh?" I looked up from my phone to find Tom staring at me intensely—not a seductive *"look how hot my baby momma is"* type of intensity, more of a *"have you contracted a terminal illness?"* intensity.

I tugged on my shirt, feeling self-conscious. "What?"

"You OK?" he finally asked. "You looked stressed out."

Well that's an understatement.

I contemplated telling him about Kenneth and Kevin but decided against it—not exactly sure why. Instead, I told him about Spencer, the visitors, brown bags, and my narcotics theory (with no mention of murder).

When I finished, Tom leaned forward and placed his arms on my desk. "I highly doubt it's drugs, Cam. No dentist is going to risk their license by selling illegal scripts out of their apartment in the middle of a Monday. And even if he were, there's not a chance he'd bag them up."

Good point.

"I do agree that the situation sounds suspicious," he continued. "You should call the police and make a report. After that, stay out of it."

"What?" I scoffed. "How can I stay out of it if it's one of my residents?"

"Easy. Stay out of it. Let the police do their job and you do yours—which does not include staking out apartments with our kid."

Another good point.

"Cam, you *do not* want to get yourself mixed up with a potential drug dealer or with anyone doing anything illegal. OK?"

"Fine," I said without conviction.

"Good." He cleared his throat and shot up straight, nose high in the air like a beagle on a hunt. "Hold on. Cam, are you *smoking*?"

"What? No! Ugh." I grabbed two cans of industrial air freshener. "Chase promised these would work. Maybe I didn't use enough."

"Who's Chase?"

"Maintenance guy." I aimed the cans high in the air and pressed the trigger, releasing a rainfall of manufactured fragrance. The bottle promised "tropical rainforest" but smelled more like cough syrup. To be fair, I'd never been in a real rainforest.

"Take it easy, Cam." Tom coughed and waved his hand in front of his face. "It's not that bad."

"I've become desensitized." I walked backwards out to the lobby, the cans high above my head, spraying every square inch until nothing more spurted out of the nozzle.

Wow, head rush.

Stars danced in my peripheral vision.

Need. Fresh. Air!

I crisscrossed over to the door and flung it open, hesitating while my eyes adjusted.

"That's it! I want a day do-over," I whined.

"What's wrong?" Tom came and stood beside me,

looking out at the two police cars double parked in front of the office with their red and blue lights flashing all around screaming *Look at me! Look at me! I'm here again!*

I placed my hand on Tom's shoulder for support, my head still fuzzy from the tropical rainforest. "Stay here. I'm going to find out what's going on."

"Remember what I said," he hollered after me. "Stay out of it."

I pretended not to hear.

Two police officers were standing near the gate, while two others took reports from a group of angry-looking residents in the carports. Of course, Silvia and Harold were standing close by observing the situation, Silvia with a disapproving shake of her head, Harold with his judgy little eyes. A group of residents began to gather around her.

Seriously, doesn't anyone work during the day?

"And then she said she was going to talk to them…" I heard Silvia telling a pudgy fellow with a bushy gray beard and a Lakers jersey on. He looked like an off-duty Santa. "She walked into their apartment, and not five minutes later, I heard the headboard banging against the wall again, while she was in there."

A woman decked in expensive yoga gear gasped, bringing her hand up to her mouth, while the pudgy Lakers fan winked at me.

But…what…no…um…ugh.

Not right now.

One disaster at a time.

I approached the officers at the gate. One was a muscular, older man with a bulldog face, and his partner was a tall younger guy, with a long neck and a large Adam's apple. Really large. As if an actual apple was stuck in there.

"Hello," I greeted. "I'm the apartment manager. Can you tell me what's going on?"

Bulldog spoke first. "A car was reported stolen."

"Stolen?" I wheezed, as if the air had been pulled out of my lungs. So much for Joyce's food-poisoning-police-radar theory!

"It happened sometime during the day," said Adam's

Apple, his apple bobbing up and down, up and down, up and down in a distractive rhythm. "You see anything?"

See anything?

So happy he asked, I proceeded to tell them about Kenneth, what I'd witnessed with Spencer, my theory, and I may have mentioned I was third choice—call me selfish, but I was having a hard time letting that one go. Bulldog scrawled in his notebook until I finished. He nodded to Adam's Apple, who nodded back then turned around to speak into the radio on his shoulder.

"I can take you back to Spencer if you like," I offered. Might as well question him now. Make an arrest. Put this murder to bed and concentrate solely on keeping Kevin clothed.

Bulldog finished speaking to his shoulder and nodded to Adam's Apple, who nodded back once again. My eyes bounced between the two men, trying to decipher their nods. "We'll turn over this information," Bulldog said, flipping his notebook shut.

"What about—hey!" A finger jabbed my arm. A short woman with more lipstick on her teeth than her lips inserted herself into my personal space, her finger pointed and ready to poke again. I took a step back. She took a step closer. "Can I help you?"

"You the new manager?" she asked with a thick accent. Her dark hair was pulled into a sleek bun, and she wore a red flamenco-inspired dress.

I rubbed my shoulder. "I am."

"We've got everything we need," Adam's Apple said as he, Bulldog, and the two other officers strolled back to their cruisers. "We have your contact information if we have any questions."

"Wait one second, offi—ouch! I am not going to talk to you if you keep poking me," I warned the woman.

"Manager," she snapped, her finger ready to dig into my bicep again.

"What can I help you with?" I asked as sweetly as I could, rubbing my sure-to-be-bruised arm.

"My car is gone, and I have my salsa class!"

My stomach dropped. "I am very sorry about that." I held my hand up, ready to strike if she came at me with her finger again. "You can submit the police report to your insurance company, and I'll see what I can do about upping security in the carports."

She took a step closer. I took a step back. She took another step closer and lashed me in her native tongue, her hands flailing above her head. Even if I wasn't fluent in Spanish, I caught the gist.

"Please, calm down," I said, knowing full well it was a pointless suggestion. If someone stole my car, I'd be… Who was I kidding? No one would steal my car.

"I can't calm down," she continued in English. "I have no car! I have salsa class tonight, and I pay good money for my salsa, and we have a competition this week, and now I can't go. So I lose my money for the class, and I lose my car. We don't need more security. We need Yoyce. This never happened when she was here, and suddenly you show up, and Kenneth is dead, and my car is gone. I think it's no coincidence."

"I can assure you I had nothing to do with any of it." I rubbed my arm and looked over at the group of angry residents huddled around Silvia and Harold. The sideways glances my way were a not-so-subtle hint I was still the topic of conversation. Great. "I'm sorry. I didn't catch your name?"

"Daniella." She crossed her arms and looked at me expectantly.

"Daniella, what time is your salsa class?"

"Seven."

"OK." I sighed. "I'll give you a ride."

CHAPTER TWELVE

———

*Landlord shall not be liable for physical assaults or property
damage caused by other Tenants or Tenants' guests.*

Thursday, October 6th
Dear New Apartment Manager,
*Accept this letter as my official thirty-day notification. We will
be moving to a safer apartment complex with a more competent
manager. You can return my full deposit within twenty-four
hours of our departure.*

Sincerely,
Rachael M. Manfeld

I'd been the sole apartment manager for seven days.
Seven days. And the place had gone to hell. *Hell* (or so I'd been
told by many). It had to be some kind of world record.

To my knowledge, there hadn't been any new
developments in Kenneth's case. I'd witnessed seven more
individuals leave Spencer's apartment, all with the same brown
bag, all looking over their shoulder, all leaving out the back
walkway. I'd called the police to report my finding so many
times I was on a first-name basis with the dispatch operator.
Penny had a three-month-old baby girl and a fiancé named
Pedro. I was one call away from being a bridesmaid.

Rarely did anyone call me back. One officer arrived,
humored me, and knocked on Spencer's door. Spencer wasn't
home, and that was the end of that.

As if a murder, grand theft auto, and drug dealings
weren't enough, two washing machines broke, which "never

happened when Joyce was here," and just about everyone lost their minds. Then Kevin dumped a bag of kitty litter down his toilet. To fix his toilet, we had to shut off the water to the back half of the building. No water for twenty minutes. This was the icing on the "I hate my new manager" cake.

Our Rent or Run rating had risen to a 50% run rate—the highest in the neighborhood. The management had dropped to 2.5 stars, and safety to 3.5—the lowest in the neighborhood.

I hate that app.

Patrick had received several complaints about my "terrible management style." The biggest complaints (aside from the crime I seemingly brought with me) were that I "hated the elderly" and I "threw away other people's hard-earned property" and was "antireligious." There was also a rumor that I had a threesome with Clare and Bob, which, when you think about it, contradicts the first complaint.

Life would be easier if I carried on Joyce's tradition of never leaving the apartment (but then I couldn't continue being Daniella's personal taxi. The woman had salsa every night). Joyce, I'd learned from Daniella, didn't even leave to show vacant units. She would hand prospective tenants the key and let them wander around. I couldn't manage like that. I walked the property. I showed apartments. I enforced the rules. If you leave a dead plant on your front porch, I will throw it away. If you hang a giant crucifix in the laundry room, I will remove it. If you tell me the reason you haven't paid your rent is because your arthritis is acting up and you are too old and the office is too far, I will show up at your door.

I didn't make the rules. I was simply paid to enforce them.

Patrick couldn't overlook the fact that I hadn't collected all the rents. Despite being served three-day notices, rents were still being withheld as reparation for an "unsafe complex and incompetent manager." It was my job to explain to the residents that that's not how life works. This would make residents mad, and they would call and complain to Patrick, and thus the cycle continued. Evictions were expensive, according to Patrick, and collecting rents was a basic job responsibility, according to Patrick. He was nearing the end of his rope. I could hear it in his voice.

According to my employee contract: *If Employee is terminated within the first thirty days of employment, Employee agrees to vacate the Premises within twenty-four hours of the time of termination.*

I was no longer swimming.

I wasn't treading either.

I was drowning.

It felt as if a pair of imaginary hands were squeezing my lungs and using my head as a punching bag. If I lost my job, my options were limited. *Where would we go?* Amy rented a room from an older woman in Burbank, a retired set designer with velvety couches, expensive glass décor, white carpet, and at least twenty rescue cats. Even if I could bunk with Amy temporarily, a white-carpeted house was no place for a child, especially mine, and I was allergic to cats in a can't breathe, puffy face, pass-the-Benadryl kind of way.

Neither of my parents was in a financial position to help. My dad was a struggling plumber by day and an under-paid high school basketball coach by night. My mom was a secretary at a meat packing facility. Neither would turn me away if I showed up on their doorstep. Of course, then I'd be forced to come clean about Tom. Tell them that on top of being unemployed, flat broke, and a complete failure in life, I was also a liar. My pride was still too intact for that option.

Worst-case scenario: Lilly could live with Tom while I scraped enough money together for a motel. When I was nearing eviction from Crap-o-la Apartments, Tom hadn't offered to let me stay with him should we officially get the boot. He of course said Lilly could, but not one mention of me. I got it. He was a womanizer and made no secret of it. He was an attractive young lawyer (although a broke one, which I doubt he mentioned), and as if that wasn't enough, he was a doting daddy. Women swooned. He'd met half a dozen short-lived flings while playing with Lilly at the McDonald's play yard. My presence would prove a challenge because although a doting dad was an attractive quality, the doting dad's baby momma living with him was a glaring red flag. Even if the baby momma was on Alcatraz.

My only real option was to keep my job, and I was prepared to do whatever it took.

I closed the office door and squeezed past the boxes working as my kitchen table. It was late. Lilly had long since gone to bed, allowing me time to finish up work. I'd kissed her sweet face earlier but didn't dare check on her now for fear of waking her up. I zigzagged through my unpacked apartment, toward the blue glow of the television. Amy was nestled on the couch watching an episode of *The Real Housewives from somewhere*. She had arrived on my doorstep late Monday night in complete ruin after giving her boyfriend of two years the "marriage ultimatum." He ultimately decided he'd rather date a model from the Valley named Jessica instead.

I did what every best friend would do: I removed all social media outlets, hid her phone, provided an ample supply of ice cream, trash-talked her ex, kept my problems to myself, and allowed her to watch my kid while I worked.

Really, she's lucky to have me.

"You're the one with a drinking problem," one blonde housewife on the television yelled at another blonde housewife. All the other blonde housewives gasped, their diamond-encrusted fingers clutching tight to their pearls and champagne-filled flutes.

"I'm so confused. I thought she had a drug problem. Or is that the other one?" I asked Amy. She didn't answer. "You awake?" I leaned over and put my chin on her shoulder. "Amy! I said no." I plucked my phone out of her hand. "I've been looking for this. I told you, online stalking is only going to make things worse."

She sat up and tucked her skinny legs under her, pouting. "I wasn't stalking *him*." We made a pact to never say her ex-boyfriend's name again. "I was looking for you."

"Here I am."

She rolled her puffy eyes. Her pink and blue greasy hair had dreadlocked, looking as if it were trying to escape from her head. The sleeves of *his* sweater were pulled down over her hands, working as a Kleenex when needed. "I was looking *for* you. I was trying to find this Chase guy so we can get more info. I want to see what he looks like."

"Why?" I squeaked. "I don't think of him as anything but the maintenance man, and even that's a stretch." Not to mention I'd already looked him up on Facebook, Twitter, Instagram, Snapchat, and every other social media site I could think of with no luck. As it turned out, Chase J. Hudson was a popular name (I may have also looked at his employment file—he lived in Long Beach, had no criminal history, good credit, and excellent references. Which was odd because he was terrible at his job).

"Sure you don't," she said with a wry twitch of her lip as she tossed a throw pillow at me. I caught it with my face. "I've never seen you so googly-eyed over a boy before, and I love it." She laughed for the first time since "Jessica from the Valley."

"Gee, thanks," I said.

"You know what I mean." She wrapped a dreadlock behind her ear. "For the longest time you've been stuck on Tom, whom we both know is never going to settle down, and when he does, it will probably be with some model named *Jessica,* like, from, like, the Valley. Tramp."

"I told you I don't like Chase. He's a colleague…ugh." I may be able to lie to myself, and I may be able to lie to my parents, but there was no lying to Amy. She knew me too well. I buried my head in the pillow and face-planted into the couch. "Why are guys who aren't attracted to me so attractive?"

Amy wrapped her long, bony arm around my waist and dropped her head next to mine. Spooning me in *his* snot-covered sweater. "If I knew the answer, I wouldn't be here," she whimpered, digging her face into my shirt and snarfing up a snot bubble. "Why do I need this stupid boy?"

I flipped to my back. "You don't *need* any boys," I said with conviction. "You were Burn Victim Number Three in a *Grey's Anatomy* episode and Dead Girl Number Four in *Zombie Time Machine.* You don't need any boys. You deserve a man."

Amy sat up. "You're totally right." She ran her hand under her nose, leaving a streak of snot on her left cheek. "We're hot, strong, independent, confident women. We don't need boys. Boys who are going to say how much they love us then follow their peckers to younger pastures." An evil smirk spread across her blotchy face. "Let's get revenge."

I'd underestimated my pep-talking abilities. I laughed,

happy she'd finally entered the anger stage of the breakup grief cycle. Hopefully the "get off my couch and resume personal hygiene" stage came next. As it stood, I was one day away from giving my best friend of twenty years the "shower ultimatum."

"Funny you should mention revenge." I spoke slowly, drumming my fingers along my chin. "I just so happen to have recently learned how to remove door locks and disassemble a toilet."

Bam! Bam! Bam!

A pounding on the window forced me off the couch and onto the floor, wedged between two boxes, where I assumed the fetal position. It was Spencer and his druggy friends. They came to take our wallets, zip-tie our hands, and impregnate us.

I was sure of it.

Amy poked her head over the side of the couch. "Some lady is crying outside your window. I think she wants to speak to the manager."

"Is she pregnant?"

"Would you like me to ask?"

I thought about it. "No, it's probably the washing machines." Or so I hoped. "People take their laundry very seriously around here." I crawled out of my barricade, slipped on a pair of sandals, and found the tear-stain-faced woman pacing outside my window. She wore an off-the-shoulder black shirt with *Pink* written in pink lettering across the front, showing off the stars tattooed down her neck and across her shoulder. She ran up to me and wrapped her thick arms tight around me, soaking the front of my shirt with tears.

I'm a human Kleenex.

I patted her back, unsure of what to say.

She took a step back. Mascara horseshoed her dark eyes while tears slithered down her cheeks. "I'm so glad you're home. I'm locked out, and I called the emergency line and had to leave a message. I tried getting in, but I can't get the window to open, and the locksmith is still an hour out. I know the lease says I'm not supposed to bother you unless it's an emergency, but I really need to get in." She drew a shaky breath. "Can you let me in? It's Apartment 39."

"Of course." I was readily accommodating to anyone

who had actually read the lease. "I'm so sorry. I didn't have my phone on me." *Damn it, Amy.* "Let me grab my keys, and I'll meet you there."

She nodded a sorrowful nod. I'd locked myself out numerous times and never cried about it. She did live next to Kevin though. He could come outside naked, and she'd have nowhere to hide. So I got it.

I grabbed my keys and hurried to the third courtyard, bypassing many a disgruntled tenant along the way. I slipped on imaginary blinders and trudged through the battleground, dodging the sideways glances, glaring eyes, and under-the-breath insults hurled at me. Narrowly making it to the back staircase unscathed.

Up the stairs I went, past Kevin's door, and found the woman on her knees, her cheek pressed against the faded brown door. "I'm so sorry, lumber," she sobbed, stroking the weathered wood slowly with her fingers. "My lumber…"

Umm.

She was apologizing to the door.

Made sense. Kevin's neighbor would have to be crazy to still live there. I leaned over the woman's head and used the master key to unlock the door. She hurried to her feet and pushed it open, revealing a brown-eyed toddler on the other side.

"There was a kid in there?" I asked, shocked. Wouldn't that have been worth mentioning?

"Lumber!" she scolded the little boy. He was covered in marker and flour and makeup and chocolate (hopefully chocolate), like the rest of the apartment. Black lines were scribbled down the lower half of the walls and continued across the carpet. Flour mounds clumped together in doughy blobs all over the couch and the television and the kitchen table that, coincidently, looked to have received a fresh coat of pink nail polish.

The mom in me felt terrible. The apartment manager in me began tallying up the charges…*paint $250, carpet $800, linoleum $450…* It would have been cheaper to break the window. "You don't ever lock the door on Mommy like that, ever… My television!" She released a high-pitched yelp. I cringed. The commotion could summon Kevin. He'd been quiet all day. It was quite nice. "My table!"

I stood in the doorway, rocking from heels to toes. Probably not the best time to let her know about the repairs she'd need to make. "Er…I'm going to head back now…" She didn't notice me. She was too busy inspecting the finger painting on the wall. "I'll just…close this door for you. Have, er, a good night."

I tiptoed to the stairwell, placing as little weight on each foot as possible to prevent the walkway from creaking. The old building made it difficult to get anywhere unnoticed. I held my breath as I passed Kevin's door and ever so carefully dropped my foot onto the first step.

Still quiet.

Next step.

Golden silence.

Another step.

Nothing.

I released my withheld breath. The black door remained closed and quiet. Almost too quiet. A calm-before-the-storm type of quiet.

The only sounds were coming from Lumber's hysterical mother and muffled yells from below. Alice and her Boo were arguing. I strained to make out what they were screaming about, because I'm nosy. Intense fluctuations, shrieks, and thunderous grumbles then the slamming of a door.

"You think I wouldn't time you," Boo yelled.

At least I think that's what he said.

Then another voice, possibly Alice. "You're…planting…ducks."

Hmmm, that can't be right.

My snooping skills needed some work, but it sounded like things were working out for Alice about as well as they were for me.

Then came the loud, wet rumbling of someone about to eject a wad of phlegm. It came from below the stairwell.

Crap.

I pretended I was examining the railing, shaking it to be sure it was sturdy, and not eavesdropping on tenants, because that wouldn't be right. Especially if I were to be caught by another tenant.

Leaning over the railing as part of my "inspection," I found a shoeless, shirtless mass of white muscles with a buzzed head shooting a snotball into the flowerless flowerbed beside him.

I crouched down and shoved my face between the bars of the now-determined-to-be-sturdy railing. Teardrops were tattooed under the guy's eyes, semiautomatics and revolvers down the man's arms and across his chiseled abdomen, stopping at the waistband of his basketball shorts and continuing down the exposed skin of his hairy calves. He had surprisingly dainty feet for a man his size and well-groomed toenails.

I'm not generally one to judge a book by its cover. However, if I *were* a judging-a-book-by-its-cover type of person, I would say this book was a murder-mystery, nightmare-inducing, unhappy-ending thriller. This guy was scary. He was scary all the way from his "I'm gonna kill you" stance to his "I can kill you with these" muscles to his "I'll kill you with one of these instead" tattooed artillery. Was it a coincidence I found a gun in the dumpster much like the one pictured on his left pectoral? Was it by happenstance that this guy stood in the same location where all of Spencer's clients had arrived and left? Was it a coinkydink that (according to an episode of *CSI*) teardrops under the eye could represent murders committed or murders attempted?

Methinks not.

I gulped, trying desperately to coat my suddenly parched throat. Scary Guy brought a nearly burnt-out cigarette to his mouth, took in a long draw of nicotine, and discarded the butt in the aforementioned flowerless flowerbed. In paragraph six on the eighth page of the *House Rules*, it states I can serve anyone caught littering on the property with a twenty-five-dollar fine.

He stuck his sausage finger up his nose and dug around until he found what he was looking for and, after a quick inspection, flicked it into the flowerbed as well. Next he folded a stick of gum into his mouth and tossed the silver wrapper into the flowerbed.

That makes fifty.

I dashed down the remaining steps. Confronting the man was the best idea since I'd left my phone in the apartment and logic was still trotting its way to my brain.

I waltzed up to Scary Guy, who turned his head, puffed his chest, and flexed his guns. Two tiny pupils glared down at me. He'd been much shorter from my aerial view. I cleared the imaginary mucus from my throat to buy time. Surely, a smarter person would have thought this out prior to advancing. "What apartment are you in?" I asked in a shrilly voice. I was going for authoritative, but I sounded more like SpongeBob.

"Who are you?" he grunted, blinking, as if I were a side dish he hadn't ordered.

I balled my fists to keep them from shaking. "I'm the apartment manager. Now, what apartment do you live in, or who are you visiting?"

"I'm visiting Mike," he said quickly, without missing a beat.

There were at least five Mikes who lived here—that I knew of. "Mike? Really? Which one?"

"Mind your own business Mike, that's who." Scary Guy was getting mad.

"Mind *my* own business?" I was getting equally mad. "Does the name Kenneth Fisk mean anything to you? Missing a backpack by chance?"

The donkey finally trotted in with my logic. *What the hell are you doing, Cambria? This guy is twice your size!*

Scary Guy locked his jaw and squared his shoulders. He stopped looking at me as the side dish he hadn't ordered and more like the main entrée he wanted to devour. *Crap.*

I took a big step back, crashing into whoever stood behind me. A pair of arms wrapped around my chest, pinning my arms to my side. My adrenaline pumped, thrusting my heartbeat into overdrive. Half a dozen self-defense YouTube videos began playing through my memory.

Thumb into trachea.

Head to nose.

Back kick to balls.

Fingers into eye sockets.

Got it.

I went into attack mode.

My attacker pivoted, bobbed, and bounced around

behind me like some kind of super ninja warding off all my attacks. Hands grappled at my flailing limbs until they landed on my lower back and pushed me forward.

I fell into a wooden pillar holding the upstairs walkway up and wrapped my arms around it, the splintery wood clawing at my forearms as my momentum swung me around to face my attacker.

Our eyes met.

I froze, stock-still and confused and scared and seconds away from peeing my pants.

Deep breath in and *ahh!*

CHAPTER THIRTEEN

———

No alcohol permitted in Common Areas.

"Why are you screaming?" Chase asked between breaths. He picked his black hat up off the ground and slapped it back onto his head.

"Why am *I* screaming?" I huffed, still hugging the pillar, scared to let it go and unsure if my legs were capable of holding me upright. "You were attacking me!"

"Calm down, everybody." Larry zigzagged in slow motion between us, flipping his stringy gray hair over his shoulder. "Everyone needs to calm down. Caaalm dooown. Let's figure this out diplomatical-baly…diploma…just be at peace before we start throwing punches." He wobbled to the right and to the left then spun around. "Why were you beating on the maintenance man?" he asked me.

"Me?" I gasped and pointed to Chase. "He grabbed me from behind!"

Chase rolled the sleeves of his black hoodie up to his elbows, shaking his head. "You ran into me and started flapping around."

"It's true!" yelled a tween standing on the upstairs walkway. She had blonde pigtails and wore a green shirt doused in sparkles and shorts the same size as my underwear. She leaned over the railing, holding out her phone, and snapped her gum. "I totally got it all on video."

"You what?" I let go of my pillar.

Larry gave me a look of warning and pointed his finger in my general direction. "Shhhtay in your corner," he said.

I went back to my pillar and looked over Larry's head at

Chase. "What are you doing here?"

"Number 38 is locked out, and her kid is inside. The emergency line forwarded to me because you didn't answer." He took a step closer.

Larry cut him off, his arms outstretched like a drunken bird about to take flight. "Shhhtay in your corner," he slurred.

"I already got sixty views on Snapchat!" the tween yelled. "Oh, wait! Make that seventy. They all totally think the chick is having some kind of seizure and the guy is way hot."

I rolled my eyes. "Of course they do." Larry kept bobbing his head like a chicken, blocking Chase from my view. "Honestly, Larry, I'm fine. We're fine. Feel free to go home and sleep it off."

Larry gave Chase a sideways glance. With a nod of his head, he cleared the space between us by stumbling to the side. Chase and I exchanged a should-we-escort-him-home-or-continue-arguing look.

I went for the latter. "I was talking to… Crap!" I looked around the courtyard Teardrops of Death (my new nickname for Scary Guy) was gone, and Larry looked to have fallen asleep.

"She was talking to crap!" Sparkly Tween screeched with laughter and stretched her arms over the railing with her phone tight in her hand. "This is totally going viral."

"No more video," Chase warned in a deep, stern voice.

The tween blushed and brought the phone to her chest, pouting her pink, glittery-specked bottom lip.

"Tell me you got video of the guy I was talking to before?" I asked her.

"What guy?"

"No!" I ran out to the carports and down the uneven driveway, looking into every stall as I sprinted past. If Sparkly Tween hadn't seen him, he must have slipped out the back. Except he was nowhere to be seen.

"Cambria, stop!" Chase grabbed my arm and spun me around. "What are you doing?"

I yanked my arm out of his grasp, panting, and plopped my hands onto my thighs, catching my breath. That was a lot of running. "You let that guy get away! He…could…have…come…" *Ouch, side cramp.*

"Dammit, Cambria. Despite what you may think, watching crime shows does not make you a cop. That guy had prison tats all over him, and you decide to confront him? As if he's going to do what? Confess to a murder? You have no idea he's done anything. A couple of days ago, you had Spencer pegged as a criminal. Really, Cambria? Common logic told you that you should get into this guy's face? He's twice your size!"

I gnashed my teeth and took a deep breath in through my nose. He made sense, and it ticked me off. I hated it. I hated every word of it. "Chase, as crazy as it may sound, I'm trying to help Kenneth *and* save my job because no one else is taking anything I say seriously. This place, apparently, was the safest compound in all the land until I showed up. I have six move-out notifications on my desk. Six!" I held up six fingers to drive the point home. "I'm doing my best to provide for my family and keep a roof over our heads, which isn't easy when you're dealing with murders and parrots and washers and nudity and guys with teardrop tattoos. I'm so close to not only losing my job but my home. So forgive me for doing everything I can. I'm sorry that upsets you. Why don't you go somewhere and fix something?" My bottom lip began to quiver. My waterworks grenade was about to detonate. *You will not cry, Cambria. You will* not *cry.* I was already coated in the snot and tears of others and was not about to add in my own, not in front of Chase.

A feeling of vulnerability crashed down on me. It was neither a familiar nor pleasant sensation.

With nothing left to say, I turned my snot-covered body around and walked away, leaving Chase speechless. I didn't expect, nor did I want, him to follow me. All I wanted was a tub of French Vanilla and a clean shirt.

My apartment door was wide open. Amy was propped up against the doorjamb, all showered and preened and smiling. Her pink and blue tendrils lay perfectly blown out below her shoulders. My red shirt, which she apparently decided to borrow, was tucked into her own boyfriend jeans. Her face was freshly painted with eye shadow, mascara, bronzer, and pink gloss. She seemed to have hurdled the last stages of the breakup grief cycle while I was out apartment managing. "You were gone forever," she said, exasperated. "I was really worried."

"So you got dressed?" I cleared the threshold, ramming my shin into the corner of the box working as a side table. "Ouch!" I kicked the stupid box, crushing its contents, which sounded a lot like glass. "My life!" I groaned, kicking the box again.

"Well, hello there. Did you lock yourself out?" Amy purred.

I turned to find Chase sheepishly waiting at the door, his hands shoved into his front pockets.

Good grief. "Amy, this is Chase, the maintenance man," I said, rubbing my shin.

Amy's eyes reached an abnormally wide circumference. "Chase?" she squeaked. "I didn't...I didn't even know you had a maintenance guy." She shrugged indifferently then turned toward me and mouthed *so hot.* "Well then, it looks like I have to be leaving. If you would be so kind as to give me back my phone, I'll be out of your hair."

Her bony behind had become one with my couch, and now, when I'd rather not be alone, she decided to detach herself from my furniture and make a miraculous recovery. It was far too fishy and very un-Amy-like. I couldn't press her too hard with Chase looking on. "What are you doing?" I asked under my breath.

"What we talked about," she said with a wink, and unleashed a mischievous smile. "Gimme. Gimme." She wiggled her fingers.

With a sigh of surrender, I dislodged her phone from behind the cable box. "Thank you," she sang, plucking the phone out of my grip. "So nice meeting you. Chase, was it?" She flashed her three-grand veneers and sashayed past him.

I leaned out the door. "I don't have bail money," I hissed through clenched teeth.

"Text ya later," she called out and rounded the corner out of sight.

I stifled a groan and tossed my attention over to the boy hovering in my doorway. "What's wrong now?" I asked all snappily, folding my arms over my chest.

"I didn't mean to upset you," he said.

Really?

It was like saying "I'm sorry your feelings are hurt" or "I'm sorry you're upset." It's an apology without admission of wrongdoing—thus not an apology at all. Under normal circumstances, I'd reject the lame attempt. However, his puppy-dog-eye accompaniment won me over.

"Chase, the situation upsets me," I said, dropping my arms. "I think the teardrop guy knows Spencer, and if I could have only kept him quarantined until I called the police, then he and Spencer could have been questioned. Now I can't call the police and say, 'Hey, I found a guy with sketchy tattoos, and even though I haven't seen him do anything illegal, I suspect him of murder.' They'll think I'm crazy."

Chase bit his bottom lip, holding in a smile, as if I unintentionally told a dirty joke he shouldn't laugh at.

"What?" I asked.

"Cambria, you were going to keep him quarantined?"

"Hell yeah I was. Never underestimate a woman on the verge of ruin."

He gave me a *touché* look. "I get your intentions are good, but you need to let the police do their job. You have no idea what they've done, who they're looking at, what leads they've followed up on. They're not going to let a murder slide under the radar. And they're definitely not going to share sensitive information with you. Shouldn't you think things through more fully?"

I nodded reluctantly. *Guess I can give him that.*

He looped his thumbs into his pockets and leaned against the doorway, looking past me. "I see you've settled in."

I tucked Einstein behind my ear. "I'm taking more of an unpack-as-necessary approach. I did hang one picture in the hallway though." I exhaled and waited. If we were engaging in small talk, it would be his turn; if we were done, I was in need of a pint of ice cream to help with my stress and a Diet Coke to help with my headache. That drug box was still hiding. Granted, I hadn't put much effort into locating it.

"Sounds efficient," he said with a smile. I appreciated the fact that he didn't try to sugarcoat the truth with some weak I'm-sure-it-will-all-work-out crap like Tom would have. I needed a little more pessimism in my life. I wanted to sulk and eat ice cream and cry, not be optimistic. "For reals though," he continued, dropping the smile. "You sure you're OK?"

"I'm fine," I lied.

He regarded me through squinted eyes, as if reading my thoughts. My stomach got all fluttery and my legs all liquidy. There was no time for gushiness, butterflies, and sexual fantasies. I was nearly homeless.

"OK, guess I'll talk to you later. Night," I said, swinging the door shut. There was no time to deal with feelings either.

I weaved through the cardboard maze in my living room to the kitchen, picking up toys along the way like a human Pac-Man, with a Diet Coke and a pint of Chocolate Malt ice cream as my prize. Both were consumed immediately upon completion. The rich chocolate combined with the sweet carbonation made my tongue happy…my stomach, not so much. Ouch.

I leaned against the counter, rubbing my ailing abdomen. My mind churned through the events of the day. In hindsight I should not have confronted Teardrops of Death. I should have stalked him instead. Follow him around to be sure he came from Spencer's apartment. Telling him I was the apartment manager wasn't the best idea either. Let's just say, for example, he decided to brutally murder me in my sleep. He'd know exactly where to find me. Crap.

I pushed a pile of heavy boxes in front of the door and sank to the floor behind them, folding in half and pulling my knees close to my chest while my mind took a terrifying trip down Worst-case Scenario Lane.

At eleven thirty Amy answered my thirty-two text messages, confirming what I suspected. She had gone to a bar that, according to Facebook, her ex had checked into. She planned to "casually" bump into him while flirting with everything on two legs to make him jealous. (This was her idea of revenge. My toilet plan was better.) The ex wasn't there, and she, according to the text messages that were getting drunker as the night went on, met a guy named "Rock." He had "broom" eyes, olive skin, and was around five foot ten, two hundred "plounders" with a "rescuing" dark "herring" (whatever that meant). She followed him to a party and sent me the description so I'd be able to identify her abductor if she went missing.

Because I wasn't stressed enough already.

My head began drooping around midnight, feeling especially heavy. It was a fight to keep conscious. Then came a tap on the door. I clambered up to the peephole.

Chase? Again?

I turned off the alarm. Removed the boxes. Unlocked the bottom lock. Flipped the deadbolt and opened the door. "Chase, what are you doing here?" I asked. His hoodie and hat were gone, replaced by a black collared shirt and a more styled mess of hair.

"When you said you were fine, did you really mean you were fine and not doing that thing girls do when they say fine but mean the exact opposite?" He looked down at the butcher knife clutched in my hand. I mean, I had to have protection just in case.

"Oh, um, I was just cutting...*avocados*," I said, hiding the knife behind my back. "Like I said, I'm fine. Just wanted some guacamole."

"Do you want some company?"

"Yes."

CHAPTER FOURTEEN

———

Landlord reserves the right to initiate eviction process or give notice to vacate if Tenant turns out to be a Grade-A Douchebag.

Sunlight shot onto my eyelids like a laser, forcing me from a deep, dreamless slumber. I threw my arm over my face and rolled to the other side of the bed, except it wasn't there. It was in the bedroom, and I was on the couch. I landed on the floor.

I forced my lids open. Chase was asleep on the other side of the couch with his feet crossed and resting on my cardboard coffee table. His head hung to one side while his nose whistled with each heavy breath he took. The old me, the PMS (Pre-apartment Management Situations) Cambria would have been aching to nestle under his free arm. He looked so cozy. Despite his lack of handy skills and the fact he scared Teardrops of Death away, he was a fine specimen of a man. He'd be almost pretty if he shaved and combed his hair, maybe too pretty. I enjoyed the scruffiness. It made him even sexier in an I-woke-up-like-this kind of way that PMS Cambria would have been drooling over. Unfortunately, I wasn't PMS Cambria anymore; I was ATBOW (About To Be On Welfare) Cambria, and I had bigger issues to deal with.

I scooted off to the bathroom to perform my usual pee, weigh myself, and declare the diet-starts-tomorrow routine. My mouth tasted like morning, and goop had embedded itself into the corners of my eyes. In the mirror, under the still-crooked vanity light, my face looked sunken and my waist smaller, even if the evil scale refused to show any changes. Dark, puffy bags girdled my eyes, and I was so pale the auburn freckles scattered across my face looked like blackheads.

What the?

I leaned in closer.

Is that…yes it is.

Chocolate. There was chocolate crusted to the corners of my mouth. I'd spent hours talking with Chase until we fell asleep. *Hours.* We had polished off a gallon of Chocolate Mocha Swirl ice cream as we chatted, touching on my year at Fresno State. Lilly's cuteness. I learned he grew up in Long Beach, didn't have too much family, and went to a junior college for a couple of years only to drop out to be a maintenance man. He was not terribly forthcoming with information. He mostly asked me a lot of questions. We had glossed over many subjects, and never, not once, did he mention I had chocolate on my mouth. *Not once.*

Well that's embarrassing.

I splashed warm water on my face, except more water went on the mirror than on my tired mug. Time to get dressed. Lilly would wake soon, so I only had time to change. Jeans off. Semi-clean jeans on. Snot-crusted shirt off. Semi-clean blue Mossimo shirt… *Oh no…* Voices came from the other side of the wall. It was a familiar grumble… *Crap!*

I bolted out to the living room where Chase, Lilly, and Tom were all gathered. Lilly perched on top of a box with Minnie Mouse in her hands. Chase stood with his hands in his front pockets and face pointed to the floor. And Tom in his usual business attire—gray suit, white shirt, black skinny tie—looked quite debonair and extremely mad.

"Mommy," Lilly giggled. "Where's your shirt?"

I looked down at the shirt in my hand and said a quick prayer of thanks my bra was still on. "What are you doing here, Tom?" I asked while pulling the shirt over my head.

"Picking up my daughter for her doctor's appointment. They squeezed her in. Don't you recall this conversation?" he answered all lawyer-y.

"Of course I remember." *Totally forgot.* "Er, Chase, this is Tom, and Tom, this is Chase." I might as well make introductions in case that hadn't already happened.

Chase nodded without taking his focus off the carpet.

"Chase?" Tom said slowly. I could see the wheels in his mind turning. "Chase. OK, that's right." He looked at me with a scathing grin spread across his face. "The 'maintenance man.'" He made air quotes around maintenance man, which would be correct since Chase didn't do a whole lot of maintenance. But I doubt that's why he air-quoted it.

We all stood there. "Awk-a-ward." Lilly broke the silence from her perch.

"Go put on the pink dress that's on your dresser." I manually turned her by the shoulders and pointed her toward the hallway. "Stay in there until we call you out." That should keep her busy for a while.

"I'm gonna go do some *maintenance,*" Chase said, his hands still shoved deep into his pockets, eyes trained on the floor. He walked around Tom, who refused to move and gave Chase the evil stare-down his entire journey to the door.

We watched the door close behind Chase. We watched Chase hurry past the windows. We watched Chase walk toward the carports, and as soon as he disappeared…

"What is wrong with you?" Tom and I said in unison.

"You're a hypocrite!" we yelled.

I gasped.

He gasped.

I stared.

He stared.

He who spoke last wins. We remained at a standstill, glaring at each other, blue on hazel, until Tom caved. "OK, I'll say it. Last month, when you came and got Lilly, and I had whatever-her-name-is at my house, you lost your mind, even when I explained that Lilly was still asleep and never saw whatever-her-name-was. You went nuts!"

"I can't believe you're bringing that up," I snapped. "That's so different. You bringing some random woman home to have a sleepover in the room next to my child is totally reckless. I stand by my decision to go nuts. Chase and I fell asleep while talking because…" I took a gulp of air, knowing if I said Chase was there because I was scared, he wouldn't believe me. If he did, he'd want to know why. Then I'd say on top of the potential drug dealers there was also a murder and a car theft. Then he'd want to know why I was putting our child in harm's way. Then I would say I wasn't. Then he would argue that hanging around an apartment where a resident was murdered was more dangerous than having a woman over while Lilly was asleep. Then I would call him immature because he was right, and I hate when he's right and I'm wrong. Then he would tell me I was overreacting. Profanity would be involved. Then he would storm out after I said something totally irrational. I finished the entire argument in my head. It was not how I wanted to spend my morning. I didn't know what else to say, so I pretended to cry.

Tom was unmoved. "That's not going to work this time. I had to jump through hoops to get you to forgive me and allow Lilly back over at my place."

"Oh, come on." I laughed a mocking laugh while wiping an imaginary tear away. "Hoops? Really? I asked you to please not have any more sleepovers while Lilly was there."

"But you can have sleepovers with your 'maintenance man.'" He air-quoted again.

"Would you stop that? He really is the maintenance man, and we fell asleep. That's it."

"Look, Cam. You can get whatever you want maintenanced on your own time. That's fine with me. Double standards are only your thing."

My mouth fell open. This reaction was not in his character. Mine, yes, but not his. "How have I ever, aside from this one time, had double standards? And I don't even have double standards now. We fell a-sleep talk-ing." This was getting ridiculous.

He pressed his mouth to a straight line and stared at me until his face began to relax. "Fine. I don't know how. I don't store everything that has ever happened in the history of us in my brain like you do. Lilly, let's go!" he hollered down the hall.

Lilly skipped out in her pink sundress, plastic Cinderella dress-up shoes, a leopard-print clutch, and a purple beanie. "I'm ready," she said. "It twirls, Daddy. See?" She spun around, giggling, unfazed by our fighting.

"Looks beautiful, Lil. We have to go." He swung her up onto his hip. "I'll bring her back later," he said brusquely.

He was crossing the line. "Like when later?"

"Like when I'm not so *i-r-i-t-a-t-e-d*...or around four thirty." He left, slamming the door behind him.

Oh no you didn't. I swung the door open. "There are two *R*s in irritated!" I yelled. Tom and Lilly were nowhere in sight, but I have last-word issues.

That's it!

I called Patrick on the number reserved for emergencies. My life was falling apart; that was emergency enough for me. It rang twice before a sleepy moan answered. A quick glance at the clock told me this emergency could have perhaps waited until after seven. It was too late though. I was committed, as I suspected he had caller ID.

I gave Patrick the CliffsNotes version. Starting with Spencer. (I had hoped to gather more evidence and another witness before explaining my Spencer theory, but time had run out.) I told him everything, even about the move-out notifications, which, as I suspected, were what really got his attention.

He loudly cleared the morning rattle from his throat. "This guy you saw last night, you're sure he didn't come from Kevin's apartment?"

"I don't believe so. I think that, when you look at everything as a whole, there's a strong possibility the guy came from Spencer's apartment." I began fidgeting with a paperclip, unwinding it and rewinding it, unwinding and rewinding, determined to stay strong and not get all wimpy and unnecessarily chatty.

He exhaled. I imagined him rubbing his temples like he did the one—and only—time we met in person. "Spencer's on a month-to-month and has been there less than a year, so we can serve him a thirty-day notice and be done with it."

"Kick him out? But I don't know for certain. It's a theory."

"Then what do you suggest we do?"

"Ummm..." *Good point.* "What about an eviction instead?" Thirty days seemed like plenty of time to, oh, I don't know, plot revenge on the apartment manager. I began unwinding and rewinding the paperclip faster. Unwinding and rewinding.

"Thirty-day notice is cheaper and usually faster. You don't have to give a reason and don't need evidentiary support. We'll have Chase serve it."

"Why Chase? I don't have a problem doing so myself."

"I want the notice served without *any* conversation. He'll know he has thirty days to move, and he doesn't need to know why." It was a nice way of telling me I have a big mouth. Justified. *Bada-bing-bada-boom.* "Let me know when Chase gets there, and I'll have my lawyer send over the paperwork."

"He may still be here. I'll check."

"Still? That reminds me, I got a message from the emergency line, so I'm assuming you or Chase didn't answer right away. Did it get taken care of?"

Note to self: Don't ever let your phone out of your sight. Ever.

"I'm sorry. My friend had my phone. It was taken care of."

"Did Chase come?"

"He did." I thought back to our little mishap in the third courtyard and wondered if it was worth mentioning—or if I should wait for the video to show up on his Facebook feed.

"Cambria, Chase is hourly, and emergencies are overtime. Now he's there this early in the morning? I need you to be mindful of the bottom line."

The paperclip broke in half. "Oh, no. I took care of the emergency, and Chase is only here this early because he spent the night."

Didn't mean to say that.

"Spent the night?" His voice took on a curious tone.

"Yes…no…yes. It wasn't a sexual thing." I slapped my forehead.

Dear Ground,

Please swallow me up next time I try to speak.

Sincerely,
Cambria

There was no recovering from the sex comment. "Go ahead and send over the notice, and I'll have Chase serve it," I said, my voice small. "Please."

CHAPTER FIFTEEN

————

Tenant agrees to not engage in any illegal activity while occupying the Premises, ever, like, ever, ever.

An hour later the fax machine popped out the notification. I was rolled into the fetal position on the teal carpet, agonizing over the conversation with Patrick. *It wasn't a sexual thing?*

My big mouth was my own worst enemy.

I reached up and grabbed the paper off the machine.

Thirty-day Notice

Spencer Bryant is hereby required to vacate the premises in which he resides thirty days from this date.

Cambria Clyne
Apartment Manager

That's it? One sentence and a line for my signature? *He needed a lawyer for this? Screw criminal law. This is what Tom should be doing.*

My phone chirped, and I pulled it from my back pocket, still reading over the very short, very unofficial-looking notification.

It was a text from Amy. Finally.

Alive Rock was a bore at home just woke stop texting me hungover

Nice. I slid the phone back into my pocket. Amy was fine. I could cross that off my Things-to-Stress-About-Today list.

Next up: Facing Chase after Tom's embarrassing performance. I could only imagine what was going through his head. Here he was, doing me a favor, and he's rewarded by what seemed like an overzealous ex-boyfriend, which was so far from the truth.

I found Chase in the maintenance garage. The room was a hodgepodge of every tool, screw, saw, and plunger imaginable. Only a single light bulb hung from the cobwebbed ceiling. It smelled like mildew, and the air was thick and clammy. Chase was using a toilet as a chair, working on an air conditioning unit. He bit his bottom lip, concentrating on his task. I cleared my throat to grab his attention.

He was too engrossed in his work to notice. "Hey, Chase," I finally said after three more throat clears. My esophagus was beginning to burn. "Fancy meeting you here" was my oh-so-clever icebreaker.

He smiled and wiped his brow with his forearm. "Because it's not like I'm the 'maintenance man.'" He hooked his fingers into quotation marks.

My face went flush. "I'm so sorry about this morning. Tom isn't normally that rude. It was a misunderstanding."

"Misunderstanding?" Chase repeated with a nod of his head. He unwrapped a new filter for the AC unit and deposited the plastic on the floor. I instinctively picked up the trash and threw it away for him. Cleaning up after his maintenancing had become part of my undisclosed job duties. He stuck the filter in. "I'm assuming he's your ex?" he asked.

"Oh, no, no, no...not really, kind of, no. He's Lilly's dad. He was only mad because I give him a hard time about bringing girls around Lilly, and he...anyway, he wasn't jealous or anything like that."

He cocked his head my way. "Could have fooled me."

"Well, he did. I think he was trying to prove a point. Again, I'm sorry, and thank you for hanging out last night."

"No problem." He replaced the front panel of the air conditioner and flipped it on. It purred to life, spurting out cold air. It felt heavenly. He smiled. "You know what? I think I might have fixed this." He sounded surprised. It was cute.

I went to pat him on the back, stopping midway. I only

recently learned how to keep myself from dissolving in his presence. Physical contact was not a good idea. I opted for a thumbs-up instead. "Congratulations. Look at you being all maintenance-y." I held out the thirty-day notification. "Here's one more item of maintenance-man business for you. Patrick would like you to serve it because I have a big mouth."

He wiped his hands on his jeans and grabbed the paper, quickly scanning the information. "You're really giving Spencer a thirty-day?"

I leaned against the workbench, folding my arms. "I know, right? I thought the same thing. Apparently a thirty-day is easier and cheaper than an eviction, and Patrick cares about his bottom line."

"You want me to do this right now?"

"I do. And, um, I'm going to watch you give it to him from a secret location." I felt uneasy. Maybe because this was my first Notice to Vacate. Maybe because I didn't have strong proof of wrongdoing. Maybe because I was worried Chase would end up like Kenneth. Maybe it was all three. The bushes near the breezeway would provide the concealment I needed to watch.

"You're going to hide? Where? Behind a bush?"

Did I say that out loud? "Maybe. I'm only thinking about...er...you. I'm thinking about your safety. What if he goes crazy and pulls a knife or a gun or tries to take you hostage. I'll be watching to make sure things don't get out of hand." This would be my excuse if Patrick asked why I was not in the office while Chase served the notice. "We could have some sort of signal."

"Signal? Because if you saw him with a gun, that wouldn't be enough of a signal?" He laughed—it was a pleasing sound—then flashed a smile. He sure had nice teeth—white but not bleach white. They were natural white, like he flossed, mouthwashed, and brushed twice-a-day-like-the-dentist-recommended-but-no-one-ever-did white. All were perfectly aligned except for his lower incisors that curved inward slightly—I wanted to suck on them.

Wow.

It was an odd, surprising desire, yet so strong. I couldn't

recall ever wanting to suck on someone's tooth. *What is wrong with me?*

"You really do watch a lot of crime shows," he noted, flashing his incisors again.

I looked at my shoes, willing my face to remain its pale freckled self and not go red. "I do." *Concentrate, Cambria.* "I won't be able to hear what's happening. So if the service goes well, you could…scratch your chin. And if it's going south then…pull your ear?" It sounded stupid even as I was saying it.

As Chase headed to Spencer's apartment, I dashed to the breezeway to assume lookout. I plastered my back against the wall and took small side steps as if walking the ledge of a high-rise building. Einstein clung to the ivy twisting up the breezeway, and the bristles scraped my exposed skin, but blood and bald spots were not going to deter me.

As the end of the wall neared, I pried Einstein from the ivy and crouched behind a bush. Chase was at the door, hand positioned and ready.

Knock.

Knock.

Knock.

My stomach clenched tighter each time Chase's fist made contact with the door.

Knock.

Knock.

Knock.

Chase looked down at the paper then up at the door, as if determining if it was worth another trio of knocks or not. I yawned.

Deciding to go for it, Chase raised his hand just as the door opened. Spencer stood in the doorway wearing dark blue scrubs with a messenger bag crossed over his chest, a steaming travel mug in one hand and keys in the other. Without so much as a "hey there," Chase handed Spencer the paper and left, scratching his chin as he walked away—the signal. Spencer pushed his round glasses back up the ridge of his nose and read the notice again and again, shaking his head as his eyes ventured down the page. He turned it over to stare at the blank side for a while then read it again, closing the gap between his face and the paper, still shaking his head as if he were utterly confused.

After a painful amount of processing time, Spencer sprinted after Chase, the contents of his mug splashing down the front of his scrubs. He didn't appear to notice or care. Chase responded to his name by throwing his hands up. I imagined he was saying something like, *"I don't know anything."* Then Spencer said something, I guessed along the lines of, *"Dude, man, what's up with this, dude?"* Because in my head, Spencer talked like one of the old surfer guys who hang around their VW vans along the Pacific Coast Highway while smoking pot, even if he didn't look like one at all. But, hey, not supposed to judge a book by its cover.

Chase shrugged. Spencer readjusted his glasses and said one more thing, eliciting another shrug from Chase, which prompted another readjustment of his glasses and a glance my way. There's no way he could see me.

Right?

"Cambria," a low, very un-surfery voice called.

Wrong.

I stood and began sidestepping away.

"Apartment Manager, wait." Spencer leapt over a bush, releasing the last bit of the hot contents from his mug, and met me at the wall.

Note to self: You suck at inconspicuous-ity.

"I don't know anything," I said, raising my palms up as if he'd said "Freeze!"

"But your name is on the bottom." Spencer pointed to my name and signature scrawled along the allotted line.

Chase stood in the walkway behind Spencer making a *W* with his arms. He then began pulling on his ear—the signal. *Got it.*

"Well?" Spencer pressed. He looked as if he might explode.

"Come on, man. Just read the notice," Chase said, sounding more surfery than Spencer.

Spencer frowned, pushing his glasses up again. *Will someone buy this man some Nerdwax?*

"I *did* read it. It is one sentence," he said. "You don't have any basis to ask me to leave. You should be the one leaving. This place is on a grease pole to hell, Cambria, and you've only been here, what, a month?" *Two weeks.* "Everyone agrees," he continued. "We've all been talking about it. You're trying to micromanage and fix what wasn't broken. Joyce was an excellent manager, totally laid-back and let us live without management breathing down our necks. I don't even feel safe leaving my car in the parking lot anymore. Neither do a lot of people here. Now this. I'm not leaving. I just settled in. This is what happens when some money-hungry right-wing nutjob..."

I wasn't sure how we landed on politics, but he was really starting to tick me off.

"It's your illegal side business!"

Oops.

And this is why Patrick didn't want me to serve the notice. Pretty sure he specifically said not to give Spencer a reason for the thirty-days.

Nice one, Cambria.

Chase slapped his forehead.

Spencer's mouth fell open, like a scrub-wearing trout. I backed farther into the wall, and Einstein reattached to the ivy, clinging for life. Then, Spencer hopped back over the bush and disappeared into his apartment, slam-dunking his notification into the common area trash can on his way.

Chase made some sort of huffing sound, probably thinking something like, *Cambria's detective skills are superior. She was obviously right!* Except he didn't look at me, tell me I was right, or even make any more noises. He turned around and walked away.

Was that a chin scratch or an ear pull?

CHAPTER SIXTEEN

———

Tenant's guests are not permitted to use parking area without a guest parking permit.

Incident Report

Friday, October 7th
Chase handed Spencer Bryant the thirty-day notification and walked away. Spencer ~~found me~~ sought me out to ask why he was being kicked out. ~~I told him about the illegal behavior I'd witnessed. He did not deny it, and therefore I was right. I remained quiet as instructed.~~ I provided minimal information.

I placed the incident report into Spencer's thick file, not feeling as content as I'd hoped. Which didn't make sense. Based on Spencer's reaction, he was involved in some kind of illegal activity. I was right. I loved being right. So why wasn't I satisfied?

I wiped the back of my hand along my dripping forehead. The ceiling fan was useless against the suffocating heat. The office was an oven. My shirt was a sopping mess. Einstein was in a hopeless state. An unpleasant smell permeated the air, and I worried I was the source of it. Using a pack of Post-its as a fan, I peeled off a single paper square to sponge up the sweat pumping out of my skin.

I swiveled to face the window and gazed through the open blinds out to the courtyard. *It's so lovely.* Most would think it ordinary. No color, no flowers, the wood warped and rotting, the iron railing chipped (but secured).

To me it was beautiful, far from ordinary. In comparison

to the places I had lived, it was practically the Four Seasons. Once the community was crime-free, it would be a delightful place to raise Lilly. A large patch of grass to kick a soccer ball around or blow bubbles, the sparkling pool perfect for hot summer days, the conveniently located laundry rooms, Teardrop of Death...

I sat up.

Teardrop of Death was strolling through the first courtyard. His biceps bulged under a white short-sleeved shirt. His flip-flops flapped against the pavement with each step he took, echoing through the courtyard. One hand held a phone to his ear, while the other fidgeted with a key ring around his finger.

I twisted the blinds shut and stuck my finger through a slat for a less conspicuous view. Teardrop stopped at the row of mailboxes near the lobby and stuck a key into a box. His massive torso blocked my view. Based on his location, he had opened a mailbox belonging to a resident in the third courtyard.

He collected the mail, the phone now sandwiched between his ear and shoulder. He wasn't a resident—at least his picture wasn't in any of the files I'd breezed through. Pretty sure I would remember him. Which meant he was a comfortable houseguest. In paragraph two on the second page of the *House Rules* it says, *Tenant may not have houseguests for more than three days without written permission from the manager.*

I took a burst of photos with my phone and released the blind slat to take a look at them—ten pictures of TDoD's back. Not exactly incriminating. I could turn them over to the police. Maybe they'd seen the back of his head before?

If I could just get one picture of his face.

I slipped my finger between the slats again. As if he'd heard my request, Teardrop's face was pressed up against the window.

Note to self: You suck at inconspi... Scratch that... Note to Self: Review previous notes to self.

With a yelp I brought my phone up for a quick snap of his face and dashed into my apartment. I slammed the door shut, twisted the lock, and fell back against it. The gasps of my own breath sounded foreign in my ears. A fear-and-adrenaline cocktail pumped through my veins and intoxicated my brain.

Ding.

It was the bell on the counter. Teardrop was now inside the office. The bell specifically says "ring for service" not "ring for victim."

Ding.

Ding.

Ding.

He was being rather polite with his...

Boom!

I fell into the kitchen counter while the thunderous *Booms* of his massive fist beating against the door continued. He must have climbed over the counter or gone through the office door—either way, *House Rules* say only employees beyond the counter. It was clear Teardrop of Death was no rule follower.

Boom!

Boom!

Boom!

I ran to my bedroom in search of the office phone and found it on the back of the toilet. The key to any emergency situation was to remain calm and to call 9-1-1 from a landline. *Right?* My shaking thumbs clumsily punched in the numbers. I slammed the phone to my ear and ran out to the hall.

"Nine-one-one, what's your emergency?" a disembodied male voice asked.

Deep breath in, slow breath out. "I'm the apartment manager," I started, struggling to keep my voice from reaching a high-pitched *holy hell* octave. "I have a man—tall, white, muscular, twenties, Teardrop and gun tattoos—who is banging on my door because he caught me taking his picture."

A crash against the door startled me, and I smashed into the single picture I'd hung in the hallway. A 10x16 of Lilly's smiling face crashed to the ground where it exploded into hundreds of tiny pieces, spewing glass across the hallway and out to the living room.

"Ma'am? Ma'am?" the operator asked. "Hello?"

"I'm...I'm..." *Breathe.* "How long until the police are here?"

"Very soon. Ma'am, what is your name?"

"Cambria Jane Clyne." He needed my full name for the death certificate.

Then it happened.

Silence.

An unnerving silence louder than the pounding. I dropped the phone and raced through the crunchy terrain of the short hall that seemed to grow a mile with each step. Then came the squeak of the old hinges on the door. If I had unpacked all the boxes like I was supposed to, I would have had a clear escape path.

But I didn't.

Dropping to all fours, I slid behind a box and curled into a ball. My heart thumped so loudly I feared it would give away my location to Teardrop, who was walking around in the kitchen. I scooted closer and pressed my forehead against the cardboard, looking at the upside-down scribble along the bottom—*Drugs*. Drugs! If I weren't about to die, I may have laughed, taken two Excedrin and a long swig of NyQuil.

"Hello! Apartment Manager?" Teardrop called out.

Thumb to the eyeball. Knee to the nuts. I ran through my attack plan.

Step...step...step...

I pulled my knees in tighter, steadying my breathing.

Step...step...step...

He was getting closer. My heart grew louder and felt as if it were about to leap out of my chest and run away screaming.

Step...step...step...

Knee to eyeballs...thumb to nuts...wait, that's not right.

Step...step...step...

"Freeze!" A brigade of heavy-soled shoes stomped through the door and filled my cramped quarters.

I uncurled my shaky limbs, feeling thirsty, nauseated, cold. I was a flimsy mass of confusion as the adrenaline drained and the shock took over. Somehow, I ended up outside with a bottle of water in my hand and Officer Bulldog, who insisted his real name was Officer Stanwall, at my side. He kindly requested I stop calling him as such then questioned me on the incident.

"You said you saw him getting mail?" Officer Bull...Stanwall asked in his burly, very bulldoggy voice.

"Yes. I took a picture. It's on my phone…somewhere." I took a swig of water.

His pen flew across his notepad, and with a lick of his finger, he flipped the page and continued. "He said he used the keys on the desk to open the door because you wouldn't answer."

Water dribbled down my chin. "Wait. What?"

"Did he say anything when he entered your apartment?" Officer Stanwall asked.

I thought for a moment. "He said…'*hello.*'"

"Stop what you're doing! Stop! Cambria! Came-bree-aaaa!"

Why?

Why?

Whyyy?

"Cambria!" Kevin ran across the grass in his bare feet, wearing a pair of blue-checkered boxer shorts and a frown. "Cambria!" he yelled again as if I were a great distance away and not a foot from where he stood.

"Who are you?" Officer Stanwall asked.

Kevin's mouth fell open, revealing all his metallic molars. He placed his hand over his furry chest. "Who am I? I'm the owner of this building."

Stanwall looked to me for confirmation, and I nodded. "His parents own it," I said, which earned me a sympathetic brow raise from the officer.

"What did you do to Wick?" Kevin hissed.

"Who's Wick?"

"My friend," he said as if it were obvious. "I sent him here to get my mail and ask you for a parking pass. What did you do to him?"

Stanwall's bulldoggy face trained on Kevin. "You know the suspect?"

"Suspect?" Kevin threw his hands up as if declaring a touchdown and paced the walkway. "I don't believe this. He got here last night, and she's been harassing him since. Arrest this one." He pointed his hairy-knuckled finger at me.

The plastic water bottle crinkled in my clenched fist, and it took all the restraint I had not to throw it at his head. "Your friend broke into my apartment, and he has a teardrop tattoo," I said through gritted teeth. This was beyond ridiculous. Mental disability or not, a woman could only be pushed so far.

"So you're prejudiced against teardrop tattoos?" Kevin huffed, shaking his head. "I know lots of people with teardrop tattoos. I was on the phone with him the entire time. When you didn't answer the bell, I told him to go into the office and knock on your door, and when you didn't answer, I told him to knock louder. Then he heard crashing, so I told him to go in." He looked at Stanwall and cocked a thumb. "This one was taking his picture. She's a perv who sleeps with old people."

My water bottle went sailing over his head, only because I missed.

Officer Stanwall planted himself between Kevin and me. "We don't need any of that," he said with exaggerated patience. "His story checks."

I opened my mouth—to say what, I wasn't sure. It felt like I was starring in an M. Night Shyamalan movie about some parallel universe, except no one bothered giving me a script.

"So you're not arresting him?" I asked, too snippily for my own good.

"He's been taken in for violating his parole," he answered, still standing between us.

"What was he on parole for?" I demanded.

"Parole for none of your damn business!" said Kevin.

"Let's all calm down," Stanwall tried.

Kevin's face went tense. "You're fired," he furiously whispered under his breath.

"That's enough," Stanwall ordered in a deep, rough voice, causing both Kevin and me to jump. I resisted the urge to salute. "I'll take you in if I need to," Stanwall barked at Kevin with a cautionary glare. His eyes softened when they landed on me. "You OK?"

CHAPTER SEVENTEEN

————

Tenant must give 30-day intent to vacate in writing before vacating. Yelling "I'm moving" is not sufficient notification.

Am I OK?

That question echoed through my head later while sitting at my desk holding Officer Stanwall's card, staring at the silver and gold police emblem. *Am I OK?* I'd answered Stanwall with an involuntary nod of my head as Kevin tromped back to his delusion hideout, grumbling and puffing the entire journey. *Am I OK?* Teardrop of Death, aka Wick, hadn't come from Spencer's apartment. He came from Kevin's. A question Patrick specifically asked before making the decision to give Spencer a thirty-day notice, and I said no. I had, true to form, overreacted. Accused a man of being a murderer solely based on his looks and my own theory. Which got me thinking.

Could I have been wrong about Spencer? Misread the situation? Ignored the real source of the crime?

It was too coincidental for murder *and* a car to be stolen within the same week. They were connected. I was sure of it. Which meant the killer was either visiting or, heaven forbid, a resident. Spencer had a lot of foot traffic—one or two of those feet had to belong to the killer. Right?

But what did I know?

I'd been there…*one*…*two*…*has it really only been two weeks?*

Felt like a year.

So I'd been there *two weeks* and had only thus scratched the surface of who the residents were. I knew Silvia was the complainer. Larry the over-sharer. Kevin the nudist. Ty the new parent. Mickey talked to himself. Apartment 3 obnoxious. Apartment 38 unruly toddler. Grandma Clare was…*active.*

Was I missing someone?

I spun around and pulled out files for Apartments 2 thru 39 and looked through each one more closely—occupation, credit score, delinquencies, incident reports. Next, I flipped through the maintenance logs—garbage disposal fixes, A/C units. Apartment 5 once attempted to install a bidet at 2 a.m. and flooded his apartment. The pool overflowed last year when Bob forgot to close the valve. Larry's head got stuck in the upstairs railings on New Year's Day. Why that was written up as a maintenance request was beyond me. Lack of things to report, I supposed.

I came to the conclusion that the most acrimonious thing to happen over the last decade was when Kevin threw Joyce's vase through the window.

The problems started the exact same day I did.

If I didn't know that I had nothing to do with it—I'd think I had something to do with it.

So was I OK?

Not sure.

The day was turning into a compilation of my failures. There was a killer on the loose. I appeared to have brought the crime. My job was on the line. Tom wasn't answering my texts or calls. Chase had disappeared. Then there was the fact that Kevin fired me. Common sense said he didn't have the power to do so. Still, he had to have a little influence.

To top it all off, when I went to print the incident report for Kevin's file, the printer was out of ink—magenta. My attempts to explain to the machine that I only needed white paper with black print didn't work. The hateful piece of machinery was going to hold my incident report hostage until I replaced the cartridge.

Was I OK?

No, I guess I wasn't. And there wasn't a thing I could do about it. Except sulk.

But before I could sink into a sulking oblivion—fun as that sounded—the lobby door chimed, and I knew it was Chase before I even saw him. He had a distinct, sexy man smell. A musky mixture of salty skin with a hint of soap. One of my favorite smells (second only to that sweet newborn baby smell). Under normal circumstances, his aroma would have me in a puddle of lust. Except I was already a puddle of petulance, and petulance and lustfulness are a deadly combination. There was an entire *20/20* episode dedicated to it once called "Women Who Murder" or something like that.

"Cambria, are you OK?"

"That *is* the question. After careful consideration I've come to the conclusion I am not."

He opened the door to my office and walked in, the man scent growing stronger. "What happened?" he asked, placing his hands on the armrests of my swivel chair, leaning in close. I breathed from my mouth only and kept my eyes away from his sexy incisors.

"I'm out of magenta ink." This, I could tell from his expression, was not the answer he expected. "And the guy with the teardrop tattoo came into my apartment looking for a parking pass, but he was arrested, so Kevin fired me." I flapped my arm in the general direction of the printer. "If I had magenta, I'd give you the incident report to read. It's a real page-turner. Or, well, it's only one page, single-spaced."

Chase pushed off the chair, walked to the printer, and yanked the cover open with ease. Something I attempted to do several times while the vile machine mocked me with its beeps and error messages. I had then given up and thrown my stapler at it. He pulled out the magenta cartridge, gave it a few hard shakes, and replaced it. The machine hummed back to life and spit out my report.

I gave a halfhearted chuckle. Even the office equipment was against me. "First the air conditioner and now the printer. You're on a roll today."

He ignored me, his beautiful green eyes darting furiously down the page.

"This is ridiculous." He flicked the paper in his hand. "Give this to your ex." He tossed the report across the desk, shaking his head. "Better yet, email it to Patrick and copy Tom. I guarantee you this will be the last straw. Kevin was already close to getting kicked out after what happened with Joyce."

"What? Why would I give it to Tom? So he could use it against me if we should ever have a custody hearing?" Chase's mind was elsewhere. "Chase?"

He returned to the conversation. "You know his story, right?"

"Who? Tom?" *How long was I in the bathroom this morning?*

He shook his head. "What? No, Kevin."

"I know he has a mental disability, went to rehab recently, and threw a vase through his window. I read Joyce's incident report."

Chase placed his forehead into his palm and laughed a hearty someone-told-a-hilarious-joke laugh. I was beginning to question the sanity of every person in the community.

"Mental health is not a laughing matter," I said, not amused. Not amused at all.

"Kevin doesn't have a mental disability." He leaned against the desk. "Cambria, you know he's gay, right?"

I shook my head. His sexual preference had never crossed my mind.

"I didn't think so," Chase continued. "Joyce called it a mental disability because that's what his parents called it. He's an only child, and when he came out of the closet, sometime during his teenage years, his parents kicked him out and cut him off. Patrick found him living here in the storage closet and put him up in a hotel for a few days while he talked to Kevin's mother. She's the one who said Kevin could live here rent-free as long as he didn't contact the family. From what I've gathered, Kevin is extremely lonely. And that guy from last night? Turns out he was from San Bernardino, and he's not supposed to leave the county without notifying his parole officer. They met at rehab, and he came out to visit Kevin. I know some stuff went down with Joyce, and Kevin was pretty close to getting kicked out, but Patrick paid her off to not sue and sent him away until she moved. Once Patrick hears about Kevin telling his friend to enter your apartment, I think he'll have to kick him out. That's why I said copy Tom. You have legal rights as an employee."

That was a lot of information to digest.

How terrible.

"Poor Kevin," I thought out loud.

Chase bent down and lifted my chin up with his finger, catching my eyes with his, holding me in place. "What happened in his past sucks. It does. Still doesn't give him any right to treat you the way he has."

"No, but it's a change of perspective," I muttered, Chase's finger still forcing my chin up. "How'd you know Tom was a lawyer—"

Chase's calloused thumb ran gently across my cheek, derailing my train of thought. His other hand went to my shoulder, his fingers spread, taking up the entire space between my shoulder and neck. The warmth of his touch beckoned every nerve ending in my body.

I felt the wisps of warm breath escaping his parted lips and feathering against mine. I felt the distance closing. I felt my eyes closing. I felt the desire so desperate to be fulfilled that it ached. I ached all over. The distance closed, and his lips brushed against mine. I could already feel our tongues dancing in sweet unison, savoring the taste of his mouth.

I parted my lips, an open invitation. His lips parted, accepting, moving in closer…nearly there. My heart beat in triple time. Almost there…

He pulled back like a hand on a hot stove, his back pressed against the door, his hands shoved deep into his pockets.

No! No! No!

I sat there with my mouth still hanging open, the feeling of his lips still hot on mine. Desire swimming around my head.

His chest rose and fell as if he had just sprinted a marathon. "I better get going," he announced, not making eye contact. The door opened, and he left. *He left.*

What happened?

I sat there, a sexually frustrated figurine. Confused. Mad. Aggravated.

What the hell just happened?

The familiar clanking against the linoleum freed my joints. "Apartment Manager," Silvia hollered over the counter. I turned slowly, weighted by the intense crappiness of the entire freaking day. "They're at it again," she moaned. Harold flapped. I stared. "Did you hear me? They're doing it again. I will move if this doesn't stop."

I continued to stare until "I'm OK with that" fell out of my mouth.

If Silvia could move her face, she would have scowled. Instead she scoffed and fluttered her eyes like she had an eyelash stuck in there. "Fine then, Apartment Manager. Consider this my thirty-day notice," she snapped. Harold bobbed his head up and down in agreement.

I shrugged an I-don't-care shrug, because I didn't. Someone at the property should be getting some, and it obviously wasn't going to be me. Why not let the senior citizens enjoy each other in peace? Honestly, I was jealous. "It has to be in writing. Drop it off when you're ready." I smiled a patronizing smile. "And the name is Cambria, not Apartment Manager."

CHAPTER EIGHTEEN

———

Tenant shall only use Premises as a residence, not for a business.

To say things weren't going well would be a gross understatement. I should have taken this as my cue to keep my attention on the job and my butt in my chair. But I couldn't. I'm a fixer. I have a *need* to fix things. Even things that didn't want to be fixed—like Kevin.

My Grandma Ruthie used to say, "We all have a backstory, and you can't judge anyone until you've read theirs." This was in reference to my cousin, Stephanie, who had blue hair (before blue hair was cool) and black nails (before black nails were cool) and purple-stained lips (not sure if that has ever been cool). Her nose ring was connected to her lip ring by a thin, silver chain. Black *O*s decorated each earlobe. When I was older, I'd learned that various other sensitive areas of Stephanie had been privy to a piercing gun as well.

Her shoulders slumped forward, and her face remained shuttered. When I spoke, she would pretend not to notice, or she would call me names, roll her eyes, make fun of my hair, and turn her back on me. I hated her. I hated being forced to converse with her. I hated when Grandma Ruthie would pull out her "everyone has a backstory" speech when I'd tattle on Stephanie for being cruel.

It wasn't until I was sixteen, while sitting in a cold, metal folding chair, looking at a 16x20 of Stephanie's shuttered face atop an easel with an urn next to it, that I finally understood what Grandma was saying. Stephanie had ended her life after a long, silent battle with severe social anxiety and depression. I never knew. I had filed her away in my mind, shoved in a folder labeled *arrogant* and *mean*, and brushed her off. I never knew she was suffering. I never bothered to read her whole story.

And now I knew Kevin's. Leaving him alone was the opposite of how he should be treated. Knowing he'd been sent away, abandoned by his family, told he had a mental disability since adolescence—it didn't sit well with me. His behavior didn't sit well. I wasn't entirely sure it wasn't substance-induced either. Time to try rehab again?

If Kevin had a friend, someone who cared, then perhaps he'd be more inclined to keep his clothes on and not steal Girl Scout Cookies. At least I hoped he wouldn't. Didn't the saying go "the kids who need the most love ask for it in the most unusual ways"?

Or was it "the most unloving ways"?

What I knew for certain was the man-child needed a person in his corner. I was ready to take the role. Kevin was not going to end up like Stephanie. Not on my watch.

Pep-talking myself, I climbed the steps up to the black door and knocked. After ten more knocks Kevin, still wearing only the checkered boxers from earlier, flung the door open.

"Can't you read the sign?" He pointed to a freshly posted note taped above the knob: *Management Not Allowed.*

I smiled, pretending not to notice. "I have a proposition."

"Does it have to do with you moving out ASAP?"

"No, it doesn't. It has to do with us."

He shook his head before I even got the words out. "Not interested," he said, swinging the door closed.

I shoved my foot into the doorjamb, and the door bounced back open off my blue Converse sneakers. "I want to propose a truce. We don't have to be enemies. I'd like to be allies." He perked up. Now I had his attention. "Come grab a bite to eat with me sometime after payday. Let's work together. I know how much this property means to you. You're valuable here, and I'm not just saying that because you tried to fire me. I genuinely want to be your friend. What do you say? Friends? How about next Saturday?" It would give me time to come up with how he could be more involved in the property without having him actually involved.

Kevin's mouth twitched upwards into a crescent. My heart lifted. Everyone needs someone in his or her corner.

I was right, I thought, just before the door slammed in my face. The wood stopped an inch from my nose.

Or maybe not.

I stared at the red, spray-painted number, debating if I should knock again or obey the sign. My shoulders sank with defeat.

Perhaps it's time to start listening?

I headed back down the stairs, my mood sinking with each drop of my foot, rejection swimming around my head like a shark preparing for the kill. So much rejection—first by Chase, who'd pulled away so fast you'd think I was contagious. Now Kevin. Of course there was also Tom, and how could I forget about Patrick who'd rejected me twice before settling.

My life had crumbled into small, unrecognizable pieces. Much like the picture frame that once hung in the hall. I'd felt despair at various times in my life but never like this. I'd always been able to reframe my thinking, focus on my resources, and find a thread of hope to cling to and figure out the problem.

I was losing grasp of that thread.

Cutting through the grass, I hugged my chest, my eyes secured to the ground. Engaged in my pity-party-for-one, I hadn't noticed the footsteps approaching and nearly face-planted into Spencer's chest. He was holding his lease out as if he were about to make a public decree. Without saying a word (might as well start listening to Patrick), I sidestepped to the right, out of his way. He shuffled over. I sidestepped to the left. He shuffled over. I turned around and walked in the opposite direction, and he jumped in front of me. This whole keeping-my-big-mouth-shut thing was becoming rather difficult.

"Please listen to me?" Spencer finally said, pushing his glasses back up the ridge of his nose. He was still sporting his coffee-stained blue scrubs with *Dr. Spencer Bryant, DDS* embroidered above the pocket and blue Crocs with white socks. "I've been reading over the lease, and I believe I've taken care of everything. I'd like to show you. If things are up to par, would you consider not going through with the thirty-day notice? I just moved here, and I'd like to stay. I really hate moving." He flipped to the ninth page of the *House Rules* and pointed to the paragraph he'd highlighted. *No Water-Filled Furniture Allowed in the Apartment.* "It says *in* the apartment, so I put them on the patio. And I got rid of my stingrays and won't be selling them anymore. So there isn't any illegal activity going on either. I'd like to show you."

Huh?

Not speaking was no longer an option because I had to ask, "What are you talking about? What's a stingray?" *Code for oxycodone, perhaps?*

Misreading my confusion, he placed his thumbs and pointer fingers together to make a diamond. "They have a diamond head and are bottom-dwelling marine rays. They're fresh water, and I realize they're illegal here in California. I didn't think it would be that big—"

"Spencer," I cut him off, more confused than ever. "I know what a stingray is. Tell me what a *real* stingray is."

He stared at me with a blank expression until it hit me. "Holy crap!" I gasped. He wasn't selling drugs or guns or pregnancy tests. He was selling fish...or...er...stingrays. "No, no, no. Spencer, I saw several people coming and going from your apartment carrying brown bags. You can't put water in a brown bag." He was a dangerous criminal. Dangerous criminals don't sell stingrays. They generally don't wear Crocs with socks and have DDS after their name either...*ugh.*

"I put the plastic bag in the brown bag so no one sees. Look. I'm sorry. I assumed Joyce knew and didn't care. I moved my setup with my smaller, legal fish. Can I please show you?"

My tongue felt thick, and I struggled to speak. "Um... I... Fine, sure, whatever. Hold on." I surrendered, mostly out of curiosity. "Give me one second, and I'll meet you at your apartment." I turned around and slid my phone out of my back pocket and composed a text to Amy.

About to enter Apartment 36, Spencer Bryant, in case I die or go missing.

I hit *Send.* If Spencer turned out to be the criminal I'd made him out to be (and oddly, I hoped he was), Amy would be able to identify my killer.

Spencer's apartment smelled like chicken nuggets, Old

Spice, and latex. A card table with four plastic folding chairs was set up in the dinette area. No furniture aside from a circular futon in front of a too-large-for-this-room television, at least seventy inches, mounted to the wall with a waterfall of black, red, and blue cords behind it.

He'll definitely need to patch that before he moves.

No pictures on the wall. Nothing on the kitchen counters. The scratchy tan carpet was filthy, littered with specks of dirt, crunched leaves, and tiny papers.

I followed him through the hall, past the linen cabinets, and into his room. A green comforter lay heaped on the floor next to the bare queen mattress. Clothes, sweat-ripened socks, scrub tops, boxers, grease-soaked napkins, pizza boxes, and books were sprawled across the floor. A lone picture of Han Solo with his blaster pointed, hair feathered, and face smoldering was hung on the wall.

"This way," Spencer said, sliding open the patio door.

I stepped outside. "You've got to be bleeping kidding me." *Fish tanks.* Five long fish tanks lined the perimeter of his rectangle-shaped patio. Not the beautiful tanks with the colorful fish, fake treasure chests, artificial plants, and aqua pebbles lining the bottom. Just tanks filled with water, a pump, and dozens upon dozens of light and dark blue fish.

Fish!

"These are frontosas," Spencer said proudly.

I stared at him.

"It's a type of African cichlid," he explained. I had no idea what that was. "I breed them, they're absolutely legal, and I only sell them to my ichthyologist group."

Ichthyologist group?

"Did you sell the stingrays to the ichthyology group as well?

He nodded, proudly. "It's a group we started in dental school."

Fish-loving dentist.

I was wrong. Spencer had nothing to do with the murder. He had nothing to do with the backpack and the stolen car and the pregnancy test. He wasn't impregnating anyone. He was too busy making fish do it.

My phone vibrated in my back pocket. Amy. "Hello," I answered, peering into one of the tanks holding a school of fish with humps protruding from their smug little fish heads.

"Cambria, what is wrong with you! Who is Spencer Bryant, and why are you going into his apartment if you think he's about to kill you?" I suspected she didn't remember texting me the exact same message last night.

"Don't worry. I was wrong."

Spencer knelt down and sprinkled red flakes into the tank holding the smallest fronto-whatever. The fish flurried to the surface, grabbing the food and swimming back down to the bottom. I wanted to cry.

"You were wrong about what?" Amy asked. "Who is Spencer?" I could hear the hangover in her voice still.

"He's a tenant. A dentist who sells *fish*." The word left a bitter aftertaste.

"Like real fish, or is this code for something?" she asked.

"Nope, like little Nemos."

"Frontosa," Spencer corrected, standing upright and dusting the fish food off his hands.

"Seriously?" Her voiced perked up into a sober range. "A dentist? Huh. Is he single?"

I rolled my eyes and looked around at the fish tanks and then back up at Spencer and then into his room with the Han Solo poster and sheetless mattress. "I'm going to take a stab in the dark and say yes."

"Oh really." I could hear the smile in her voice. "Give him my number."

"No."

"Come on."

"No."

"Please."

"Not a chance."

Spencer took a step toward me. "You know I can hear both sides of your conversation, right?"

Uhhhhhhh...

"I'll call you back, Amy." I shoved the phone into my back pocket, clasped my hands in front of me, and gave Spencer an apologetic smile.

Awk-a-ward.

Spencer brought his hands to his hips. "Your friend said that you thought I was going to kill you?"

I opened my mouth, about to spit out a pathetic attempt at an explanation, then opted for the truth. "I saw people leaving your apartment with bags and assumed it was drugs and that you had something to do with Kenneth Fisk's murder."

Spencer stood frozen.

"I told the police to look into you as a possible suspect," I added, to, you know, make the situation more uncomfortable.

Spencer finally came to. "If you thought I had something to do with Kenneth's murder, then why did you willingly come into my apartment, alone."

Good question. "I am a poor decision maker" was my answer.

"A fair assessment." He pushed his glasses back up the ridge of his nose. "At least that explains why the detective came to my office to question me. I thought it was weird she didn't come here."

"They questioned you!" I said, happy to know the police followed up on my lead.

Spencer's eyes narrowed.

"I mean…" I cleared my throat. "They *questioned you*?"

"Yes, they did." He crossed his arms over his chest. "I had to take time away from a patient to be grilled for almost thirty minutes."

Spencer was clearly upset, but I had to ask. "What did they ask, and what did you say?"

He dropped his arms. "Monday is my early day. I left for work about 5:45 and saw Kenneth walking in a hurry toward the back stairwell. I waved to him, but he was on the phone, and I don't think he saw me."

The message on the answering machine was left at 5:45 a.m.! Which meant Kenneth was on the phone, leaving the message when Spencer saw him. Kenneth had already witnessed whatever it was that warranted the call, and if he was walking toward the back stairwell, that something happened back there.

"You said *all* this to the detective?" I confirmed.

"Of course. I have nothing to hide."

I glanced at the fish tanks.

"Besides this," he added. "Look, I had nothing to do with Kenneth Fisk. I gave all my information to the detective. I moved my tanks to the patio. Do you think I can stay? Because you obviously don't have a reason to kick me out now."

Ugh, that.

"I'll get back to you," I said, not looking forward to the conversation where I tell Patrick that Spencer's fishy behavior is actually fish.

"And by the way," said Spencer. "I *am* single." He flashed a smile and pushed his glasses up the ridge of his nose.

"I'll let her know."

Note to self: Turn volume down on your phone.

CHAPTER NINETEEN

———

Landlord is entitled to at least one mental breakdown during the length of the rental agreement.

I felt like a scarecrow—hollow and made of only straw and clothing. No bones to keep me vertical. No brain to process the monumental mess I made. I lay on my bed, spread out like a strawy starfish, with my newly retrieved *drug* box open and on the floor beside me. I watched the blades of the ceiling fan spin around and around and around and around into a blur.

To recap.

Me: Teardrop of Death is a murderer!

Reality: Teardrop of Death is Kevin's boyfriend.

Me: Spencer is selling drugs!

Reality: Spencer breeds fish.

I'd say I should stick to my day job, except I wasn't exactly killing it there either.

Patrick: Don't tell Spencer why he's being served a Notice to Vacate.

Me: OK!

Reality: Tell Spencer everything then set him up with my best friend.

What a mess.

I flopped my straw-filled head to the right and got a sideways glance of the armoire still standing in the middle of the room. "I should have taken your lead and never left my apartment," I told it, as if speaking to Joyce. "I should have asked more questions about Kevin, about rent collection, and the job. I have no idea what I'm doing, and I have a sinking suspicion it isn't even that hard of a job. I was wrong about

Spencer. What was I thinking? That someone who sold drugs would bag them up like a grocery store? 'Would you like your narcotics in paper or plastic?' Who killed Kenneth? Who stole Daniella's car? And why did it all go downhill the day I started? Why did Chase make a move and then pull back? Why do I try and fix things? Why can't I listen? Why do I make a mess out of everything I touch? Why am I talking to an armoire? Ugh." I flung my arm over my eyes.

I've lost my mind.

The office cordless phone rang. I felt around for it with my free hand then brought it to my ear without looking. "This is Cambria."

"Patrick here."

"Hi, Patrick. How are you?" I tried to sound as cheery as one who talks to furniture could be. I knew why he was calling. He'd spoken with Kevin, and now I had to tell him I was wrong about Teardrop and Spencer.

"I heard the police were in the office today?" he asked curtly.

"What did Kevin tell you?" I thought it best to hear what version he'd given Patrick before I added in my own account.

"Kevin? I haven't heard from him. What did Kevin do that warranted a visit from the police?" Now he sounded irritated.

I gnawed at my thumbnail while weighing my options. "Nothing," I finally said, surrendering to my conscience. While I believed Kevin telling anyone to go into my apartment without my permission was wrong, I couldn't imagine what would happen to him if he were kicked out. I couldn't live with that. He needed to stay, especially if there was a substance abuse situation. This was even more clear to me after a swig of Benadryl and a tub of ice cream.

"Did they come to question Spencer?"

"Well, here's the thing about Spencer." I ran my hand along the rich fabric of my comforter, procrastinating. "The thing is he actually *was* doing something illegal. He was selling stingrays."

"Is that some kind of narcotic?"

"No, it's actually a real stingray. The ones with diamond-shaped bodies who dwell at the bottom of the ocean... I mean, this type is in fresh water, so in a lake. I don't think he had anything to do with all the crime. He stopped selling the stingrays and moved his fish tanks to the patio and would like to stay."

"What about the man from last night?"

"Well, here's the thing about the teardrop tattoo guy. Turns out he was visiting a friend for the night only. He lives in San Bernardino. It looks like he doesn't know Spencer and wasn't even here last week."

"OK. If the setup is fine, and you don't think Spencer is involved in any criminal activities, he can stay. I don't care. One less vacancy to add to the pile." Patrick's voice was tense. My stomach hurt. "I received a call from Silvia Kravitz saying you kicked her out because she complained? She also gave me another story I don't care to confirm about you and her neighbors. She told me the police were in your apartment?"

That woman was seriously getting on my nerves. "It was a misunderstanding."

"Misunderstanding?" he repeated. I nodded yes, forgetting he couldn't see me. "At what point do we step back and evaluate when this all started? I've never had so many calls from tenants in all my years of property management. Since you started we've had a murder, a car theft, and now we have a seventy-five-percent run rate on Rent or Run *and* 2 stars in both safety and management. Now we've got a crowd moving out next month, putting you at a—" His fingers tapped at a calculator. "—eighty-percent occupancy rate? It's a bad situation. Now I have this application for an Alice Burns with a copy of a student ID card sitting on my desk. Where's her license? How do you know this is really Alice Burns? You have no photo identification? The picture on her student ID is small and grainy."

I continued to gnaw on my thumbnail. "She said she lost it, and she's only a roommate."

"Only a roommate?" he repeated, growing angrier. "Roommates still live there. Roommates still pay rent. Roommates are added to the lease. Per your time card, you went over the application process with Joyce. This should not be news to you."

I slapped my forehead.

"Were you even aware Vincent Romero had a three-month deposit?" Patrick continued. "We only collect three-month deposits from applicants who have iffy credit. He's been a model tenant from what I see, but the point is, I have to trust my managers to look into these things. To look at the bigger picture, collect the rents, maintain at least a ninety-five percent occupancy rate, a low Rent or Run rate, and do a decent screening of applicants. Before I get the application, you should have already verified employment, past rental history, and done a Google search. I'm still missing some rents. When Joyce was there, she never had a single eviction. Not one. In twenty-five years." He exhaled into the phone. "I'll be there tomorrow morning so we can chat more about this in person."

I'm fired.

CHAPTER TWENTY

_____

Landlord agrees to fulfill all reasonable maintenance requests within a reasonable amount of time as long as the Tenant is reasonable.

It felt as if I'd been punched in the stomach. After everything I'd been through, I was fired. Why else would Patrick come down for a "chat"? It's the twenty-first century. We can chat via phone, Skype, FaceTime, text. No need to speak in person unless it was to serve termination papers. I took a bullet, figuratively, for Kevin, and where did it get me? Fired.

Tears clogged the back of my throat as I stormed over to Alice's apartment. I was not going down without a fight. Nope. Not me.

I passed Mickey, who was arguing with himself, and then Alex and Trent, who were arguing with each other. Larry was on his upstairs balcony, nursing a Bloody Mary as he sat in an old-school aluminum lawn chair with yellow and white webbing. The resident from Apartment 7 marched by, avoiding eye contact, with a stack of moving boxes in her arms.

I continued with determination to Apartment 39. Chase rounded the corner, coming from the carports, scrolling through his phone. I pretended not to notice him, keeping my eyes on the destination. Remaining employed was more important than dealing with whatever that was that happened.

With his focus still on his phone, he stopped in front of Alice's door, cutting me off. "Excuse me," I said curtly because I was livid—mostly because he kissed me and then ran away, and partly because I had texted him several times since. Once asking what happened. Another text with a maintenance request for

Nearly Naked Grandma Clare's garbage disposal. Another asking if he received my text about Nearly Naked Grandma Clare. And the last text was an accident. I meant to send myself a grocery list, but it went to Chase instead. No replies to any. I had hoped it was because he didn't have his phone on him.

Chase looked up, startled, then shoved his phone and hands in the front pockets of his jeans—his signature stance. "Oh, hi." He glanced over his shoulder at the door then at me and moved out of the way.

Oh, hi?

I scooted past him, careful not to inhale his scent or touch him in any way. "Did you get my text messages?" I muttered, mostly to the door because somehow talking to wood had become my norm.

"I did. I'll take care of it," he said, lingering. Rocking back and forth from his heels to his toes.

I raised my hand to knock, waiting for him to leave. *Is he waiting for a formal order?* "Can you go do that now?" I asked.

"Yes, I can." Still lingering. Still rocking.

I dropped my hand. "Is there something you'd like to say, or are you hanging around here for a particular reason?"

He thought for a moment. "Nope, nothing to say. I'll go take care of that now." He turned and reunited his face with his phone.

Yeah, why don't you go do that.

I knocked again and waited.

The click of the deadbolt sliding free preceded the clink of a chain being unhooked. A man about my age popped his head out. He had thick features, a shaved head, and long, crooked, yellow teeth.

"What?" the head asked in lieu of a salutation.

This must be Boo aka Vincent. I'd never met him before, never seen him walking around the property. I recognized him from the picture in his file. According to the lease, no one else lived here. "Can I speak with Alice, please?"

"Who?"

I shook my head, remembering. "Sorry, Wysteria. Can I speak with Wysteria, please?" It's hard enough to keep all of the residents' names and apartment numbers straight, let alone their stripper names too. "Is she home?"

"What's wrong?" came a soft voice from behind.

I turned around as Alice emerged from the carports. She had on tight jeans and a black hooded sweater, her hair stringy and greasy and haphazardly wrapped in a knot on the top of her head. Her hazel eyes were hammocked in a bed of dark bags, and her face looked sunken and pale with blotchy spots on her cheeks and forehead. This wasn't the bubbly Alice sucking on a Tootsie Pop I'd a month ago.

Alice's eyes darted from me to Vincent, whose head was still sandwiched between the door and frame. "What do you need?" she asked, tugging the sleeves of her sweater over her hands, which pulled it down around her neck and revealed three large finger-like bruises.

"Alice," I whispered, covering my mouth with my hand. "Your neck."

She sunk her neck into the sweater like a turtle. "I'm fine," she muttered.

I turned to Vincent. His thick features remained unchanged. I looked back to Alice, who slipped her hands into the front pocket of her sweater and eyed the ground. "Do you need help?" I asked under my breath.

"She's fine," Vincent moaned from the doorway, sounding bored with the conversation.

"I'll help you get out of here, Alice." I was furious I'd somehow missed this. Too busy focusing on everything else. This was my job as an apartment manager. *I think.* My job description needed some fine-tuning. I wasn't exactly sure what it was. It *was* my job as a human being to not ignore abuse. "Let's go, right now," I pressed.

Alice's eyes turned angry. "I'm not going anywhere. Mind your own business." She pushed past me, ignoring the ample unrestricted space around me and knocked my shoulder with hers.

I reached for her arm. She withdrew it quickly. "Don't touch me," she warned with a glare that could kill. She turned sideways and squeezed into the narrow gap Vincent allotted her.

"But, I need your driver's license," I said as the door

closed. Far too many doors had been closed in my face. It was growing old. I knocked again, and again, and again. "Alice? Wysteria? Vincent?" I tried all the names I could remember. "My Boo? Hello? I need your...driver's...license," I begged through the faded lumber. "Please open. I can help." I pressed my forehead to the door and whispered, "Please?"

Nothing.

I spun around and pressed my fingers to my temples. This could be a classic case of my jump-to-worst-case-scenario mind at play. Those could have been hickeys on her neck. If there was one thing I'd learned in the past twenty-four hours, it was that my gut could not be trusted. *Hello Spencer and his fishy brothel.*

I was overdramatizing the situation. Alice was fine.

I, however, was not.

I tucked escaped strands of Einstein behind my ears and numbly padded back toward my apartment. Kenneth's door was open. The Donation Truck company arrived sometime after three and got to work. Two men dragged Kenneth's mattress out of the apartment. Another man came behind with the *books* and *kitchenware* boxes in tow. Poor Kenneth. I may not have been able to figure out who killed him. Now, I could only hope the police were better at their job than I was at mine.

Back in my apartment, I stood in my square kitchen and gazed at the chrome sink with the plastic still wrapped around the spray nozzle and the brand-new paper towel holder that didn't hold any towels.

I yanked open the silverware drawer, releasing a fresh-paint aroma, bringing me back to one week earlier when I had walked through the apartment for the first time since it had been renovated—the feeling of excitement, the freedom, the endless possibilities, the relief. Oh, the relief. The relief was palpable, as if I could reach out and grab it, cradle it in my arms and kiss it.

Now it was gone.

I pulled out the silverware tray and deposited it into an open box on the floor. Then came the spatulas and whisks. Next the apron Grandma Ruthie had made me the Christmas before she died. The dusty cookbooks my mother insisted I take with me when I moved. The basket of Taco Bell sauce packets and the chopsticks still in their plastic casings. I tucked in the cardboard flaps, grabbed a brown crayon, and labeled the box *Taco Bell Sauce* because if I'd learned anything from this last move, it was the importance of labeling the essential items.

Out of the corner of my eye, I caught the top of Lilly's head bouncing across the bottom of the windows overlooking the courtyard. Tom followed behind, carrying a Happy Meal bag from McDonald's. I grabbed the remote control, found an episode of *Mickey Mouse Clubhouse* on the DVR, and pressed *Play*.

Oh how I'll miss you, cable.

I met the duo at the door and bent down to give Lilly a kiss. "Did you have fun?" I asked.

She nodded, running her tongue over her ketchup mustache, and held out her prize from her Happy Meal, a Spiderman frozen midjump with his wrist poised and ready to web. It brought me back to the day I'd interviewed with Joyce. I'd glossed over everyone's warnings, so desperate for employment and so enamored by the cute co-worker that I'd failed myself. I'd failed my little family. I'd failed my daughter.

"I love it," I said, tapping her nose with the tip of my finger and eliciting a carefree giggle. "Hey, I turned on a show for you. Can you go watch it while I talk to Daddy?"

"*Chắc chắn.*" She giggled and bounced into the apartment, oblivious to the fact her life was about to be turned upside down. She settled on the couch, ironically hanging upside down, and sang along with the opening song. I shut the door, leaving a small gap to still keep an eye on her.

Tom hooked his aviators over the top of his shirt. He'd gone casual—khaki shorts, yellow shirt with the purple Lakers' logo painted across the front, and sandals.

"What's going on?" he asked casually.

I blinked. "What's going on?" How he managed to so easily forget about the world's troubles was incomprehensible. My mind was like an iCloud, storing every detail of every good, insignificant, and bad thing that had ever happened in the history of my existence. It was all shoved in some mysterious file, hovering above my head, ready to be brought back up on a whim. "What's going on is this morning. What was that?"

He nodded, as if remembering. "Oh that. Yeah, I might have overreacted a little. I swear I know that guy, and I don't like him. I don't trust him. I don't want him around my kid." He shrugged an unapologetic shrug.

He was being completely unreasonable. This must be what it's like having a conversation with me when I'm upset. "Tom, you don't know him. Therefore you have no reason to not trust him or not like him. You don't have any right to storm in here and act like a jealous ex-boyfriend, because you're not." I winced, pressing my hand over my abdomen. The numbness had worn off. I felt everything—specifically the burning campfire of stress in my stomach.

"Cambria, I wasn't acting like a jealous ex. I was acting like you do."

Ugh. I dropped my face into my hands. I didn't have the energy to argue. "Tom, I just can't right now," I mumbled into my palms, and before I knew it, I was crying. The dam broke, and tears burst out. Snot seeped out of my nostrils. Spit pooled in my mouth. Every hole in my face leaked fluid.

"Um, uh," Tom stammered. I could see between my fingers his feet dancing around on the cement. "Is this a trick or for reals?" I didn't answer. "Cam?" I hated when he called me *Cam.* Then he cupped his arm around my trembling shoulder, and that, I didn't hate so much.

"A tenant was murdered the day I got here, and I have no idea who killed him. A car was stolen. The washing machine broke. Now I'm losing my job," I said in between sobs. "And I might need you to take Lilly while I figure out where we're going to live." My salty tears slithered down my cheeks, landing in my mouth. "I don't have any money or credit, and I can't go back to Fresno because I said the stupid gay thing, and now I can't go without saying I'm a liar, but I am a liar. And I'm probably going to hell now, but I have to say so because I have no idea what I'm doing, and I'm talking to furniture."

Tom didn't say anything. He just kept rubbing my shoulder. I leaned into his embrace, nestled under his armpit. When my sobs turned to a manageable cry, he asked, "I'm not really sure what any of that means. Who was murdered?"

"Kenneth Fisk in Apartment 21," I sniffled.

"And why didn't you tell me about this?"

"I don't know."

"And why are you losing your job?"

I ran my fingertips under my eyes, catching the smudged makeup and tears. "My boss is coming to *talk* to me tomorrow. Kenneth Fisk was murdered the day I got here. Then a car was stolen. I almost kicked out the wrong guy, I got the owner's son's boyfriend arrested, I don't have all the rents, and everyone here hates me. Need I go on?"

"OK," he said slowly, as if carefully choosing his next words. "Were you involved with the murder?"

"What? No! Of course not." Honestly.

"Then how does this make you a liar who's going to hell?"

Oh.

I looked down, chewing on my bottom lip. Was this the right time to reveal my stupid lie? I didn't have the money for a Motel 6, let alone a new apartment. I should receive compensation for the time I'd worked thus far, which wouldn't be much but would hopefully be enough for gas to Fresno and an oil change (my little genie bottle, lamp-looking thing had been lit up on my dashboard for the last six months. My car would probably explode somewhere on the Grapevine). Going home was my only real option, and I was going to have to explain myself then, so I might as well start now. I took a deep, shaky breath. "I sort of told my family you were gay, and if Lilly and I move there, I'll have to tell them I've been lying."

Tom's arm fell off my shoulder and slapped back to his side. I turned to face him, still chewing on my lip. He put on his angry face. "You're not moving to Fresno with my kid. You're not moving to Fresno period."

Really?

Not the part of the story I anticipated him getting upset over. "Tom, it's much cheaper there, and I could stay with my mom while I find another job. It wouldn't be forever, but what am I supposed to do? Live on the streets?"

Tom brought his hands to his hips, giving me a you're-being-ridiculous look. "You think I'd let you live on the streets? And why am I gay?"

Here we go. "Well, it's a funny story, really. So you remember when I found out I was pregnant, and I said 'I think we should try to be a family'? And you were all 'I don't want to date you' and I was all 'Ouch, my heart.' Well, when I told my parents, I kinda implied we were dating when I got pregnant and that you sorta came out of the closet, so we broke up. Then it all got so out of hand. I was heartbroken, and it sorta made us look better. I don't know why. I'm beginning to think there's something wrong with my head. You should know my parents are very supportive of you."

Tom's mouth hung open. His brows pressed down to a *V*, and his hazel eyes stared straight through me. He then closed his eyes and shook his head as if waking from a dream. "I don't ever remember having that conversation about dating."

He sure was sticking on the less poignant points of my stories here. "I was paraphrasing," I told him.

"Cam, we barely knew each other. It took me a while to get my head around being a dad. I thought you were trying to do the right thing. I never knew you were heartbroken over it."

For a lawyer he was rather unobservant. "Does it matter now?"

He thought for moment. "Yeah, I think it does," he decided.

Lilly stuck her face in the gap in the door. "The show's over!" she announced.

"I'll be right there," I told her.

"But it's over nooowww," she whined.

"Lilly, I'll be right there," I repeated. She heaved herself to the floor.

"Lilly," Tom said sternly. "We're talking. Go sit on the couch and wait for us to finish."

"OK, Daddy," Lilly quickly obliged.

I rolled my eyes.

"Cam, you'll stay with me until we figure everything out. You're not going to Fresno. You're not going to be homeless. You're certainly not staying with the 'maintenance man.' Are you even sure you're losing your job? You have a tendency to jump to conclusions."

"Really?" I didn't know what else to say. "Thank you," I

added, locating the thread of hope I'd lost grasp of. My stress lifted, a little, taming the campfire in my stomach. "My boss is coming tomorrow. I'm pretty sure he'll fire me. Wouldn't you? I was already his third choice. This place started going downhill the moment I started. I mean, literally, within an hour..." A thought pecked at my subcranium...*the moment I started.*

"By the way, the doctor doesn't think it's allergies, and he didn't seem too interested in the article you wanted him to read," Tom said.

I gazed up. "Huh?"

"The doctor," he repeated. "He said it didn't look like an infection or allergies. If anything it's a cold."

"Oh, right." The doctor's appointment. Slipped my mind. "What can we give her for a cold?"

"Tylenol. Kids her age can't take cold medicine."

Cold medicine?

Cold medicine...cold medicine?...cold medicine!

I got it.

Less than an hour after I started, Kenneth was found dead in the dumpster, beside him was the backpack, the gun, the wallets...and the pregnancy test...the positive pregnancy test. Pregnancy...holy mother crap of bleeping nuggets...Pregnancy. Cold medicine. Dumpster.

I grabbed Tom by the shoulders. "She's pregnant!"

"Who are you talking about?" He looked so freaked out, I had to laugh.

"Why are you laughing?" The concern lacing his words was even funnier than the fact I so blindly missed the obvious.

"You can't buy cold medicine without an ID!"

"Now you're scaring me."

I placed a hand on Tom's chest. "Can you please stay here with Lilly? I have to talk to someone. I'll be right back."

CHAPTER TWENTY-ONE

———

Tenant shall not keep any items of a dangerous, flammable, or explosive nature on the Premises.

"She's pregnant," I thought out loud, nearly singing it. Ty from Apartment 12 gave me a double take, repositioning the car seat draped over his forearm, protectively placing himself in front of his newborn. I caught my reflection in his dark glasses as I whizzed by in a flash, not even bothering with a polite smile. I had a murder to solve.

Through the ivy-laced breezeway and into the third courtyard I went. Determined. Silvia descended the stairwell in front of her apartment, her heels clanking against the worn stone steps, still wearing her silk floral robe. The same one she'd been sporting all week. Harold was in his usual spot, bobbing his head around, his claws digging into Silvia's shoulder. Her bulging eyes met mine. I didn't waver though. I pressed forward, maintaining eye contact.

She stopped at the base of the stairwell, one age-spotted hand resting on the railing, the other balled into a fist. I stared into her mucus-colored eyes as the distance closed between us. I once read if you should ever encounter a lion, you should stare directly into its eyes to prevent being attacked. I applied the same approach to Silvia.

It worked.

She broke eye contact and stepped around me. I ran up the stairs to Apartment 22 and knocked with both hands continuously, impatiently, feverishly, and all other related adverbs. "Clare? Bob? It's Cambria. I need you, please!" I shouted.

I heard Silvia huff from below. "I knew it," she hissed.

I snapped around and leaned over the railing. "Yeah, and it was awesome!" I yelled. "Maybe you should get some. Then you wouldn't be so miserable when everyone else does."

She gasped, bringing her hand to her chest. Harold turned around, flashing me his backside.

"What was awesome?" Clare stood in the doorway wrapped in a white terrycloth robe, holding her hand up to block the incoming rays of the setting sun from her eyes. "What's wrong?"

"Hi, Clare, I'm sorry to bother you. I'm looking for Chase. I need to speak with him right away." She stared at me, blank of any recollection. "He's the maintenance man. Is he not here fixing the garbage disposal?" I asked.

She continued to stare at me.

"Never mind. I don't really need him." I pounded back down the stairs, past Silvia, who huffed and puffed as if she were about to blow my house down. No time. I was on a mission. It was so obvious!

My determined march slowed to a yielding shuffle. *Was it obvious?* Had I jumped to conclusions again? Was I about to blow this entire situation out of proportion? I'd been so wrong lately.

Or had I?

My gut told me something was lurking behind the corner, waiting for me to get comfortable before jumping out and revealing him or herself. Isn't that exactly what happened? I was asleep, warm in my bed, tucked under my comforter, when I was summoned to meet Kevin. Spencer, technically, was selling illegal items out of his apartment just as I'd thought. Did I anticipate it being stingrays? No. Would any reasonable adult assume it was marine animals? No. Wick was in fact on parole. Therefore he was a criminal, and therefore I was not overreacting when I'd approached him. OK, maybe when I had called the police and hid behind a box. But who knows what he was on parole for?

I was right all along…in a roundabout sort of way.

I was going for it, I decided. Resolute and fast, I rounded the corner. Kevin stood under the archway below his apartment, wearing cargo shorts and a white tank. I almost didn't recognize him with so many clothes on. He brought a cigarette to his mouth and took a long drag.

Kevin's presence was problematic. I hadn't included him in the plan I'd devised during the one-minute walk over. Chase would have been helpful. Kevin, not so much, especially considering he'd snapped the olive branch I'd extended. Though he never did call Patrick to tattle. If he were serious about firing me, wouldn't that be his first item of business? Telling Patrick what happened?

Perhaps the olive branch remained intact?

I tapped his shoulder. He jumped and spun around, dropping his cigarette in the process. I brought my finger to my lips before he could say anything. "Shh," I whispered.

His face contorted into all-consuming anger. His jaw tight, eyes narrowed into furious slits, hands clenched into fists.

Or perhaps he left Patrick a message?

Then it happened. His jaw relaxed. His hands went limp and were promptly brought to his clothed hips. He lifted his brows high to the middle of his forehead and shrugged. "Well?" he whispered back.

It took me a moment to process the shift in his demeanor. He had not stormed away, taken off any clothing, called me a tramp, or slammed a door in my face (granted, there wasn't one around to do so with). "Well…how are you?" Might as well start with pleasantries.

"Fine, you?" It was the most normal conversation we'd ever had. He stuck his pinky into his ear and gave it a jiggle, pulling back to inspect his findings. For the first time I noticed the diamond studs glittering on each earlobe. His auburn sideburns were peppered with strands of white hair. His face had rather strong, masculine, well-defined features. He was, I realized for the first time, attractive. It's amazing what you notice when not actively avoiding staring at someone's exposed genitalia.

"Kevin," I said in a hushed tone, trying not to sound too amazed. "You really do look good in clothes. You should wear them more often."

He looked down, pulling at the bottom of his tank. His

mouth twisted to the side as if deciding if making the effort was worth it. "Eh," he finally said, mirroring my hushed tone. "You here to see," he said, jerking his head toward Alice's apartment.

"Yeah, why? You know something?"

He looked around. "It depends on who's asking."

This was the Kevin I'd come to know and love, and by love I meant tolerate, and by tolerate I meant I hadn't smacked him upside the head yet. Which had to be some kind of world record. "Me, Kevin. I'm asking you," I answered in an angry whisper. "I don't have time for games."

He looked taken aback. "Calm down. I was only joking."

Joking? *Joking?* Was I talking to Kevin's reasonable identical twin brother? "Oh, sorry. Can you please tell me if you know anything?"

He folded his arms over his chest and looked around again. Confident we were alone, he leaned in and whispered, "I know everything about this place and everything about everyone." He winked.

"Ugh. I'm done. I've got bigger fish to cook."

"You mean fry?" Kevin corrected.

"Whatever," I said, pushing past him.

The carports wrapped around the building and backed up to the patios of first-floor Apartments 39, 22, 36, and 19.

I would have an unrestricted view of Alice and Vincent's patio from the carport roof, and if the blinds were open, the bedroom.

The crime started the day I arrived. Alice was the only one to technically move in on my watch. She said her name was Alice, yet everyone calls her Wysteria. Makes sense to use a stripper name. Or did it make sense to use a different name if you were using a different identity? She said she'd lost her license, yet she had a bag with medicine because her "Boo was totally, like, sick with a gnarly cold." You can't purchase cold medicine anymore without swiping your driver's license! And I learned from my crime shows it's because you can make meth with cold medicine, so the stores track who's buying cold medicines in large quantities. Ha! See? Chase shouldn't have given me such a hard time about watching those shows when that knowledge is clearly coming in handy now. So Alice had lied. She'd never left her license at a club. Her name wasn't even Alice. It was Wysteria. She knew we would run background and credit reports, and any criminal hits would show up. She only turned in an application because Joyce had asked her to, and she didn't want any negative attention.

The clincher was her appearance. The day we met, she was bouncy and colorful. The new Alice (or whoever she was) was layered in clothing on an extremely hot day. Her face was pale, her eyes sunken, and those dark spots looked an awful lot like pregnancy melasma (I'd suffered through it my entire pregnancy with Lilly).

Alice had left the office, and not thirty minutes later, I'd found the wallets and backpacks discarded in the dumpster. She didn't a have a purse or wallet with her. The application and photo ID were folded into quarters, as if stored in her pocket. Did I think she killed Kenneth Fisk? Maybe. It seemed unlikely she'd be able to haul him to the dumpster herself. Which meant she had help.

Kenneth Fisk *was* last seen hurrying toward the back stairwell. The stairwell right above Apartment 39. What if Kenneth witnessed something happening in Apartment 39—a theft, drugs, something illegal—and called to report this to Joyce but was killed before he could finish his message?

Could Wysteria or Boo be into something illegal?

It was, once again, a theory. A theory that I wasn't about to tell anyone—police, Patrick, Chase…until I had hardcore proof.

The carport roof was much taller than I anticipated. Chase and his accompanying ladder would have been helpful. I squatted down and with all my might sprang upward with my arms outstretched, hoping to catch the top of the carport.

Not even close.

Note to self: You are not Michael Jordan.

That said, it didn't stop me from trying two more times. I leaned against the rough stucco surface of the too-high wall, catching my breath.

"Here," Kevin said, appearing at my side. A freshly lit cigarette hung from the corner of his mouth. He stood in a braced position with his fingers intertwined.

"You sure?" I asked, cautiously inserting my Converse'd foot into his makeshift lift. I was heavier than I appeared. At least that's what every nurse said as I stepped onto the hateful doctor's office scale. "You're solid," they'd say, and I'd want to punch them in the face.

Kevin wrapped his thumbs around my shoe for extra support. "I'm sure," he replied, keeping his cigarette balanced in his mouth. "They've been selling coke in there for a couple of months now. The guys are pretty cool. They don't make it here. They get it from somewhere else," he said, as if it should make me happy. "It's decent stuff, best I've ever had. Grabbed an eight ball from them this morning."

My mouth fell open. My frontal lobe worked frantically to decipher which disturbing piece of information to process first. "Kevin," I scolded, removing my foot. "You just got out of rehab."

"I didn't stay. Checked myself out and went to Mexico instead."

Good grief. "Promise me you will not touch whatever you bought from them." I noticed his dilated eyes. "Too late?"

He brought his thumb and forefinger together, leaving a small half-inch gap between them. "Just a wee bit," he said, stifling a giggle.

And yet another piece to the puzzle—Kevin acted the way he acted because he was on drugs. Again, it should have been obvious. To be fair, I did have a hunch.

"Do you know if they had anything to do with Kenneth Fisk's murder?" I whispered.

Before he could answer, we heard Apartment 39's sliding patio door opened and shut.

Kevin, I mouthed, pointing to his hands. He returned them to their boosting position and squatted down to better bear the weight. I placed one foot into his hands and jumped up with the other. Kevin lifted me until I managed to hook my hands on the edge of the roof.

"You're heavy," Kevin quietly wheezed, his face turning apple.

"Just a little farther..." I inched my foot up the wall until I could leverage it on the ledge as well.

What a sight this must be.

With every ounce of strength pulsing through me, I made it to the top of the carport roof.

Note to self: Work out!

I paused to look up at the gorgeous full moon while I caught my breath.

Then it was back to business. I army-crawled across the roof to get a better view of the patio.

The bedroom blinds were closed. Dark trash bags filled to maximum capacity were piled two deep next to the sliding glass door. The patio was littered with broken plastic chairs, crinkled papers, and food containers. Paragraph three on the third page of the *House Rules* says patios are to remain free from trash, broken furniture, and wood-burning barbecues. There was also something in there about not being in possession of illegal drugs or involved in the distribution of them.

In short, I had plenty of grounds for an eviction.

From the reflection off the sliding door, I saw Vincent leaning against the wall directly below me. The patio door slid open, and I flattened myself against the roof. Footsteps approached. I held my breath. The footsteps stopped below, out of my line of sight. "Boo, are you, like, mad at me?" It was Alice. Her voice was small, submissive.

"I told you not to leave the apartment," Vincent said, his voice angry.

"I was just, like, walking around. Getting some air."

"Yeah, last time you *got some air*, you took a damn car and police were crawling all over this place. What part of *lay low* do you not understand?"

Alice took Daniella's car?

"I told you it was just to get away from Rev, not you."

"Don't play me," Vincent warned.

"I'm not," she said. "Rev's crazy. Why does he have to stay here?"

Who the hell is Rev?

"I told you, it's just until we get enough money to pay off my debt."

"We don't need him," she said. "We can figure it out on our own, Boo. I told you I'd help."

"Like you helped last time?"

"I told you, I didn't know," she grunted.

Know what?

There was a long break of silence.

"I didn't do anything. It was all Rev," Alice said, her voice louder.

"Dammit!" A trash bag sailed to the other side of the patio. "Rev is the only reason I'm not in prison right now."

"But it wasn't you, Boo. It was all him. Don't blame yourself."

Blame himself for what?

For Kenneth?

"Shut up. I'm done talking about it...I have to go," Vincent growled. "I expect you here when I get back."

"You're meeting Malone at Alcove right now, right?" Alice asked, her voice even louder.

"You on my phone?" He punched the wall. That had to hurt.

"No, no. I just...like, I heard Rev say something."

"Just you remember, if I go down, you go down too. Get inside."

I heard them walk across the patio, so I dared to lift my head. Vincent's hand was wrapped around Alice's waist as they disappeared into the apartment, sliding the door closed behind them.

I reached into my back pocket for my phone and quickly texted myself. *Vincent meeting Malone now at alcove. Rev. Alice is Wysteria. She stole the car. Vincent should be in prison. But why? Did he kill Kenneth?*

I would wait, I decided, for Vincent to leave. I would wait for my feet to hit solid ground before I called the police. This was huge!

The moments ticked by. The moon grew brighter and higher. Finally, Vincent left. The car parked directly under me in the carport roared, and...

Ack!

It happened in an instant. One second I was lying on the carport roof, and the next second I was on the patio floor, with a pair of crazy, angry eyes glaring at me.

CHAPTER TWENTY-TWO

———

Tenant will, at Tenant's cost, keep Premises in good, clean condition.

I took a quick assessment of all limbs and organs. Everything was accounted for, and nothing throbbed. Hurt like hell, yes. Throbbed in a need-to-replace-a-kidney kind of way, no. I lay in a bed of stuffed, black trash bags with a hand wrapped tightly around my left ankle. The hand belonged to a man with a sprawling spider web tattoo across his neck, angry jaw, strong limbs, and eyebrows so blond they blended in with his face. I gulped. He made Teardrop of Death look like Mary Poppins.

"When are you going to learn to not be so damn nosy?" the man asked through gritted teeth.

"Right now," I assured him, kicking my free leg. Without taking his eyes off my face, he grabbed my other ankle. "Help!" I screamed. "I'm being hel—" Before I knew what was happening, he was sitting on my legs, pinning me down, and his large, flat palm landed over my mouth, silencing my cries for help. I licked his hand. *Blech.* It tasted like fish.

"Who are you really?" the man snarled. I had a hunch this was crazy Rev Alice/Wysteria and Vincent were talking about.

I also had a hunch the spider web across Rev's neck was what Kenneth was referring to when he yelled "Spider web!" on the message. *Gulp.*

"Who do you really work for?" he asked, clearly rhetorically, since his hand prohibited me from answering.

Keeping his hand over my mouth, he slid off me and

moved around behind me then hoisted my torso up with his free hand, holding me against him. Then he dragged me backwards through the patio door, my legs flailing the entire journey.

Frantic, my eyes dashed around, taking in the surroundings. A dark-spotted popcorn ceiling. Rectangles cut into the drywall along the bottom. The furnace was missing. A variety of colorful stains dotted the dingy carpet. As he dragged me over empty McDonald's containers and flattened In-N-Out cups, a Taco Bell wrapper stuck to the bottom of my shoe. The apartment smelled like burning plastic with a hint of the *Tropical Rainforest* I'd used in the office. Even in my current distressed state, I could see why Joyce asked for a high security deposit.

My tour continued down the short hallway. More rectangles. More stains. Into the living room we went. I could see the kitchen from there—the wall that separated the two had a hole so big a child could stand in it. All the kitchen cabinet doors were missing, leaving only the skeleton of what was once many-times-painted-over cabinetry. The apartment was void of any real furniture, only a few plastic patio chairs and a card table.

The spider-webbed assailant kicked a box blocking his route, sending it sailing across the room. We ended in the dinette area beneath a window adorned with thick, black curtains.

My fight-or-flight mode was alight and blazing, even though my attacker was twice my size and at least that much crazier. I had a hunch he was just as stupid as he was high. My arm was released, but my mouth was still muzzled. His hot breath at my neck triggered a tsunami of fear.

"You a narc?" Rev growled. I tried to shake my head, but his hand was too tight over my mouth.

"Nooooo!" I muffled into his palm.

He didn't hear me.

I kicked and thrashed around, fighting with everything I had until his hands landed on my neck. His eyes bore in to me, like two black marbles. My vision blurred. My heart thundered.

I can't breathe!

The world tunneled…then came a knock on the door. Rev's head snapped, eyes faded from black to brown. He loosened his grip around my neck and returned a hand over my mouth. I grappled to stay conscious.

Another knock on the door.

"Hold on!" screamed Rev.

He grabbed a handful of zip ties conveniently left on the ground. This must be the hostage room, I figured. "Put your hands together behind your back. If you don't listen, I'll go after the kid. Lilly, isn't it?" he hissed into my ear.

Lilly!

Saying her name out loud didn't spark the compliant fear he'd intended; it ignited a fiery rage. With an accelerated rise and fall of my chest, to give the illusion his threats were working, I pressed my wrists together as instructed. Around went the shiny white tie, securely cuffing my hands together.

Another knock on the door.

I hoped it was the police coming to rescue me and take away Crazy Rev before I, literally, dismembered him. Threaten my kid, and I will kill you. I will rip off your balls and choke you with them. Dead.

Two more rapid knocks.

If not the police, I'd even settle for Kevin, or Silvia Kravitz. How she lived so close to drug dealers and only found the time to complain about two old people having loud sex was mind-boggling.

"Who is it?" hollered my assailant, agitated.

My breath hitched as we waited to see who our visitor was.

"It's maintenance," came the two most beautiful words I'd ever heard. Chase, despite our earlier kerfuffle, had come to rescue me. My hero.

"Not now, man," Spider-Webbed Assailant said, not detoured by my drill-toting knight in shining armor.

"Come on, man," Chase begged. "I've got to get to this before I leave." He was quite convincing, I'd give him that. I was ready for him to drop the act, though, and kick the door open. Or use his copy of the master key.

Spider-Webbed Assailant clenched his jaw.

Chase pounded on the door. "Open up! Or deal's off." This sent my assailant into a blind rage. He grabbed a roll of duct tape.

"Not one word," he warned, ripping a piece of tape off

with his teeth before slapping it over my mouth. He walked to the door, his fists balled tight and forearms flexed.

"Deal's already off," he declared upon opening the door.

I shimmied my arms under my butt, pulled my knees together and looped them through my arms. *OK, Cambria, you can't screw this one up. Up high over your head, elbows together, good. Now, bring them down quickly and chicken-wing your arms out to the side.*

It didn't work.

Again.

Nope.

The guy on YouTube made this look so easy.

"Come on, man, just give me a taste of whatever you got," Chase said in an uncharacteristically lazy drawl. He was either playing a role to trick his way into the apartment or I'd missed a Titanic iceberg of a detail in the case I already solved.

OK, Cambria, last time. Arms up high over your head, elbows together, bring them down quickly and chicken-wing your arms out and... Snap! My hands were free (thank you, internet!). I ripped the tape, taking my lips with it, or so it felt, and scrambled to my feet. My Jell-O-y legs carried me to the living room where I found Chase standing with Rev, in no rush to rescue me.

"Cambria?" he asked, confused.

"Chase, what..." My eyes ventured down to the tiny white baggie in his hand.

No.

I felt sick. I felt betrayed. I felt the need to inflict bodily harm. The rage burned so deep I no longer had control over it.

"You bastard!" I lunged toward him, knocking him into the wall. I shoved him against the wall again and again and again. He didn't put up a fight. My assailant didn't try to stop me either. He was actually laughing.

Just then, the door flew open, and in stormed a heavily armored man with a rifle pointed at my face. "Freeze!"

Now here's my knight in shining armor. Finally!

A gang of police officers dressed in black and carrying guns barged through the door. One gun pointed at Rev, who knew the drill and was already down on his knees with his hands high in the air.

"Hands up!" yelled my not-so-friendly knight. "I said hands up."

"You don't understand!" I released Chase, turning around to explain.

"Hands up!" he repeated.

Chase fell to the ground, clasping his hands behind his head instead of putting them up—*he can't even follow the police officer's instructions.*

"I said hands up, now!" the rifle-toting officer yelled.

This isn't happening.

"Look," I tried to explain again. "I promise I'm not—"

"Up!" Now there were three guns pointed at my head. Obviously, they were not in the mood to listen. I dropped to my knees, bringing my hands up as high as they would go.

A policeman pushed me to the ground. "Ouch! I didn't do anything," I pleaded with the man whose knee was in my back. He forced my hands together and slapped a cold, metal cuff over each wrist. "I'm the victim here. I promise I didn't do anything!" He led me through the door and out to the spectacle in the carports—dark SUVs, squad cars, a German Shepherd being escorted around by a policewoman, scores of people watching. I half expected a news crew to show up along with a helicopter.

"Cam!"

I heard the familiar voice and looked over my shoulder to scan the crowd. Tom stood behind two police officers. Lilly was balanced on his hip, her face digging into her daddy's shoulder. "Don't say anything! I'll meet you there!" Tom yelled.

This was really happening, I realized. I was being arrested, real handcuffs and all. My feet felt as if they were made of cinderblocks, and I dragged them to the police car. One hand on my head, and I was pushed down into the back seat.

Kevin came flying through the crowd. "No! Stop! That's my apartment manager," he screamed. Sometime, during all the fuss, his clothes had disappeared. A police officer wrapped his arm around Kevin's bare waist. "Let go of me! Do you know who I am?" Then he was on the ground, hands pulled behind his back, and on went the cuffs.

I dropped my head back against the seat, listening to the

world collapsing around me.
This wasn't part of my theory.

CHAPTER TWENTY-THREE

———

Tenant shall be liable for all legal expenses if Tenant should have Landlord falsely jailed.

My chauffeuring police officer had dark, creamy skin, a dusting of black hair over his top lip, and a boyish face—like a twelve-year-old dressed in a policeman's costume. Instead of a badge and a gun, he should be carrying a pillowcase going door-to-door saying "trick-or-treat."

He led me through the back door of the police station and down a long busy hallway. We stopped at an unlabeled steel door, and the officer, to my surprise, removed the handcuffs and instructed me to wait in the chair. The room was small, warm, and gray. Two fluorescent tubes hummed from the ceiling, filling the small space with bright light. I sat at a table long enough to double as a bed, with an empty chair across from me.

My neck ached. I inspected the red marks on my wrists, the raw burns from the great zip-tie escape that turned out to be everything *but* great. No doubt I'd be sitting at home instead of in an interrogation room if the police had found me tied up. I hadn't been booked, at least not yet. No fingerprints. No mug shot—for which I was grateful. I had caught a reflection of the train wreck that was my face and bird's nest that was Einstein in the cruiser's window. Call me vain, but I wanted at least a decent-looking mug shot if I had to get one. Those follow you forever.

It struck me as odd that I'd been so dramatically paraded out in cuffs and shoved into the back of a police car only to be questioned. The information of my innocence must have come to the police while we were en route to the station. Now I'd be forced to give a full statement before I could go home.

Or so I thought.

The door opened. It was the ill-fitted-suit detective from the day I found Kenneth Fisk.

She stared at me so intently my palms began to sweat. Then she paced over to the opposite chair, remaining on her feet, one hand on her hip, the other holding a manila folder. "I'm Detective Angela Spray," she said with a forced grin. "Do you remember me?"

I flattened my hands on my thighs to keep my legs from shaking.

The detective cocked her head, staring at me with an unreadable expression. "Rough day, huh?"

I nodded.

She took a seat and leaned forward casually, as if we were two long-time friends about to have coffee. "Some tea? Water? Soda?"

I shook my head.

"I have a few questions for you so we can clear this up. OK?"

I nodded.

"I need you to answer verbally, please."

"Yes."

"Can you state your full name?"

"Cambria Jane Clyne," I answered so softly I could barely hear myself.

"Thank you, Cambria." She paused, slowly drumming her fingers on the tabletop. Painfully slow, starting with her pinky and ending with her pointer finger, only to start the rhythm over again. My stomach clenched. If she was trying to create a comfortable environment, one to make it easy for me to share the details of the traumatic event, then she was really sucking at it. "It's been a hard time for you, Cambria. Laid off, an eviction filed against you, new job isn't going so well, and money is tight. You've got to be feeling desperate, needing to provide for your daughter. Then there's the added stress of being a single parent."

Again, not feeling comfortable here.

"I talked to your buddy Rev," she said.

My heart flipped. "He's not my buddy."

"No? He's not? That's interesting." She spoke slowly

then cleared her throat, much like I did when I was mentally preparing my next words. "He said you killed Kenneth Fisk and asked him to take care of the body for you."

I nearly fell out of my chair. "What! I never even met Kenneth Fisk."

"Rev said that you came to make a purchase before work, Kenneth confronted you, and you killed him."

"Wh…wh…wh…" I forgot how to make words come out of my mouth. "I called the police to report it!"

"I know." The detective placed her elbows on the table and stared into my eyes. "It's a good tactic." She clasped her hands together. "Pretty genius really. Calling the police, making reports, and telling them about this tenant who is engaging in criminal activity when you yourself were the one working with one of the biggest drug dealers in the city. Takes all the focus off you. I get it. You're in financial ruin and have to take care of your child, can't afford to get caught."

"What?" I squeaked. "I didn't have anything to do with Kenneth Fisk, and I've never done a drug in my life!"

"Then why were you in Vincent's apartment?" She stiffened, like a dog ready to attack. "Why were you in the middle of a drug transaction?"

What is happening? "I was on the carport roof, and Rev pulled me down and dragged me into the apartment. If you spoke to him already, then you should know this."

"You were on the roof?"

"Yes. I climbed up there to see if I could find anything incriminating. I thought maybe Alice had something to do with… As a matter of fact, I know Alice or Wysteria, whatever her name is, did have something to do with Kenneth and the backpack."

The detective leaned back, staring at the ceiling as if her next question was written across it. The fluorescent lights buzzed and flickered, only adding to the intimidating ambiance. "You climbed an eight-foot-high stucco wall?"

"No, I got a lift up from Kevin."

"The one we arrested? The one so strung out he could barely walk?"

I felt faint. "Look. I had nothing do with this. I'm just the apartment manager. Rev was holding me against my will. Since when is the victim treated like a criminal?"

"When we arrived you were engaged in a one-sided physical altercation with Chase Hudson. How was it you were being held against your will?"

"I was mad at him because he'd been lying to me."

"Lying to you about what?"

"About his involvement."

"His involvement in this case?"

"Sure, the case, the drugs, whatever. I was mad that he was buying drugs from Rev."

She nodded her head, as if answering an internal question. "Tell me this, Cambria. If you're just the apartment manager, innocently caught up in this, then how did you know Malone's exact location?"

"What?"

"Malone's location." She pulled a sheet of paper from the manila folder and read it out loud. "*Vincent meeting Malone now at alcove. Rev. Alice is Wysteria. She stole the car. Vincent should be in prison. But why? Did he kill Kenneth?*

His inner circle is tight-lipped. He keeps a low profile, nearly impossible to locate. And you expect me to believe you just so happened to come across this information?"

I was confused beyond comprehension. "How did you even know I..." Crap. *Did they tap my phone?* "Wait. No, no, no. I'm not supposed to be talking," I thought out loud. Tom said not to say anything. Keeping broke, innocent people out of jail was what he did for a living. I was both broke and innocent. "I want to see my lawyer. Right now."

She stared at me. "You're not involved with Malone at all but already have a lawyer?"

I clasped my hands together to keep them from shaking. "Thomas Dreyer is my attorney. He's here waiting for me." *I hope.*

CHAPTER TWENTY-FOUR

———

Landlord will be out of the office for personal or business reasons periodically during the term of the Lease.

My requesting to speak to an attorney didn't make Detective Spray very happy, and she had no qualms about letting me know it either, not by verbalizing her displeasure but by leaving me alone in the small, gray, hot room for several hours…or days…maybe weeks. There was no clock, no window to gauge the time. It felt like an eternity before Tom barged through the door. He'd ditched his Lakers shirt and sandals for a black suit, blue tie, blue shirt, and loafers.

I ran straight into him, throwing my arms around his body and burying my head into his chest. I'd never been so happy to see anyone in my entire life.

Tom pulled me back, with his hands around my shoulder blades. "Are you OK?" he asked, his hazel eyes running over me.

I was in an interrogation room having just been cuffed and searched and stuffed into the back of a police car, and he had to ask "Are you OK?"

I suddenly lost confidence in his lawyering abilities.

"No I'm not OK!" I yanked my shoulders out of his grasp. "What took you so long?"

After waiting in this horrid room for ages, my patience had worn thin. I was about to be tried and convicted for something I didn't do. I'd spend my life in prison with a crazy cellmate named Betty who'd never shower, steal my stuff, and be doing time for a crime so heinous I'd be forced to sleep with one eye open.

Leaving someone like me with a wild imagination in a

small room should be deemed cruel and unusual punishment.

"I dropped off Lilly with Mrs. Nguyen and changed. I had these clothes in my car. Trust me, I hurried."

He took a seat, placed a black leather folder on the table, flipped it open to a notepad, and clicked his pen. "Sit down and let's figure this out."

I plopped down in the chair.

"Right now, they're only questioning your involvement. You haven't been booked yet, but if you are booked, you're looking at possible charges of possession with intent to distribute." Tom said matter-of-factly, as if he were telling me the score of the Dodgers game or what he ate for dinner. "There's also question of your involvement with the murder of Kenneth Fisk. Cam, this is serious."

My heart thundered in my chest. I nearly flew over the table. "Of course it's serious!" I stood and paced the room, squeaking my Converses from one corner to the next in three steps.

"I told you not to say anything," Tom said.

"I didn't know I was being questioned. I thought they were just taking a report."

"And they didn't read you your Miranda rights?"

I ignored him, still pacing. "I can't believe this is happening to me. Me! I couldn't have murdered him. The timing doesn't work. I was with Amy. I was with Mrs. Nguyen. This is a complete injustice. I was being held hostage—he tried to kill me!" I held out my wrists to show him the fresh red marks.

Tom grabbed my hands and pulled me closer to inspect, touching the wounds as if making sure they were real. "Cambria," he whispered. He rarely used my full name, so I knew I'd struck a nerve. "Sit down, and tell me everything from the beginning."

I fell down into the uncomfortable chair and launched into my story. "I was on the carport roof when I overheard Alice, or Wysteria—she could go by both or neither—and Vincent, the resident in 39. They were talking about Vincent meeting Malone at Alcove in a few minutes. I don't even know what that means. He left, and so did she, I guess. Unless she was hiding. I didn't see her in the apartment. I sent myself a text message with all the information." I crossed my legs and uncrossed them, unable to get comfortable in the chair. Or in the situation. "The detective was talking about the text I'd sent myself. Do you think they've been watching me? That they tapped my phone?"

"I don't think so," Tom said, jotting down the information on his notepad. "They probably found your phone when they searched the apartment. Plus they've got Rev and Vincent both down the hall saying you're a loyal customer and that's why you took the apartment management job. Also, they're both sticking to the story of you killing Kenneth Fisk."

"What?" I was up on my feet again, pacing the floor, wringing my hands. This had gotten out of control so fast. "I didn't do anything! Chase was the one buying whatever it was they were selling."

"Cocaine."

"Yes, Chase was buying cocaine. I was trying to leave, but then the police officer came, and I...*ugh*." I fell back on the chair.

Tom dropped his pen. "I told you I knew him. I've seen him down at the courthouse before. I knew it."

"Fine, you were right, and I was wrong. Would you like to write that down on your notepad?" He took me up on the offer and wrote it in the margin. "As I was saying, I wasn't involved. I was trying to get away, except...*ugh*." I buried my face in my hands. "Instead of leaving I started beating the crap out of Chase."

Tom chuckled.

"It's not funny."

He sucked in his bottom lip and clicked the end of his pen against his temple repeatedly, staring down at his illegible notes. "It would only be funny if he was hospitalized," he added under his breath. He stared down at his notes again, nodding his head. "They didn't read you your rights, and detaining you for this long is a direct violation of your fourth amendment rights." He reached across the table and grabbed my hand, giving it a reassuring squeeze. I wondered if he did this with all his clients. "Hang tight. I'll be right back."

CHAPTER TWENTY-FIVE

———

As previously mentioned, Landlord reserves the right to at least one mental breakdown during the Lease term.

A room of any size turns into a miniature suffocating box—let alone an actual miniature, suffocating box—when you're awaiting vindicating news. The internal battle to remain upright and sane was becoming harder to win. I was ready to confess to just about any crime if they'd let me out. In an effort to stay lucid, I concentrated on the flood of questions spinning through my head at hyperspeed—*Where did Alice go? Did Vincent get away? Was he arrested? If Kevin had called the police, wouldn't they have known I was being held against my will? Would they have sent a SWAT team? Who was Rev, and where did he come from? Why would he and Vincent both say I was the one who killed Kenneth? Was this their plan all along? To pin this on me? Did the police really believe them? Was Vincent the father of Alice's baby? Or Rev? Or this Malone person? Did Joyce know about Vincent?*

I thought about the cute maintenance guy who had betrayed Patrick. He betrayed the property. He betrayed all the residents.

He betrayed me.

I felt used. Sick. Confused. How could I have gotten everything so backward? He knew how I felt about him. I'm not that good of an actor, and I'm obviously terrible at hiding. He used my gag-worthy girly emotions to his advantage. It was humiliating.

Still, call me stupid, but I held on to a thread of fraying hope that Chase would not mention my name in his confession.

He never did remove Joyce's smoky armoire from my room, and he installed my medicine cabinet backwards. Seemed the least he could do was confirm I was nothing more than a nosy apartment manager who was desperate to keep her job. Unless...

Oh no, was Chase the father?

This could have a very soap opera-y ending.

The door opened, and Detective Spray walked in. My throat tightened. My lips went numb. My stomach knotted. Her expression remained unreadable, but the door was open. Was this an invitation to leave? Was I free to go?

Then Tom appeared at the door. His face was drawn and worried, but his familiar scent was calming—woody, citrusy with a hint of fabric softener. He dragged a chair next to mine and took a seat, opening his leather folder on the table. *Sent text to Chase* was scrawled across the top.

"What's that?" I asked Tom.

"You said you sent yourself a text message," Detective Spray answered for Tom, entering the room and standing across the table from us. "Why send the information to Mr. Hudson as well?"

I was so confused. I didn't know what she was talking about, so I said, "I'm so confused. I don't know what you're talking about."

"You sent a text about Malone's location at six thirteen yesterday evening to Chase Hudson's cell phone. Why specifically did you send the information to him?"

Yesterday?

Detective Spray slid a paper across the table. "These are the last dozen or so texts retrieved from Mr. Hudson's phone. Look familiar?"

I took the paper and scanned the texts.

Hudson: 32 is fixed.
Clyne: She just called to say her toilet is still backing up. Can you refix, plz.
Hudson: Will after lunch.
Clyne: Nvm. Took care of it.
Clyne: Not sure what happened just now? Why did you leave?
Thanks for fixing the printer. But can you look at 22 g/d?

Clyne: Excedrin. Soap. Bread. Peanut butter.
Clyne: Sorry! Disregard.
Clyne: Did you look at 22 garbage disposal? Plz.
Clyne: Hello?
Clyne: Vincent meeting Malone now at alcove. Rev. Alice is
Wysteria. She stole the car. Vincent should be in prison. But
why? Did he kill Kenneth?

I read the report several times over, shaking my head. "I must have texted Chase by accident. I meant to text myself. I've done this before, texting him by accident. See?" I pointed to the grocery list. I remembered I was *this* close to adding tampons to the list. "I promise you that I thought I sent this to myself and was planning to call the police once I got off the roof. I didn't know who Malone was. I only knew something bad was happening in that apartment, and I suspected someone there killed Kenneth Fisk." I slid the paper back to Spray. "Rev pulled me off the carport roof and into his apartment, strangled me, zip-tied my hands, and I was only able to escape because Chase knocked on the door and distracted him." Tears pooled in my eyes. I blinked hard to keep them from spilling down my cheeks.

Spray was unmoved. "Was Wysteria in the apartment?"

I shook my head.

"Do you know where she might be?"

Tom snapped his folder shut and tapped his watch. "She said she doesn't know. You've got nothing on her. I think we've been here long enough. Done?"

Spray gave him a disconcerted look. "For now."

CHAPTER TWENTY-SIX

———

Tenant agrees that Landlord will seek revenge if Tenant makes Landlord's life a living hell.

With his hand pressed firmly on my lower back, Tom led me through the station to the lobby.

It smelled like BO, onions, and cologne. In that order.

We passed a man in an Ironman costume who was recounting his tale to a police officer behind a pane of bulletproof glass. It was obvious the sun had long since set and the full moon had taken center stage.

How long have I been here?

We neared an old woman seated by the exit. Her mouth was void of teeth, and a gray version of Einstein sprung from her head. Several grocery bags were piled in her lap. She looked exactly as I pictured Betty, my soon-to-be cellmate.

I don't want to go to jail.

"Can you tell me what you know?" I asked Tom.

He loosened his tie and smiled, but it was without conviction. "We'll talk about it in the car."

"No, now. Am I going to end up back here? Maybe I need to give a more detailed report of what happened. I was so flustered I don't think I got my point across."

"There's nothing you can do right now." He placed his hand on my shoulder and looked me in the eyes. "OK?"

I shook my head. Nothing was *OK*. Frankly, I was tired of that word. "I'm not *OK*. I was arrested today. One of my residents is dead, and another was dealing drugs out of his apartment. My maintenance man was buying them. So was…holy crap. Kevin. We forgot about Kevin."

"We forgot about Kevin," the old woman who looked like Betty repeated.

"Kevin?" Tom asked, ignoring Betty.

"He's the son of the owner of the building," I explained. "He was arrested too. The naked guy."

Tom nodded, understanding whom I was referencing. How could you not?

"I doubt his family would send a lawyer. Trust me. If you knew his story, you'd be all over this."

"All over this," Betty parroted, letting out a Wicked Witch-inspired cackle. "Naked. Naked. Naked. Naked."

Tom placed a hand on my lower back again, urging me away from the cackling stranger. I didn't move. "Tom, help him," I pleaded.

He grunted. "He's the owner's son?" I nodded. "What's his last name?"

"Kevin… I actually don't remember his last name. It starts with a Mc." I bit my lip, flipping through my memory bank. Kevin's file only said *Kevin* as if he were Prince or Cher. Certain people need only a first name. I'd read the family trust name on paperwork before…

Betty began spitting out last name options. "McFarlin. McDonald. McDermott…"

"I love Dylan McDermott," a woman chimed in. She had a teased pouf of red hair and bright orange lipstick. She was wearing a pleather tube top and a leopard-print short, short skirt. "He was in that show *The Practice*. You look like him, you know. Like a young Dylan McDermott." She pointed a crimson fingernail at Tom and winked.

I studied Tom's profile with a musing tilt of my head. I'd never made the connection before. "You know what? I can see it now. A little…if you squint your eyes," I said to the woman. "Oh, hold on. I got it. It's McMills. Kevin McMills."

Betty applauded and threw a starlight mint at us. It bounced off Tom's face.

"Let's go," he barked.

"But my mint," I pouted.

Tom's eyes were ablaze and jaw tight. It was the angriest I'd seen him since…well…since that morning.

"What's wrong with you, Cambria? None of this is funny. Do you realize how bad this could have been? You could have been killed. You could have been raped then killed. You could have been tortured, raped, then killed. Why aren't you taking this more seriously?" His eyes glistened. *Is he going to cry?* "I told you to stay out of it! You just inserted yourself into a major drug operation with one of LA's biggest drug lords. Do you realize the only reason I was able to get you out of here was because of some technicalities?"

I didn't answer. I didn't know how to. He was clearly upset with me, maybe because he'd spent all night at the police station or because he knew he'd never get paid for his time or because he was as tired and hungry as I was. Or maybe he truly was upset with me for putting myself in this situation. Regardless, if anyone had the right to be mad it was me, but I wasn't. I was too tired and emotionally bruised to be angry—at least not yet. And I didn't want to fight with Tom, especially after all he had done.

"Thank you for everything. I'm sorry if I put you out," I said, my voice small.

"You didn't put me out, Cam." He exhaled and ran his hands down his face. "I'll go find out what happened with Kevin. You…" He looked around the room. "Just…sit here." He pointed to an empty chair next to a man with a bloody tissue up his nose. "And don't talk to or leave with anyone."

Seriously?

Tom stalked off to speak to a policewoman behind the glass, glancing over his shoulder to be sure I was following instructions, as if I were an unruly child. His mood was out of character. He was the even-tempered, everything-is-gonna-be-totally-fine one. I was the pessimistic overreactor. If we were switching roles, he should have discussed it with me first.

CHAPTER TWENTY-SEVEN

———

Tenant forfeits security deposit if Tenant turns out to be a complete psychopath.

Tom sat behind the wheel of his 4Runner, one hand draped over the steering wheel and the other clutching the armrest. His eyes darted to Kevin's reflection in the rearview mirror, then to me, then to the road, only to repeat the rotation again. Kevin was squished in the back seat between Lilly's car seat and the window. He was swimming in Tom's Laker shirt and khakis, with his feet slipped into Tom's three-sizes-too-big sandals. He stared out the window, his face etched in sadness. Tom said people can be depressed when they come down from a cocaine binge, and Kevin was no exception. Especially when you added in the possession of cocaine, resisting arrest, and public nudity charges—he had plenty to be unhappy about.

"Hey, Kevin," I said, turning around in the passenger seat to face him. "Did you happen to see Chase when you were in there?" He continued to stare out the window, not answering. "You ever see him visiting Apartment 39?"

"He was there all the time," he said, monotone, to the window.

My heart sank. Regardless of the fact that Chase had been arrested and that the police had his phone records, I still hung on to the hope he'd mistakenly been caught up in all this. Like I was.

"I wish you would have told me," I said. "I was completely blindsided."

Kevin exhaled, fogging the window enough to write his name in it. "I didn't say anything because you were screwing each other and I figured you must have known."

I was shaking my head before he even finished his sentence. "Nope, that's not true. Nothing happened at all."

"You wanted it to then." True. Not something I wanted revealed in front of Tom, especially after his outburst over Chase spending the night.

I flipped back into the passenger seat, fidgeting with my seat belt. "He must still be high," I told Tom. He returned a halfhearted smile and pulled into the parking lot of the apartments. The SUV bounced over the uneven pavement until we arrived at the entryway, near Kevin's apartment.

The place was quiet at nearly four in the morning, and only a few windows showed signs of life—the blue glow from a television or the dull light of a lamp. If I hadn't spent the entire day in hell, I'd be tucked into my own bed sound asleep as well.

"Remember, Kevin, Sunday at ten," Tom said to the rearview mirror. "Keep the clothes, and wear a suit and tie if you have one."

Kevin slipped out the door without answering, slamming it shut behind him. He looked like a child in adult clothing shuffling along the pathway to his apartment.

Poor Kevin.

I leaned back against the headrest. *What a long, terrible, terrible day.* Tom looked about as exhausted as I felt, his face pale, the top button of his shirt undone, and tie pulled loose.

He began mindlessly playing with the keys dangling from the ignition. I noticed the bronze circular keychain hiding in the mass of keys, the one with *I Love Daddy* stamped in the middle. A gift I had bought him for his first Father's Day. I had wrapped it in blue wrapping paper (his favorite color) and attached a homemade card with Lilly's handprint on the cover. I said it was from Lilly, but of course there was no way she crawled down to Hollywood Boulevard to purchase it for him, nor did she wrap it, tie a bow, or even know it was Father's Day. Tom never said anything. *Anything.* He barely acknowledged the gift. Not even a blasé "Thanks." I was livid. *Livid.* And still bitter over it. At least I had been until I noticed the keychain hanging from his ignition, weathered from years of use. I'd never noticed it on his key ring before. Probably because this was the most time we had ever spent together since...well...since the night we made Lilly.

"What time do I need to get Lilly from Mrs. Nguyen?" I asked.

"I told her I'd call first thing in the morning to let her know when I'd be able to pick Lilly up. I checked in with her before I knew what was happening with you." Tom let out an exhausted sigh.

"Do you think I'm going to jail?"

He shook his head. "It's not you they want. They've been working on this Malone case for over a year. You were proving problematic at first because you kept calling the police and staking out apartments, but still, they figured you were harmless. Chase and Kevin both corroborated your story. Detective Spray was really stuck on why you sent that text message. It's because of that text message that they were able to find Malone and make the arrest."

"What about Kenneth Fisk? I think Rev is the one who killed him."

"I don't know. They were still looking for someone named Wysteria. They could have a few more questions for you, but you had been detained for far too..." He paused for so long I thought he had fallen asleep until he said, "I wouldn't be surprised if they contacted you for some more of that stuff."

"That stuff?" I snorted. "Did you just fall asleep?"

"A little," he confessed, flashing his signature side-smirk.

I laughed much harder than the situation called for. "Go get some sleep."

"That's the best idea you've had today." He gave a tired chuckle and shifted the car into reverse.

"Wait." I placed my hand on his arm. He tensed under my touch. "Let me get out first."

"I thought you were staying with me."

"Why would I do that?"

"I figured you wouldn't want to be alone. Plus you said you were losing your job, your apartment...your parents think I'm gay... Ring a bell?"

Oh. That. You know it's been a bad day when losing

your job slips your mind. Life had been hell since becoming an apartment manager. After Patrick found out what happened, would he let me keep my job? Would I still want it?

I didn't know.

All I knew for certain was that Tom was right—I didn't want to be alone.

"Before we go," I said, "can I go to Vincent's carport? I want my phone back." I felt naked without it, as if I were missing an appendage.

"Not a good idea."

"Why not? I have to answer the emergency line."

He gave me a you've-got-to-be-kidding-me look.

"What am I supposed to do then?" I asked.

"You're going to have to wait until we're sure the police have finished examining the area."

Now it was my turn to give him a you've-got-to-be-kidding-me look.

Finally, Tom sighed, clicked his seat belt free, and reached for the door. "I can't believe I'm doing this," he groaned. "I doubt it's even up there, but I'll go check."

"Really?" I was surprised and thankful. He was going above and beyond his lawyering and baby daddy duties. *I'll have to buy him lunch or dinner for his help.* I still had those free burrito coupons. "I promise I'll stay here and not move, ever," I teased.

Tom allowed himself a small smile. "I think I'd like that," he said, more to himself than me, looking surprised at his own words as he opened the door and slid off the seat.

I think I'd like that?

What does that mean?

I propped my elbow on the windowsill and watched Tom stroll toward 39's patio fence.

Was he throwing me a life raft? A means of escaping the Alcatraz Island I'd been trapped on since I uttered the words "I'm pregnant" nearly four years ago?

No.

He couldn't be.

Or could he?

I hadn't been down the "maybe" road with him in

months...or...er...weeks. Not wanting to get my hopes up only to have them squashed by his playboy ways. It was the family life I'd longed for since my parents' divorce twenty years ago. A real family—a mom, dad, kid all under one roof kind of family. It was easy to picture Tom, Lilly, and me all gathered around the kitchen table eating the mac and cheese I made from the dusty cookbook my mom had given me. Tom would make Lilly laugh, distracting her from her food. I'd playfully scold him but secretly love every second of it. Family vacations to the snow, all three of us clothed in mittens and scarfs and puffy jackets, building a snowman or sledding down a hill. Then there'd be soccer games, me as the coach, him as the team parent, Lilly as the star player. Family pictures at the beach in jeans and coordinating shirts. Eventually, a little brother or sister would be added to the mix...

It was a warm thought. Everything I'd ever wanted.

Then my mind took a swift left turn, and the green-eyed maintenance boy entered the picture. Chase and his ridiculously perfect hips, the way they swayed when he walked. The way his jeans hung off them in the right way. In my daydreams he didn't have to be a criminal. In my daydreams he could be an upright citizen, an excellent maintenance man, and an even better boyfriend, eventual fiancé, husband, stepfather then father. He'd be wonderful with Lilly, taking on the stepfather role with ease...

What's wrong with me?

Why couldn't I get Chase out of my head? Why would I ever entertain a thought with him in it? Ugh, I was developing Bonnie and Clyde Syndrome.

Hold on.

Where's Tom?

Too busy daydreaming, I'd forgotten what was happening. Tom was nowhere in sight. I pulled the keys out of the ignition and jumped out of the car, locking it over my shoulder with the remote. I headed to the wall, the one I had so ungracefully climbed hours earlier. Cupping my hands around my mouth, I loudly whispered, "Let's go, Tom."

Nothing.

"Psst, Tom. Don't worry about my phone." A sudden chill ran down my spine. I glanced over my shoulder, expecting to find someone, but no one was there.

I walked slowly into the carports. It was dark. Only one of the four lights worked.

Note to self: Check again about more lighting in parking area and fill out maintenance request for back carport lights.

Crap.

Note to self: Find maintenance man.

Crap.

Note to self: Make sure I don't find him attractive.

All the parking stalls were filled with cars except for Vincent's assigned space, which was empty. The cement was stained with oil, and the wall looked to have been hit by a bumper on more than one occasion.

"Tom?" I called out. The air took on an eerie vibe, causing every hair on my arms to stand up. "Hello? Tom? Hello?"

"Hello," came a familiar voice from behind.

My heart leapt so far out of my chest, it was sailing over San Francisco about to cross the Oregon border by the time I realized what was happening.

Without a heart to keep me vertical, I collapsed to the ground and…died.

CHAPTER TWENTY-EIGHT

———

RIP

Or so it felt.

Clutching my chest, I gasped for air, beckoning my heart to return. Tom wrapped his long arms around my trembling frame. "I didn't mean to scare you," he apologized, holding me tighter.

I clutched his arm, digging my nails into his triceps.

"Shh," Tom whispered, stroking the back of my head as if petting a dog. "It's OK. It's just me. You're fine."

Slowly my heart returned to my chest cavity and began beating at a normal rhythm. The feeling returned to my legs and the air to my lungs.

"You OK?" asked Tom.

"No," I snapped. "Stop asking me that." I inhaled a long breath through my nose and released it through my mouth. In through my nose, out through my mouth. In, out, in, out...

Calm down, Cambria. Calm down.

Stabilized, I turned and gave Tom a fierce stare down.

"I've got your phone," he said, holding it up.

"Forgiven." I snatched it out of his hand and unlocked the screen. Eighteen missed calls, a full voicemail box, and seven text messages (one from Amy, five from Tom, and one from AT&T letting me know I was nearing the end of my data usage). All but one of the missed calls were from the emergency line. Residents calling to complain about their apartment manager being arrested, or so I figured. One was from Patrick.

"Cambria, let's go back now," Tom said. But I was too absorbed in my phone.

"Cambria!" Tom sounded annoyed.

"What are you mad about now…" I looked up, and that's when I caught the shadowed figure coming toward us. Crap.

Tom saw it too. "Let's *go*." He didn't have to tell me twice! Er, well, actually he did.

We'd nearly made it out of the parking stall when the shadow revealed its familiar face.

Alice or, actually, Wysteria.

My skin prickled in goose bumps. "Hey there," I said, trying to sound casual. "What's up?"

Wysteria was wringing her hands. She had on the same outfit as earlier, sweatshirt and jeans. Under the glow of the one working light, the bruises on her neck and melasma on her face were faint but still there.

"I totally just came back, and everyone is gone, and there's a huge mess in the apartment." Her voice cracked.

I eyed Tom. He wasn't buying it. Neither was I.

"Sorry about that," Tom said to her. Then he turned to me. "I think I left the car running. Why don't you check on that for me?" His eyes screamed *get out now!*

"No!" Wysteria yelped. "I'm glad you're here, Cambria. You were right all along. Vincent and Rev trapped me. They were abusive and mixed up in the wrong crowd. You could see it. You know I had nothing to do with Kenneth Fisk. I'm desperate." She dropped her head into her hands and unleashed a tearless cry. It was a performance worthy of a 1990s made-for-television movie.

She could be crazy, and according to my theory, she could also be a hormonal criminal. So I humored her. "You're right, Wysteria. I know you didn't have anything to do with all of this. We're not here to get you in trouble. I only wanted my phone."

She smiled. "I knew you'd understand. I just don't have anywhere to go. I'm, like, totally broke. If only I had some way to get away from Vincent before he makes bail and comes after me."

She was beginning to tug on my heartstrings. Could I have had this wrong all along? Could she have been trapped? Was she just an innocent bystander?

"Cambria," Tom quickly jumped in. "Cambria, go back to the office and see if there's any deposit left for Wysteria." His voice was steady, his arms casually at his side. If it weren't for the use of my full name, I'd believe he was being serious.

He knew something. Something bad.

"Go, Cambria," he pressed again. I wasn't about to leave him alone. He had no idea she was pregnant. He'd end up dead. Heaven knows I nearly killed him a few times when I was pregnant with Lilly.

"I need you to come with me to help," I said.

"Cambria, please don't go. I need to explain to you what happened. Like, I had nothing to do with any of it." She was nervous. I could tell by the way she glanced around and wrung her hands.

So I humored her.

"I know the backpack was yours," I said. "You were backed into a corner, tangled in with the wrong people, forced to do things you weren't comfortable with." I paused to clear my throat and find my nerves. "Then you found out you were pregnant, took the car to get away, Vincent found you, and you were stuck. I understand. From one mother to another, let me help you get out of this mess." My goal was to tug on Wysteria's heartstrings, get her to relax enough to trust me and confess.

My plan failed.

Click.

Wysteria held up a black revolver. Much like the one I'd found in the dumpster.

"You're looking at two to four years right now, and if you pull that trigger, it's life," Tom stated, as if this were a helpful tidbit of information to give to a woman pointing a gun at your face. *Men.*

"Shut up and put your hands up, both of you," Wysteria ordered, now holding the gun with both hands. Her feet were spread wide, her eyes focused. Tom held up his palms, and I followed suit.

"Who told you that the backpack was mine?" Wysteria demanded. "Was it Vincent or Rev?"

"Neither," I said in a panic. "I put two and two together. That's all."

Her eyes flickered from Tom to me and back again, as if deciphering if she could trust us. "I wasn't trying to escape from Vincent. I love my Boo. He'd never hurt me. It's all Rev. Do you understand me? It's all Rev!"

"Rev. Got it," said Tom. "Why don't you put the gun down now."

"Why? So you can run off and call the police? It wasn't me!" she cried out. "Everything was great until Vincent got mixed up with Rev. He's the one who killed that man. He's the one who put him in the dumpster. I had no idea he was there!"

I thought back to the conversation between her and Vincent, when she insisted she didn't know. At the time, I had no idea what she was referencing. Now I knew what she didn't know.

She didn't know Kenneth's body was in the dumpster when she threw her backpack in.

This explained why Kenneth was covered and the backpack wasn't.

"You really didn't have any idea," I thought out loud with my hands still high up in the air. The debt, I remembered, and it suddenly all made sense. "Vincent got mixed up with Rev to settle a debt. Is that why you stole the wallets? To help pay?"

"Shut up!" yelled Wysteria.

"And Vincent said he would be in prison if it weren't for Rev. Kenneth Fisk witnessed Vincent and Rev dealing, called Joyce to tell her, and Rev killed him before he could?" I was still thinking out loud, forgetting for a moment that a gun was pointed at me.

"Shut up!" she yelled again.

"And when you found out Rev killed Kenneth Fisk, you tried to get away because your DNA was all over the backpack. But Vincent found you, worried you'd tell the cops what happened, and brought you ba—"

"Listen to her and shut up!" Tom cut me off. He looked at Wysteria. "Why don't you put the gun down, and we'll forget about it."

Wysteria stared at Tom as if he were wearing a unicorn costume. "Like you're going to forget about it. I mean, like, your girlfriend here climbed onto our patio. Who does that? You, like, think I didn't see you, Cambria? You think, like, you didn't set this whole thing in motion yourself? Seriously? You think, like, what, I didn't know you were eavesdropping? I saw your reflection in the slider window and gave you Malone's location so this whole thing could be over." She laughed a vile laugh. "You think I'm gonna let you go, like you'd actually forget about this? Like you're not going to call the police and tell them where I am."

"Think about your baby!" I blurted out. "You don't want to have your baby in prison."

"I *am* thinking of my baby. That's the reason I'm here. That's the reason I've done everything I can to get away from Rev." She smiled, raised the gun, and pointed it at my chest. "And I wouldn't want to have my baby in jail. You're right on that one."

In a slow-moving blur of motion, Tom leaped from my side and knocked Wysteria to the ground. A shot fired. Then another. A horrifying scream echoed around us. It took me a second to realize the shrieks were coming from my own mouth. Involuntarily rocketing from my core—screams of pure horror. I fell to my knees and stared down at the blood. My hands shaking uncontrollably. So much blood. So much...

CHAPTER TWENTY-NINE

———

In the event of a life-threatening medical emergency, Tenant is encouraged to call 9-1-1 immediately, not the after-hours emergency line.

Detective Spray was back, except on my turf now. "I know this is difficult for you," she said, forced compassion lacing her words. "Did she mention how long Vincent had been involved with Malone?" I was sitting in the back of an ambulance, my feet propped up on the bumper. I pulled the blanket the paramedic had draped over my shoulders tighter. My body shook as if I were sitting on an ice cap, not in seventy-five-degree October temperatures. The paramedic told me I was coming down from the shock and encouraged me to lie down on the gurney, but I refused. They didn't need to spend time on me. The blood soaking my shirt was not my own.

Silvia stepped in front of the detective and handed me a glass of water. "Here, drink this." I took it appreciatively, trying not to spill as I brought it to my chapped lips. Silvia readjusted her robe, pulling it around her tiny waist. It was the first time I'd seen her without Harold. "It helps with shock," she explained, sounding as if she spoke from experience. If she could move her face, I think she would have a sympathetic expression.

She was the first of the residents to pour out of their apartments after the gun went off, the one to call 9-1-1, and the one who wiped away the blood splattered on me.

"Cambria," the detective said. "Did she mention anything else about Malone?"

I shook my head.

"Did she say where she was planning to go?" She

pressed, desperate to coax whatever information she could out of me. Unlike the other police officers who had frequented the property, Detective Spray wasn't taking down copious notes on a small pad of paper. Rather, she intently studied my face with her hands settled on her hips. This was hard for her, I thought, trying to drag information out of an emotional witness.

I brought the water to my lips and took another sip. The cool liquid slid down my scratchy throat, settling my stomach. "Do you know if Chase was released?" I asked her. I told myself I only wanted to know for safety reasons. Not because I cared what happened to him. Nope. Not at all.

"She gave you nothing else on Malone?" Spray asked again.

It was clear the detective only cared about Malone. How many times was she going to ask?

"No more mentions of Malone?"

At least once more apparently.

I shook my head again. "She mostly talked about getting away from Rev."

"OK, that's enough for now, I guess. I may need to ask you more questions later."

A lump formed at the base of my throat. "I'll have to check with my attorney first," I said, turning around. Tom was strewn across the gurney inside the ambulance.

When the gun had fired, I'd fallen to the ground with a bloodcurdling scream. Then I'd gone to Tom.

He had rolled off Wysteria, clutching his arm. Blood had spread across his shirt and all over Wysteria, who lay in an unnatural position, comatose. I'd grabbed the gun and swooshed it across the cement, under the row of cars.

"Tom," I had sobbed, carefully placing his head in my lap. "You're such an idiot. What is wrong with you?" I'd ripped his shirt open to find the source of the bleeding. "Where does it hurt?" I'd asked, not seeing any blood.

"My arm," he'd groaned.

"Arm?" I had pulled his sleeve over his shoulder and found the half-inch opening where a bullet had grazed. "Oh, it's just a graze. What is wrong with you? You could have died." I had been so mad and so relieved.

Concerned voices had begun gathering around us. I had paid no attention. Instead, I'd looked at Wysteria. Pools of blood had formed underneath her, spreading across the cement. Her lower abdomen had been drenched in crimson. Tom had rolled to his side and sat up with my assistance. "What can we do?" I'd asked.

He'd winced as he rose to his knees. "Take this off me," he'd ordered, nodding toward his shirt. I'd immediately done as told (for once) and yanked the shirt off, forgetting about the wound on his arm.

"Dammit, Cam. Careful."

"I'm so sorry. You OK?" He'd given me a look. "I mean, aside from the gun wound thing?"

He'd shaken his head and used his uninjured hand to point to the shirt. "Apply that to her abdomen."

I'd done as instructed and applied pressure to the wound on her stomach, soaking Tom's shirt. He'd scooted closer, cradling his arm, and leaned down. "Can you hear us?" he'd asked Wysteria.

Her eyes had fluttered open, and she'd gasped for air, looking panicked. "Don't move," I'd told her. She'd coughed and lurched around, moaning. "Stay still."

A man in flannel pajamas had come to her side, claiming to be a podiatrist and a friend of a resident—which one, I'd forgotten the moment he'd told me. I'd only kept screaming that her feet were fine.

The firemen and the police had arrived shortly after, along with several EMTs, who'd replaced my bloody hand with their gloved ones. "We've got it," one of the EMTs had reassured me.

"Wait," Wysteria had moaned. "I really didn't touch Kenneth," she'd told me in a barely audible whisper, and I believed her.

I hadn't known what to say to that, so I'd said nothing. Scooting backward on my butt, I'd leaned against the wall. My legs and arms and hands and feet had been shaking uncontrollably as I'd watched the scene unfold, feeling as if I had been looking through someone else's eyes. The paramedics had worked on Wysteria, one holding her head still, talking to her in a calm yet firm voice. The other two had been inspecting the wound, pulling instruments out of their medic bag. Around the corner had come another man in uniform with the gurney. The wheels had rolled over the blood. A police officer had been trying to talk to me, but his words weren't making sense. Then the ill-fitted gray suit detective had walked up, and she too had been trying to talk to me. One of the fireman had been tending to Tom, whose blood-soaked shirt was at my feet.

It could have been worse. It could have been so much worse.

The sun rose, bathing the dark sky in blue and yellow hues and the ground in glistening dew. The police cars pulled out of the parking lot, one by one. The ambulance had long since left with Wysteria. I turned to Tom, who was lying in the back of the ambulance. He had a butterfly bandage over his brow while the paramedic wrapped his arm in gauze. "She wants to ask more questions later," I told him.

He gave a thumbs-up.

"I guess that'll be fine," I turned and told the detective. "Only, one more thing I forgot to mention." She looked at me, hopeful. "Rev did kill Kenneth Fisk. Wysteria told me before they rushed her to the hospital."

The corners of her mouth turned downward. "I know. I'll be in touch." It sounded more like a warning than a farewell.

She strolled off to her unmarked black sedan, removing the flashing red and blue light from the dashboard.

I know?

Then why the hell did she accuse me of it?

The blanket slipped off my shoulder as the chills subsided. The boyish-faced officer who had escorted me through the police station was standing near the entrance to Apartment 39, talking to Larry and Silvia. Larry had his arms folded over his Van Halen shirt, wide stance, and rocked slightly from side to side. Silvia had her hand spread over her chest.

"Excuse me!" I called. The boyish officer held a finger up to Silvia and Larry before dashing to my side.

"What's wrong?" he asked. I swore he wasn't a day over twelve, fifteen at most. He did look rather agile and eager though, which was exactly what I needed.

"It's my phone," I said. It was still on my mind. Pathetic, yes. "It's somewhere in the carports, and I need to call my babysitter to let her know why we are so late picking up our daughter. Could you find it for me?"

He quickly obliged. A few minutes later, I was reunited with my phone. The screen had a few cracks on the bottom but still worked. I unlocked the home screen and sent a quick text to Mrs. Nguyen.

Next, it was time to call Patrick.

CHAPTER THIRTY

———

Upon move-out, Landlord or Landlord's Agent will inspect Premises to determine the amount of deposit applied in order to return Premises to a re-rentable state.

"What's this for?" Patrick asked, nudging the plastic thimble-looking thingy with the end of his pen. There were several scattered across the bathroom counter of Vincent's apartment. I shrugged, not having a clue, and continued to snap pictures with my phone.

Patrick stalked down the hall, his yellow notepad tucked under his arm, already filled with three pages of notes. He tapped a box with his toe, shaking his head and making another note.

When I had called Patrick the morning of The Incident, as Tom and I called it, he'd answered with the voice of a man who had reached his very last straw. He'd nearly fired me on the spot before I greeted him with a pleasant salutation of, "I'm sitting in an ambulance and was just held at gunpoint and as a hostage for the second time tonight."

His response? Nothing. He'd said nothing. I would have thought he had hung up if it weren't for the female voice in the background repeatedly asking, "What happened? What's wrong? Tell me, Patrick."

Once he'd recouped enough to form words, we'd agreed to meet as planned. After I explained what had happened, I suspected he wouldn't be firing me anymore.

I was right. Instead of handing me a notice of termination (which I saw when I peeked into his bag, already signed and dated), he handed me a bonus for all my "troubles." I opened the envelope, readjusting my sore body on the ugly chair across from the even uglier couch in the lobby, and stared down at the three-thousand-dollar check with my name scrawled on it. It was enough to bring my bank account to positive and put a deposit down on a new apartment, should I choose to leave. "I'll understand if you want to look for a new job," Patrick said earnestly. He looked tired.

Biting my lip, I stared down at the money that would only go so far. "I think," I replied, "I'd like to stay. I would like to be trained though." I realized over the course of the past three weeks how little I had learned from Joyce and how little Google knew about property management. Patrick readily agreed, and it was back to business as usual (with a negotiated extra week of vacation time and free laundry, you know, for my troubles).

Back in Apartment 39, Patrick stared through the hole in the wall between the kitchen and the living room. "This never should have happened. Inspections should be done at least twice a year. We got lazy," he said, making note of such on his pad. It took nearly a week to get the eviction processed for the apartment before we could enter. Warranting two visits in one week from Patrick. The most he'd visited the community over the last five years, he'd said to me before promising to start making monthly inspections. For which I was glad. I found his company quite pleasant. "You heard from Kevin lately?" he asked.

I nodded. "He says the plan is to get him into rehab again instead of doing jail time."

I'd prodded Tom for more information at breakfast. He'd kept silent on the subject, scooping a forkful of pancakes into his mouth instead. I'd spent the night at his apartment. I had spent every night since The Incident there. Cuddled up in Lilly's bed, wrapped in her *Frozen* comforter, nearly hitting REM before my head hit the pillow.

The day after The Incident, we had both been too physically exhausted to make food, so we'd opted for IHOP.

Lilly had sat next to Tom in the booth, enjoying her pancake covered in syrup and whipped cream and chocolate chips with a cherry on top. Her eyes had grown about six inches when the waitress slid the plate in front of her, and she'd gasped and giggled and clapped as if she'd just won the lottery. I had pushed my Southwest-style omelet around the plate with my fork. My stomach had not quite settled. Tom had nudged my knee under the table with his, making sure I was all right. He'd, of course, offered to help me with workers' comp and to file a lawsuit against Elder Management for negligence or whatever. But I wasn't interested. I was ready to start a career and get out of the limbo I'd been in for far too long.

It hadn't been until the waitress dropped the check on the table that I'd realized I was living out one of my Tom fantasies. We'd been sitting at breakfast as a real family—mom, dad, and child all enjoying a meal. It had been picturesque (aside from the bandage around Tom's arm, the cut on his eye, and the dark bruise on my cheek I'd discovered when I woke). I had caught Tom staring at me over the table, and I couldn't help but blush.

A life raft from my baby daddy.

Patrick groaned, kicking part of a broken plastic chair out of the way. "What really gets me is Chase," he said, running a hand over his bare head. "I've always had a good read on people, and he struck me as a real stand-up guy. He had good references, excellent credit, no criminal hits, and he was inexpensive. You know how hard it is to find anyone to work for minimum wage? It was too good to be true, I guess. Maybe he wasn't that great at his job, but for that price, I could live with it." He jotted down a thought on his notepad.

"Aren't you glad you didn't hire his friend?" Part of me was still bitter about being third choice, especially now. Would either of his first two choices have basically solved an entire crime on their own?

Methinks not.

"What friend?"

"His friend who applied for my job."

He scrunched his bushy brows together. "No, I don't recall anyone mentioning they knew him. I was going to offer you the position the day after you interviewed. Then Chase called and told me you'd cheated on your application and he didn't think you'd be a good manager. At the time, I believed him to be a straight shooter. So I offered the job to two other seasoned managers who both turned it down, mainly because of the horror stories they'd heard about Kevin."

"Are you serious?" My heart swelled. I was the first choice? It was the confidence booster I needed to confirm my decision to stay and pursue a career in property management. And yet another mark on the Reasons-You-Should-Stop-Thinking-About-Chase list. Any sane person with a heartbeat and a brain would scream "Forget about it!" Especially when looking at all the evidence—the way he'd made an advance only to pull away (douche), the drugs (liar), the arrest (criminal), the job sabotage (even bigger douche).

CHAPTER THIRTY-ONE

———

Newly remodeled one-bedroom apartment. Gorgeous downstairs unit, easy access to the carports, large patio, wonderful location. Luxurious pool, spacious laundry rooms, stunning courtyards. $2,900 a month. Must provide two forms of identification, paycheck stubs, references...

"The entire apartment is brand new from the carpet to the walls to the kitchen cabinets," I said in my best sales-pitchy voice, running my hand along the newly installed countertop. Patrick and I had gone back and forth on color options over the last month while Apartment 39 was being restored. I pushed for color, wanting to add yellow, green, and blue hues to liven up the space. Patrick wanted grays and whites and browns—blah. We "compromised" and went with silver countertops, beige cabinets, and tan carpet. Baby steps, I told myself.

A short, curvy woman with a thin black side braid stood in the kitchen, bouncing the drooling baby boy wrapped around her chest in one of those mile-long cloth-wrap things I never was able to figure out how to use with Lilly. Speaking of Lilly, she came skipping around the corner, nearly knocking into the young mom. "Sorry about that," I said, shooting Lilly a cut-it-out look, which she completely ignored.

She waved off my apology. "No worries. I love the family atmosphere of this place." She opened the brand-new dishwasher, noting the instruction manual still inside. "Why is everything so new?"

"Fire." It was only a slight exaggeration. "It just came on the market, and I'm sure at this price point, it'll go fast. I have applications in the office if you'd like to fill one out?"

She kissed the top of her baby's head. "What are the neighbors like? Are they nice, like good family people?"

I chose my words carefully. "The neighbors are *quiet*." It was only a slight exaggeration. Kevin had been gone for a couple of weeks now and wouldn't be returning for some time. "There's a family with a little boy upstairs."

She smiled. I had her.

I locked the apartment behind us, and we traveled back to the lobby for an application. Larry cut across the lawn with a box labeled *Harold's Things* in his arms, Silvia walked behind him with Harold, supervising the move of her belongings. I'd arranged a transfer from her apartment to the vacant unit across the courtyard. It only shared a wall with Larry, and he was more than happy to have a new neighbor. They both enjoyed complaining—her about everyone and him about all his physical ailments. Perhaps they could complain to each other and keep me out of it.

Or so I hoped.

Silvia's apartment was already rented out to a wonderful couple who I was thrilled to have—Mr. and Mrs. Nguyen. Mr. Nguyen had started as our new, and much improved, maintenance man (he actually fixed the things I asked him to and didn't fraternize with felonies). I'd introduced him to Patrick shortly after Chase was arrested (and never heard from again), and the two hit it off. Of course, Patrick ran a thorough background check prior to approval, and Mr. Nguyen passed all checkpoints with flying colors. I didn't have to micromanage his hours either as his apartment counted as part of his compensation along with a salary.

Lilly was thrilled with the thought of having her SoCal grandparents back, and Mrs. Nguyen promised she'd teach Lilly how to sew. And the fact that Mr. and Mrs. Nguyen were hard of hearing paired perfectly with the loud lovemaking of their neighbors, Clare and Bob. Another win for Cambria.

Back in the lobby, I opened the door for the young mom, who was beaming at the prospect of occupying "the best apartment in the complex." She filled out the application. I took her driver's license. Checked it twice. Then one more time for good measure. Faxed it over to Patrick, and we were done. I politely shooed her out of the lobby and locked the door. I knew I was late. I knew I'd be late when I stopped to show the apartment. If I could rent it, the risk would be worth it. At least I thought so. I wasn't sure anyone else would see it that way, aside from Patrick maybe.

Lilly bounced up and down on my hip as I sped through the community. Residents either waved or scowled as we passed. Most had forgiven or forgotten about the crime sprees, my arrest, and the gunshot. The threesome rumor had lost momentum (hallelujah). Our Rent or Run safety rating was up to 3.8 stars and run rating down to 20%. The management rating was holding steady at 2 stars. Baby steps.

Only a few apartments remained vacant, although a steady flow of traffic and a motivated apartment manager (me) had already filled most of them. Patrick was impressed.

By the time I made it to Apartment 36, I could barely breathe. (I still hadn't exercised. Baby steps.) I pounded on the door, checking my watch. My phone vibrated in my back pocket. I knew who it was, and I knew why he was calling. Not answering would give the illusion I was driving to the location I should be at.

Amy opened the door. Her blonde and purple-streaked hair blown out to perfection, framing her face. "There's my girl," she singsonged and reached out for Lilly. "You ready for a fun day with Auntie Amy?"

Lilly squealed.

"Make sure you're super careful," I said, handing over Lilly's bag. "Don't let her out of your sight, and she can't have anything with soy because she has this rough patch of skin below her ear, and I think it could be an..."

Amy put her hand on my shoulder. "Breathe." She took in a deep breath and exhaled slowly, inviting me to join her. I took heed and inhaled and exhaled to make her happy. "You sure you don't want me to go with you?" she asked.

My stomach was all butterflies, and my throat felt about two sizes too small. Still, childcare was more of a concern than my nerves. "I'll be fine. Where's Spencer?"

"Right here," he hollered, emerging from the hallway in jeans and a white polo shirt. He'd made significant improvements in the wardrobe and décor department since he began dating Amy. His apartment now had a white couch and a blue love seat, decorative rug, art on the wall, and a real kitchen table. It smelled of fabric softener and cinnamon. It was only a matter of time before Amy would be submitting her own rental application to join Spencer's lease. I was thrilled.

"Where are you guys going? The park?" I asked, my phone vibrating again in my pocket.

"The Aquarium of the Pacific," Spencer said, grinning. He placed a hand on Amy's shoulder and said hello to Lilly. He had waited until their third date before springing the fishy brothel on her. Turns out he's a decent guy who treats her like a queen. She decided she could live with the whole fish thing, as long as it remained on the patio.

I fidgeted with the bottom of my shirt. "That's in Long Beach, right? I mean, that's kind of far to drive, and it's super busy… What about going to McDonald's instead?"

Amy cocked her head and gave me a look. "She'll be fine. We'll be fine. You will not be fine if you don't get out of here right now. Go."

She had a point. I kissed Lilly's head. Made one more plea for McDonald's. Was told to leave.

Thirty minutes later, I pulled into a parking space at the courthouse. As usual I crawled over the center console and passenger seat to exit the car then raced inside. I found Tom pacing the hall, his phone at his ear. My phone vibrated in my back pocket.

I wore a pair of black slacks and a blue-collared shirt, the most professional outfit I could find at Target. Amy and I had our hair blown out the day before. Einstein was so silky and long, I couldn't stop running my fingers through it. I'd spent the night before watching makeup tutorials, practicing the smoky eye. I was going for a sexy business-casual look, and based on Tom's gaping expression, mission accomplished.

I had to look my best, especially today.

Tom lowered his phone and stared. "You look…*good.*" He blinked, hard. "Why are you so late?"

"This girl showed up and really wanted to see an apartment." I smiled a sorry-not-sorry smile. "I'm here now."

He ran his hand down his face and grunted. "You have any idea how serious this is?"

I scoffed. Of course I knew how serious this was. I was the one who had to take the stand. I was the one who had to sit through hours of questions from multiple detectives to prepare for today.

"Tom, I'm ready. I can do this."

"Here's the thing. You probably don't have to now."

"What?" I'd been stressing for days and rushing all afternoon, and now I might not even have to testify? "Why not?"

Tom looked around the busy hallway and led me to a quiet corner near the drinking fountains. His hand lingered on my arm—a life raft. But if he really wanted this, if he really wanted me, then he'd have to come right out and say it. Cause I was ready to jump on the raft and paddle to shore.

"It looks like one of the detectives on the case blew his or her cover and came forward to testify. The DA said there's enough incriminating evidence to put Rev away for life without your testimony now."

"Really? Do you know who it was that came forward?"

He shook his head. "You don't need to find out either. Let's go, and you can have some peace of mind knowing you won't have to face Rev." I wasn't sure how much peace I could have knowing Wysteria's trial had not been set yet. Vincent and the mystical Malone trials had already started. No word on Wysteria. She survived the gunshot, but her baby wasn't so lucky. She would still be forced to stand trial, and I was concerned she would blame Tom or me—or both of us—for the death of her unborn child. She would plot revenge, stalk us, take us hostage—or worse, our daughter—and finish us off as she intended to do that night. My worst-case-scenario mind was clearly still alive and well.

"I want to watch," I announced, charging down the hall. "Which door?"

Tom shook his head and pointed the way. The last courtroom I'd entered was for Kevin. After a guilty plea for possession and public nudity, the judge sentenced Kevin to court-ordered rehab after a three-month stint in jail. Tom had wanted rehab only, without any jail time, but Kevin arrived without shoes or a shirt on, so he had to work with what he had.

I had high hopes the rehab and jail time would serve him well. Patrick promised Kevin would have a home to return to. I removed the cobwebs over his door and placed a "welcome" mat in front. I was still in his corner, maybe because of my cousin Stephanie or maybe because he'd had a crappy childhood or maybe because I saw Kevin as the underdog and I loved a good underdog story—it was the most relatable.

Only two days before, I had received my first letter from Kevin.

Dear Kamebria,

Hi! I hope you and your child are doing well. I am doing alright. Jail sucks, but my new cellmate is cool. I wrote Patrick and said I think you should get a raise. So you should be seeing that in your paycheck soon.

Being here has made me realize I really need to get my act together. I promise once I get out of jail, I will be a model tenant. I promise I won't play my music loudly or let sexual offenders hide out in my house. I won't pee on the mailboxes, and I will wear clothes when I swim. I'm going to be really quiet and helpful. Like you said before, I can help you manage the place! I'm looking forward to it.

I also wanted to ask you a few favors. Can you please water the plants on my patio? I also need you to go into my apartment, but don't look in the kitchen or bathroom!!!! I have a pet snake named Viper in my closet, and he needs to eat one mouse a week. I keep the mice in a brown box on my dresser. In my hallway closet I have a few plants, and I need you to water those on Mondays and Thursdays. I have a heat lamp on a timer, and I need you to make sure that is coming on. Can you please get my mail and set it on the floor by my bedroom door? I also need you to evict Larry. Make sure he is gone before I get home.

If I think of anything else, I will write you again. Thanks for the letter. You can visit again if you want.

Sincerely,
Kevin P. McMills

P.S. My first cellmate, Doug, will be calling you. He just got out last week and is looking for a new apartment. I gave him your name and number so you can hook him up. I told him all about the place, and he said it sounds real nice. I told him to put me down as a reference.

I had read the letter twice before folding it back up and shoving it into the envelope.

Note to self: Don't show anyone named Doug an apartment alone, ever.

This courtroom was much bigger than Kevin's. Men and women of all ages and races made up the jury. The judge, an older woman with dark skin and red half-moon glasses resting at the end of her nose, presided. The gallery was near empty. I chose a seat in the third row behind Scarlett Fisk, who sat surrounded by close friends there to support her. Tom sank into the chair next to me.

A hot flash hit me like lightning when I caught sight of the back of Rev's head. His hair had grown out a little since I'd last seen him, and he was now sporting a suit. He looked like a creepy Chia Pet, which is kind of redundant. My hands shook, and sweat sprinkled my forehead.

"That's it. We're leaving," Tom whispered, starting to stand.

"I'm fine," I said, slowing my breathing and trying to calm down. "Fine," I repeated to myself.

Breathe.

Then it happened. The air shifted. A scruffy-faced man took the stand, swore in, and sat. Chase. He wore a fitted dark blue suit, white shirt, and a solid yellow tie. His normally shaggy hair was slicked back and wrapped behind his ears.

The District Attorney stood behind a wooden podium, a pudgy fellow with a comb-over of silver hair. He asked Chase to state his name for the court. Chase rattled off a series of numbers instead.

Tom's jaw dropped about a foot.

Chase was no druggie. Chase was no maintenance man either. Chase was an undercover cop.

I stared in awe over the next hour as Chase recounted the events leading up to the arrests, amid peppered questions and objections from various attorneys.

Chase wasn't the bad guy. He wasn't a bad guy at all. He was the exact opposite. He was the good guy. A guy who had been protecting me all along. He'd tried to stop Patrick from hiring me to keep me off the property he knew was overrun with drug dealers. He'd been so shocked when Spencer admitted he was participating in illegal activity because he had done a sweep of all the residents and determined him harmless (which he was). He was terrible at his job because he was too busy doing his *real* job. He was disappearing and reappearing when I needed him, and after everything that had happened, my gut was right.

It turned out Chase had been working on the Malone case for over a year before he went undercover. Rev was Malone's top dealer. The detectives had been following him closely, hoping he'd lead them to Malone. Over the summer, Vincent approached Rev about making extra money to pay off a gambling debt. Rev hooked Vincent up with Malone, and the two dealt together. When Rev moved in with Vincent, Chase had a hard time keeping tabs on the two because of the location of the apartment. So he took on the role as the maintenance man at the property, having assumed the identity of Chase Hudson. He built a good rapport with Vincent and later with the Rev. Turned out Rev and Vincent asked that Chase keep the nosey apartment manager (aka me) distracted—*and what a distraction he was.*

Chase did not witness the murder of Kenneth Fisk. He wasn't on the property yet. But Vincent told him what had happened. That Kenneth saw him and Rev make a drug transaction outside his apartment early in the morning. Kenneth pulled his phone out to call the police (or so Vincent assumed, because yes, the police would have been the wiser choice). When Rev saw what was happening he "took care of him." An arrest couldn't be made because it was all hearsay. There was no proof.

Chase received a tip from an anonymous source (aka me) with the exact location of Malone. After they got Malone and Vincent, they came back to the apartment building to arrest Rev, but first they had to catch him dealing.

"When Rev answered the door, he was agitated," Chase continued. We were on hour two of his testimony. "I found the apartment manager inside. It was later confirmed during a confession by the defendant that he had taken the apartment manager hostage with plans to kill her."

Yikes.

"Once he agreed to sell me a gram, we were able to make the arrest. I'd planned on staying undercover, so I was arrested too, as was the apartment manager because at the time we weren't sure of her involvement. But she turned out to be in the clear."

For a few glorious seconds our eyes met, and that spark exploded around us. He'd blown his cover so I wouldn't have to testify. Chase, or whatever his real name was, returned his attention to the District Attorney and casually lifted his hand and scratched his scruffy chin—the signal.

Everything was fine.

CHAPTER THIRTY-TWO

———

I and/or We have read and agree to abide by the terms of this lease. In witness thereof, the Parties have executed this Lease on this day.

I took a seat at my desk. The office was quiet. I'd only just removed the *Be back at 4:00* sign from the window. I grabbed the program from Kenneth's memorial service out from my bag and placed it in his thick file, on top of the incident reports, pages of notes, my theories, and the security deposit reconciliation sent to Scarlet.

"Rest in peace, friend," I said as I closed the file for the last time.

With a sigh, I scrunched my knees up to my chest. I still had on the black slacks and gray sweater I'd worn to the memorial. Good thing because the office was a freezer—sixty-degrees outside and five degrees cooler inside. My teeth chattered, my lips were chapped, and my skin was dehydrated. Didn't help that I had just polished off a pint of French Vanilla.

Still, I knew I'd never survive a *real* snowy, blizzardy, mittens-and-earmuffs kind of December like the rest of the country was experiencing, and I was fine with it. I'd take crisp, smoggy air, bare trees, and the occasional rainstorm over frozen pipes, shoveled walkways, and slippery sidewalks. It sounded like a lot more work. Being a SoCal apartment manager had its benefits.

The lobby door opened, and Mr. Nguyen backed in, dragging the five-foot palm tree I bought for the office. It wasn't until after I paid for it that I realized there was no way I could get it home. Then in came Mr. Nguyen to save the day. Just as he did when Apartment 5 had dripping muck-colored water at three in the morning, and when the pool's heater broke, and when Larry got his ponytail stuck in the garbage disposal. He was a lifesaver. Patrick called us "the dream team" because we were.

I'd be lying if I said a ping didn't stab at my heart when I caught a glimpse of the embroidered "maintenance" above Mr. Nguyen's shirt pocket. I had a small sliver of hope that Chase, or whatever his real name was, would have contacted me after Rev's trial had ended. Show up at my apartment. Send a letter. An email. Maybe a friend request on Facebook?

Nothing.

Not one word.

He'd been whisked away after his testimony, not to be heard from again. Granted it had only been two weeks. And it was possible he was already on a new job, having done his judicial duty by ensuring Rev got the life without parole he deserved. According to Tom, Chase didn't show up at Vincent's trial, where he was sentenced to twenty-five years. Malone's was still ongoing (and seemed to be never ending). According to the various news outlets covering the trail, Chase had not yet been called to testify.

As for me, I was still hanging out on Alcatraz—catching some rays, feeding the birds, living the spinster life to the fullest. After Rev's trial the life rafts stopped…until today. Tom had sent me a text while I was at Kenneth Fisk's memorial, saying he had something "important to talk about" tonight. And he wanted to talk "alone." Which wouldn't typically mean too much except for the accompanying wink *and* heart emoji.

A wink and a heart!

Not to get all school-girly but—*eeeekkkk!*

With Tom at my side, all would be right in my world— except for Wysteria.

Wysteria's trial had been postponed again and again and again. It was bordering on ridiculous. Not only because she deserved to rot in prison, but also because there was a chance Chase would show up to testify, a very small chance. "Less than a one percent chance," Tom had said when I asked, not hiding his frustration with the question. He was cute when he was jealous.

I went to the lobby and showed Mr. Nguyen where to put the tree. The added foliage helped the ugly. Except, crap. Now everything was off-centered. "Would you hate me if I asked you to get another one?" I asked directly into Mr. Nguyen's ear. Patrick said he'd personally see to it that Mr. Nguyen got fitted for hearing aids in the New Year. Mostly because talking to him on the phone was grueling.

He shook his head. "No problem! I go now!" He was out the door before I could thank him.

I grabbed the mail piled on the ground near the mail slot and sat on the couch with my feet propped up on the coffee table. I sorted the mail—most were bills, some spam. The property management catalogue looked interesting.

Mickey from Apartment 19 walked through, arguing with himself. "Hi, Mickey," I said automatically, my attention on the magazine. He flung open the door. "Bye, Mickey." I flipped to the marketing section. "These waving inflatable tube men are only fifty bucks?"

"Those things are kind of creepy, though."

My heart skipped two beats. I dropped the magazine, afraid to look up. My mind was playing tricks. It had to be. I had no time for liquidy limbs.

"Cambria?" It was Chase. It was his voice. It was his smell. It was his sensual energy.

I rolled my sleeves up to my elbows. *It sure is hot in here.* Deep breath in, slow breath out. I gazed up.

Chase. His hair was shorter, styled, and darker—light brown. Only the faintest appearance of a five o'clock shadow brushed his jawline. The scruffy I-woke-up-like-this Chase had nothing on the groomed I-could-be-an-underwear-model Chase. He had on jeans and a red hooded sweatshirt with USC printed on the front in bold yellow lettering. I didn't know what to say, so I made a squeaky noise that could be interpreted as "Hello."

He twisted his mouth to the side. "Maybe I shouldn't have come," he said more to himself than to me.

"No…" I didn't know his name. It could be Bartholomew or Dan or Peter. It was hard imagining him going by any other name than Chase.

"My name *is* Chase," he said, as if reading my mind.

Holy crap! He's an undercover cop. He could read minds. Not literally. Part of his job was to get a read on people. I'd seen it on the hundreds of crime shows I'd watched. He had to know I was pining over him the entire time he was here. That's embarrassing.

"You OK?" he asked.

My insides were hyperventilating. "I'm fine. A little surprised, that's all." I was determined to have a normal "hey, haven't seen you in a while" conversation. Tom was on his way over with a heart and a wink! "What brings you by?" I asked casually. "We don't have any more drug dealers I need to know about, do we?"

He took a step closer, close enough to touch. *Control yourself, Cambria.*

"I wouldn't know. I'm not undercover anymore. I went to uniform with a different agency."

"What?" I suspected that meant he was a regular police officer now. "Why?"

"It was time."

"Oh." I paused to regroup. "By the way, sorry for, you know, hitting you that night. I don't think I've ever hit anyone before."

He laughed. It had a charming musical sound. "I thought it was awesome. Here you were, face-to-face with two druggies, and instead of cowering, you went all Tyson. You can definitely hold your own. I like that."

"Thanks." I blushed, biting my lip.

"So, hey." He shoved his hands into the front pockets of his jeans. "I came by to see if you wanted to go out. Maybe get ice cream?"

"Go out?" I chuckled. No matter how hot he was (and he was), I couldn't run off with him like some schoolgirl. "Chase, I don't even know the real you."

"What do you want to know?"

"I don't know… Do you have a wife and kids at home?" It had crossed my mind, numerous times.

"Do you think I'd be here asking you out if I did?"

I shrugged. People are idiots. You never know.

"No," he finally answered.

Phew.

"I've never been married. Never been close to anyone. Not a good idea when you're doing what I was doing for a living. I *did* grow up in Long Beach as I said. I *do* have nieces—four of them—and three brothers and a sister. I'm the second oldest. I *did* go to Long Beach City College, except I didn't drop out to do maintenance, obviously. I transferred to USC. I'm fluent in Spanish, Cantonese, and I can get by in Japanese. Still working on it. I root for the Angels. I run for fun. I could watch *Seinfeld* all day. I went undercover six years ago, and this is the first time I've worked in uniform. Anything else you want to know?"

"How old are you?"

"Thirty-three."

"Chicken or beef?"

"Vegetarian."

"Morning or night person?"

"Night."

"Do you have a cat?"

"No. Goldfish named Fish."

"Was that really an old injury you had the day we were spying on Spencer, or did you hurt yourself chasing bad guys?"

"Neither. I fell off a ladder getting a wasp's nest."

"Did you...wait, you fell off a ladder?" I laughed. I laughed until tears blurred my vision. "I'm sorry. It's not funny...except it is. No offense, but you weren't very good at your job. Unless that was part of the cover?"

"Hey, I fixed the air conditioner," he said with pride.

"It broke the following week."

His shoulders drooped. He looked genuinely sad, as if I'd just told him Santa wasn't real. "You know, it was a lot harder than I thought it would be. Doing this job and mine. I bet if I gave it my full attention, I'd be a good maintenance man."

"Without a doubt," I humored him.

"Yeah, the truth is I probably wouldn't." He laughed.

"*A man who can laugh at his own expense is a keeper*," Grandma Ruthie used to say.

I wiped my eyes. "Seriously, I have one more question. Did you really tell Patrick not to hire me because you were trying to protect us or was another undercover cop trying for my job?"

"To protect you."

That's what I thought.

"I was upset when I heard you got the job," he continued. "You also made my job difficult by being so…"

"Nosy?"

"I was trying to think of a different word. But, yes, nosy. Squad cars here from a different agency. You staking out apartments. Hiding on top of carport roofs." He narrowed his eyes. "I still can't believe you did that."

"You *can't* believe I did, or you *can* and wish I hadn't?"

He smiled. "I *bleeping* wish you hadn't." He leaned over and placed his hands on my shoulders. His touch was warm. His face so close I could feel his breath brush against my cheeks. Heaven help me, I wanted to kiss this man.

So I did.

Once his mouth opened against mine—all else was forgotten. It was almost ravenous. Instinct took over, and I liquefied faster than a pint of French Vanilla sitting on my counter in the 90-degree heat.

And I didn't mind one bit.

ABOUT THE AUTHOR

Erin Huss is a blogger and best selling author. She can change a diaper in fifteen seconds flat, is a master overanalyzer, has a gift for making any social situation awkward and yet, somehow, she still has friends. Erin shares hilarious property management horror stories at *The Apartment Manager's Blog* and her own daily horror stories at erinhuss.com. She currently resides in Southern California with her husband and five children, where she complains daily about the cost of living but will never do anything about it.

To learn more about Erin Huss, visit her online at:
https://erinhuss.com

Enjoyed this book? Check out these other humorous mystery reads available in print now from Gemma Halliday Publishing:

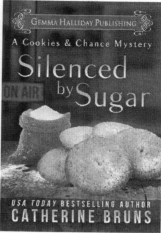

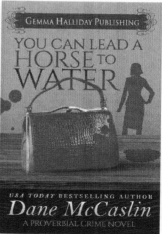

www.GemmaHallidayPublishing.com

Made in the USA
Middletown, DE
18 March 2018